PRAISE FOR

"Sasha has done it again! I devo[...] them to come out because I kn[...] should be on your must-read a[...] you are into sports romance."

"You want a sizzling soccer romance??! This is for you! I could not put this book down! I was hooked from the second I started reading!!"

"Sasha Lace has fast become one of my favorite authors! The world she exposes, the world she builds, has me glued to my screen from the first word to the very last!"

"This is everything that I love about contemporary romance: strong male and female main characters, romance with instant chemistry."

"A witty, flirty, and a little bit of everything else romantic story. The sizzle was awesome too. Read it in one sitting, it was such an easy read."

"30% in and Sasha Lace became a one-click author."

"I am loving that an author is giving women their shot in the world of sports romance!"

"Gabe needs to be added to your list of book boyfriends, he is handsome, knows what he wants and my heaven, knows his way around a woman. The spice in this was beautiful and fun. It was delicious."

"I left each chapter wanting more and more and MORE. Well written, fast read that gives readers everything they are looking for."

"As with any book by Sasha there was a point where I was reduced to a crying mess and wanted to throw my Kindle at a wall . . . which led to having to stay up all night to get to the HEA."

"Would I recommend this book? Yes! Would I recommend everything written by Sasha Lace? Yes!"

Playing the
Game

TITLES BY SASHA LACE

Playing the Field series

Playing the Game

SASHA LACE

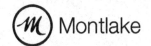

Published by Montlake, Seattle

First published as *Playing the Billionaire* by Sasha Lace in 2023. This edition contains editorial revisions.

www.apub.com

Amazon, the Amazon logo, and Montlake are trademarks of Amazon.com, Inc., or its affiliates.

ISBN-13: 9781662526121
eISBN: 9781662526114

Cover design by The Brewster Project
Cover images © lupengyu © LadadikArt / Getty Images; © IR Stone © ESOlex / Shutterstock

Printed in the United States of America

CONTENT WARNING

Parental illness and death

Grief

References to sexual harassment (side character, off-page)

Explicit sex

Public sex

For James
If I'd known writing about football was the way
to capture your interest in my books, I would have
done it years ago.

Chapter 1

GABE

ONE YEAR AGO

The bastards were camped on the doorstep again. Dad's parties attracted the paparazzi the way rain brought out slugs. Not that he minded. No doubt his publicist had tipped the slugs off. Camera flashes dazzled.

"Smile for the camera, Gabe."

"This way. That's right."

A pulse beat in my temple, but I pasted a smile on my face and paused to give the press what they wanted. Better to get it over and done with on my terms. Less chance of them sneaking around in the bushes. I had no patience for the media circus. I needed to find Emma and apologize. She was still ghosting me after I'd chuckled all the way through her latest premiere in Cannes. It was hardly my fault. She could have warned me it wasn't supposed to be a comedy.

A microphone appeared so close to my face it touched my nose. "Karen Delaney. Breakfast TV. Calverdale United at the top of the Premier League for the third year running. You had aspirations to play once. You didn't fancy putting on your boots and joining them this season?"

"Me? No." I flashed the most charming smile I could muster. "I'm too pretty for football."

I dodged past her, but the microphone butted my chest. "Micky must be happy."

"Dad's delighted. The guys put everything on the pitch this season."

I made for the front door, but she sidestepped me, blocking my way. "Rumor has it your dad's getting ready to hand over the reins. Are we looking at the next director of Calverdale United?"

My smile faltered. The *click-click* of the cameras filled my ears. Lights flashed in my eyes. Karen raised an expectant eyebrow, waiting for my answer. Fuck it. Might as well be honest. Dad would be pissed off, but maybe he'd finally get the message.

"I'm ready for the club whenever Dad's ready to let it go."

Karen lowered her voice, being purposefully mysterious. "What's stopping him?"

Good question, Karen, but I have a better one—what fucking business is it of yours?

It took everything I had to hold my smile in place. "If you'll excuse me. The party awaits."

I squeezed through the horde of press. A blast of heat and rock music hit me. The sweeping entrance hall teemed with famous faces: footballers, models, actors, musicians. My shoulders tightened. I had work for the club in the morning, but Dad had insisted I show my face at his party. I needed a drink after Karen Delaney's onslaught. Everyone was always asking the same stupid questions.

Dad kept the best Scotch whisky in his office. He wouldn't be sharing that with the plebs. Guests lined the grand central spiraling staircase. I stopped to greet a couple of the guys I'd played with on the junior team. My Prada brogues tapped on marble as I headed up and up the never-ending steps. A gold balloon fell from a chandelier and bounced off my head. Laughter and conversation chased me before it faded to a dim pulse in Dad's wing of the house.

A strange noise drifted from Dad's office and gave me pause. A rhythmic scraping and grunting seeped through the door, then a stream of high-pitched cries. Either the filthy old bastard had a woman in there or he was murdering an owl. What was he thinking? Mother turned a blind eye to Dad's affairs, but this was taking the piss. Who was it this time? Another nineteen-year-old gold digger? The old man was always a seedy piece of shit, no matter how hard he tried to maintain a veneer of respectability. He'd crawled out of the gutter and built an empire on porn and crime. Sleaze flowed in his blood.

The booze could wait. I'd leave the filthy bastard to his fun. I turned to go, but the door swung open and a pair of familiar brown eyes met mine.

Emma?

Emma's mouth fell open; her face paled. She wriggled in her midnight-blue cocktail gown, pulling the neckline up and tugging down the hem. Her hair fell in long auburn waves and a pink flush tinged her cheeks. Confusion made my brain reel. I dodged past Emma into the opulent wood-paneled office. Dad stood behind his desk, red-cheeked and sweating. He combed his fingers through his disheveled salt-and-pepper hair and tucked his crumpled shirt into his trousers.

Just the two of them.

My dad and Emma.

The office closed in around me. My guts churned. This was low. Even for Micky Rivers, this was fucking low. We'd never had an easy relationship. Micky Rivers was a self-made billionaire. He mangled his vowels like a barrow boy in an East London fruit market, but he was one of the richest men in the world. All my life, he'd been distant and formidable. He'd never been in line for dad of the year,

3

but—this? And Emma? Things hadn't been great between us for a while, but I'd trusted her.

Emma cupped my cheeks with smooth hands, her eyes wild and imploring. "I'm sorry, Gabe. You weren't supposed to find out like this."

Her scent of Chanel perfume, sweat, and guilt filled my nose. A knot tightened in my chest, but I smothered the feeling and kept my voice level. "I was looking for the Macallan. It can wait."

I headed down the landing.

Emma dashed in front of me. "Please. Don't run off like this, Gabe. Let's talk."

I'd broken all my rules for this woman. I didn't chase. I didn't do commitment. Nobody thought I was capable of settling down and being serious about anything, but this had been my chance to prove myself. I'd visited every movie set in every butt-fuck-nowhere location Emma was filming. When I'd found her toothbrush in my bathroom, I'd cleared out space for her in the cabinet. I'd even done a few scenes in her trashy reality show and let her plaster every photo of us together all over her social media. I'd wanted to show that I could do stable and mature. Not that it had been enough to convince Dad I was ready to step up. They both must have been laughing at me the entire time.

I let my gaze rove over her, and it was like looking at a stranger. Who was this woman that could do this?

"I'll handle him." My father smoothed a hand over his hair and flashed Emma a commanding glance.

Emma bit her lip, a pensive shimmer in her eyes.

"Go," Dad barked.

Emma flinched then walked away stiffly in her skyscraper heels. My chest ached so much she may as well have taken one of those shoes off and stabbed me in the heart with it. She didn't give me a second glance. Dad mopped his sweating brow with a

4

handkerchief. A ludicrous red suit with a snowy fur trim wrapped around his powerful shoulders. Heavy gold chains dangled down his front. He looked like a pimp Santa.

"It wasn't planned, but with this girl it's . . . different." He measured me with a cool, appraising look. "This is real for me. I love her."

"Bullshit. You only love yourself."

Laughter and music drifted up the staircase and made my teeth grit. Everyone would be laughing when word of this got out.

"This place is crawling with press. If you cause a scene, you'll embarrass yourself. Come on, Gabs. Let your old man off the hook." His tone was cajoling, as though I was a toddler and he'd found me crying with a scraped knee. "What can I do? How can I fix this?"

Anger swirled tight and hot in my chest, but I'd die before I let him see what this was doing to me. The words spilled out without any thought. "You can give me the club."

His mouth lifted with humor, but I held my face level. *It's no joke. You screwed me over, so I'm going to screw you.* "Give me the club or I'm going to tell everyone what kind of man Micky Rivers is: a cheat and a cold, double-crossing bastard who would betray his own son."

The amusement died on his lips and his expression turned still and serious. "Don't push me, Gabs. We've talked about this. You're still too young."

"I'm thirty in a couple of years. You made your first million by twenty."

He studied my face before he took a long breath and blew it out. "This is a big year. I've got some ideas for new signings. Let's talk about it next year."

Every time. Next year. Next bloody year. What more did he want from me? I'd done everything he wanted. I'd won the respect

5

of the team and the coaches, jumped through every hoop. He didn't trust me. The club would always be a carrot he dangled to keep me in line.

"Fine. I'm telling the press what I walked in on."

His eyes narrowed. "You'll ruin Emma, too."

I had to calm down. A tabloid feeding frenzy wouldn't be good for any of us. I had to get out of this bullshit mansion. Away from this bullshit party. I had to breathe. I dashed down the endless landing. Dad darted after me.

"Don't do it, Gabs." Dad's voice was breathless from the exertion.

He caught up with me at the top of the staircase. Loud music pulsed up to us. Guests milled at the bottom of the steps, a couple of them glancing curiously in our direction. Dad's fingers wrapped around my wrist.

I ripped my arm free. "Don't touch me."

A warning flickered in his eyes; his voice was a low whisper. "Keep it down. People are looking."

A bitter laugh escaped me. He'd just been balls deep in my girlfriend and I was supposed to shut up and get over it. I had a girlfriend who lied and cheated and a father who would betray his own son. And that didn't even hurt as much as the fact that he didn't believe in me enough to hand over the reins to Calverdale United. Why the fuck not? What did I have to do to prove myself?

Dad gave an anxious cough and glanced down the steep white marble steps to the guests gathered below. He smoothed his hair. "I'm going back to the party. I suggest you—"

Grimacing, he clutched his chest. His knees buckled and he stumbled, piling into me. My back hit the banister, but I steadied him on the edge of the steps. He gasped for breath. Shit. That had been close. A couple of inches nearer the edge and he would have been a goner. He hunched over, his hands resting on his thighs.

6

"Are you okay?"

He straightened, then slumped into me. I tried to prop him back on his feet and twist him away from the edge of the stairs. His fingers dug into my shirt and he let out a low, unnatural groan.

A knot of anxiety twisted in my gut. "Dad?"

Taking a deep, unsteady breath, he pushed away from me to grab hold of the banister. Time slowed into something strange and unreal. Dad's legs buckled. This time I wasn't in the right place to catch him. My fingers slipped over red velvet at his back. A scream drifted up from the onlookers at the bottom of the steps. My stomach dropped to my knees.

He hit the bottom with a sickening thud before I could even process that he was falling.

Chapter 2

Miri

Present Day

Jed sat opposite me in the same dingy café where he'd told me about Rosie. He'd even chosen the same booth overlooking the dumpsters and the frost-slicked parking lot. I took a sip of dishwater coffee and pasted a smile onto my face. I still hated him, but I needed him to get me out of this mess with his cousin, so I'd have to play nice.

An angry-looking bruise marred his right eye. It looked out of place on his round, boyish face. He looked the same now as when he'd sat across from me in school all those years ago and asked me to help him practice his goal kicks.

"Who have you been fighting this time?" I asked.

"Why?" He flashed a rueful smile. "Are you offering to nurse me back to health?"

That smile would have made me melt before. Not now. That ship had sailed. Then, when it was done sailing, Jed had smashed the ship into smithereens and blown it up with dynamite.

"Haven't you got Rosie to do that for you?"

His eyes slipped away. The too-loud conversation of an elderly couple tucking into their fried breakfasts drifted to my ears. The stench of bacon fat turned my stomach.

Jed attacked a greasy sausage on his plate with his knife and fork. "Tell me you've got the money."

Ice bloomed in my gut. I opened my mouth and closed it again. The speech I'd prepared had fallen out of my head. What the hell was I going to do?

I swallowed past the lump in my throat. "I need a little more time."

"There is no more time."

Jed shoveled a forkful of baked beans into his mouth and threw them down like a prisoner on death row. Rosie probably had him on a diet. She'd always been controlling around food. I couldn't help but smile at the thought that there was trouble in paradise.

"I can't help you anymore." He flashed a glance over his shoulder before leaning across the booth, his voice low. "These are bad guys, Miri. They aren't the kind of guys that you keep waiting."

His knife scraped viciously on the plate. The sound set my nerves jangling. "What am I supposed to do? It's your bloody cousin. You said he wouldn't mind helping me out with a loan. Can't you talk to him?"

"Second cousin, and he doesn't want to talk. He wants his money."

"Give me a month."

He barked out a laugh and coughed on his sausage. "A month?"

"I can't get it any faster."

He wiped his mouth with the back of his hand and pushed his plate away. "I'm done, Miri. I can't keep them away from you anymore. You'll have to deal with them yourself. I'll tell Deano that you'll pay him in a month. I'm sure he'll drop in on you to discuss."

A prickle raced the length of my spine. "What?"

Bean juice dripped down his chin like a toddler. Gross. What had I ever seen in this man?

"I can't be the go-between anymore, Miri."

I grabbed his wrist, holding him still. "Money is so tight at the moment. I can get it, but I need time."

His grim gaze drifted over me. We'd been kids when we got together. He was the first man I'd kissed. The first man I'd slept with. The first, and last, man I'd let trample my heart. My resolve hardened. Never again. He cocked his head, looking at me like I was a dog he'd found on the side of the road and he couldn't decide whether to drive on or take me to a rescue shelter. Heaven forbid he took me home and looked after me.

"Please, Jed. I need your help."

"You're a grown woman, Miri. You knew what you were getting into when you took that loan."

"I was desperate after Mum's stroke. I thought I'd be able to pay it back . . ."

Jed mussed his stupid hair in his conceited way, his lips turned downward. "I wish I could help you, Miri."

No. You don't. You haven't even asked how my mum is.

"You *can* help. I just need time. That's all."

He scrubbed a hand over his face. "I'm sorry. I am. I'm sorry." He sighed and gave me a sheepish look. "You have to stop calling me. Rosie doesn't like me talking to you . . ."

I couldn't help my indignant snort. Oh dear. Poor Rosie. Was she feeling a little insecure? That's what you get if you sleep with someone else's boyfriend. What a fool. He'd do the same to her as he'd done to me. Not that I was bitter. They deserved each other.

I reached for his hand. "Don't throw me to the wolves. I need—"

"Don't." He tore his hand away and stood. "Save it for the wolves."

◆ ◆ ◆

"She's been brighter today," Frankie said.

I dropped into my usual chair next to Mum's hospital bed. Gently, I took the spoon from her shaking hand and lifted it to her mouth.

Mum clucked her tongue in annoyance. "I don't need . . . you to . . . feed me." Her voice was slow and slurred. "And . . . stop talking . . . about me like . . . I'm not . . . here. I'm not a baby." Mum's head flopped back down onto the pillow and her eyes flickered shut.

Frankie fiddled with the piercing in her nose. Her heavy boots jangled as she shuffled in her chair. "You're usually here earlier."

Guilt prickled my neck. I hated to miss a second of visiting hours. Mum got so bored now that she was getting back to herself. "I'm sorry. I was on the pitch. I came as soon as I could."

Better to skip the part that I met with Jed rather than come straight from training. My younger sister hated my ex even more than I did.

I pulled at my filthy football kit and straightened my socks over my shin pads. No doubt my face was splattered in dirt, too. Mud and sweat seared my nose. There hadn't been time to shower.

My brother Reece burst through the door, red-cheeked and breathless. Rain smeared his thick-framed black glasses and his dark peacoat brought the November chill.

He froze in the doorway when he saw Mum. "How is she?"

"She's . . . fine." Mum's eyes flashed open. "And she's here. Don't talk . . . about me as . . . if I'm not here. Read me . . . something . . . Miri. My eyes are . . . blurry."

Frankie frowned. "I can read you something."

11

A smile pulled at one side of Mum's face. "I like . . . hearing Miri read about fashion and . . . celebrities she's never heard of. It's . . . more entertaining."

I rolled my eyes, but amusement went through me. We'd come so far. For weeks after the stroke, I couldn't imagine Mum making jokes again. I took one of the glossy magazines from the pile and flicked through it, stopping on a picture of an impossibly handsome chestnut-haired man in a well-fitted suit.

Frankie's smile turned into a chuckle. She snatched the magazine. "Gabriel Rivers. This guy is such a prick."

Mum clucked her tongue. "Language."

Reece frowned. "Who's Gabriel Rivers?"

Frankie rolled up the magazine and swatted him on the arm with it. "What planet do you live on, Reece? Everybody knows who Gabe Rivers is. He's famous for being rich and pretty and shagging anything that moves. His dad was Micky Rivers. Haven't you listened to the podcast? *Hot Enough to Get Away with Murder*?"

Reece smiled blandly. "I must have missed that one."

"Micky Rivers fell down the stairs at one of his parties. The rumor is that Gabe Rivers pushed him, but it's never been proven. Imagine that? The ruthless bastard killed his own dad and got away with it." Frankie's mouth curved into an unconscious smile. "Anyway, he's so hot, I don't care if he did it. He definitely has BDE."

Mum's brows raised. "BDE?"

I took the magazine back from Frankie and leafed through it. "Don't ask."

"Big dick energy," Frankie said matter-of-factly.

A faint smile pulled at Mum's trembling lips. "Language," she said again.

Frankie threw up her hands. "You asked."

"Well, that's okay. As long as he's hot, what does it matter if he's a stone-cold killer?" Reece pushed his glasses up his nose and shot me a wry look. "Sounds like a classic womanizer—only capable of superficial relationships because he's seeking the love he never got from a parent. I doubt he has the skills necessary for true emotional intimacy."

I rolled my eyes. There was nothing worse than when Reece went into psychologist mode. "No one normal talks like this. It's weird."

A glint of humor flashed in Reece's eyes. "I've never claimed to be normal."

"Are you saying the man just needs to be loved?" Frankie's hand shot in the air. "I volunteer as tribute."

Humor threaded Mum's voice. "Me too."

"Mum!" Frankie threw her head back and let out a great peal of laughter. "I didn't know you had it in you. Is it because I mentioned the BDE?"

Mum clucked her tongue, but teasing laughter lit her tired eyes.

I adjusted her pillow and smoothed her hair. "You should rest now, Mum."

Frankie always got everyone all overexcited. Her laughter was infectious. Mum offered me a faint smile and closed her eyes. Rhythmic beeps and the chatter from the nurses' station drifted into the silence. I scrolled my phone, checking out the fixtures for this month. We had a couple of away games but not too many. I'd still have plenty of time to be at the hospital.

A soft snore drifted from the bed and we all stilled to watch Mum sleep. The bruises on her cheek still hadn't faded. Dark circles haunted her eyes. She looked so different asleep. So . . . ill. She'd always been fierce and in control. She'd spent a lifetime working as a psychotherapist; nothing shocked or fazed her. It was awful to see her so poorly.

I looked up to find my brother watching me. His dark, feeling eyes held too much compassion. You couldn't even have a normal conversation with Reece without him analyzing every word you said or didn't say. God knows how we'd all live back together in Mum's house when she came home. They'd drive me mad.

Reece smiled tentatively. "Have you been getting any sleep?"

"Yes," I lied.

"Are you eating?"

As if on cue, my stomach growled. "I'm fine."

"You look exhausted. Breakups can be tough, Miri. You were together for a long time. Can you take a break from training?"

"The team needs me."

"They need you to be well."

I shook my head. Football kept me going. Reece didn't get that.

I smoothed Mum's blanket and rubbed the crick in my neck. "Let's get Mum home. Then everything will be fine."

Reece nodded, but he didn't look convinced.

I picked up a medical chart from the end of the bed and rifled through it as if I'd have any idea of what any of it meant. There was still so much to plan for Mum to come home. "The hospital is delivering the hoist and the bed with rails tomorrow, but I need to sort out the wheelchair. The builders are coming to do the ramps. The caregivers need to confirm their schedule, but we're on track."

Oh God. This was all adding up. The NHS covered some of the costs, but not everything.

Reece pushed his glasses up his nose. "If you need more money then—"

"I don't. I'm handling it."

His eyes were gentle and contemplative. "I don't want you to have to do this alone."

My stomach churned. I hadn't been honest with Reece about how much of a strain this was financially. Reece's money was all tied up in his fancy house. He was trying to sell it since we were moving back home anyway, but until he did, he couldn't help. Besides, as the oldest, it was my job to keep everything together. Somehow, I'd have to figure out the money. I was in too deep now to drag anyone else down with me.

I offered my siblings the most reassuring smile I could manage. "Don't worry. I'm handling it."

Chapter 3

GABE

A knock sounded on the door to the penthouse. The digital alarm read 7 a.m. Nope. I wasn't getting out of bed before 9 a.m. on a Sunday for anyone.

"Fuck off," I shouted.

The door to my suite swung open and my mother stepped in. She was accompanied by a stern-faced blonde in a smart suit. The woman looked around the same age as Mother. Although Mother was hard to age accurately. She'd had so much cosmetic surgery she could have been anywhere between thirty and two hundred. You'd probably need carbon dating to be certain.

"What do you want, Mother?"

A smile stretched her lips; her eyes narrowed. "Can't I check on my son's welfare?"

Of course. There's a first time for everything.

She gestured to the woman next to her. "This is Claire Easterly."

The blonde woman averted her gaze while I pulled on a robe. "A pleasure to meet you, Mr. Rivers."

I bit back a sarcastic retort. Nothing was pleasurable where my mother was concerned. Whoever Claire was, this wasn't going to be good news.

"It's Gabe." I shook Claire's hand and turned to my mother. "And today is Sunday. I don't work on Sundays."

Mother stiffened and pulled a magazine out of her enormous handbag. "Yes. It's Sunday. I don't want to work either, but like most days of the week, I'm spending it dealing with your mess." She threw the magazine on the bed. "I take it you've seen this?"

An unrecognizable woman stared at me from the front page. The headline read: Exclusive—My Night in Heaven with Gabriel Rivers.

"I don't know who that is."

"Well, she seems to know you . . . *intimately*."

I opened the magazine and scanned the article. A dim flare of recognition registered somewhere. The flight attendant? We'd dated a few times when I was in New York. Disappointing. She hadn't seemed the type to kiss and tell. Then again, they never did.

I threw the magazine back on the bed. "It could have been worse. It looks like a good review."

"You're a human being, not a Tripadvisor listing. You shouldn't be proud of getting five stars." She pulled out her phone and presented the screen to me. She scrolled through a blur of news stories. "There are more. A stream of women desperate to sell their stories . . ."

How was any of this my fault? "The tabloids won't get off my arse."

Mother's brow lifted a fraction. "It needs to stop."

A sarcastic smile pulled at my lips. As if I had any control over what the tabloids decided to write about me. "Fine. I'll join a monastery if you like."

Mother lowered her designer sunglasses to glare at me. Purple bruises and swelling covered the bridge of her nose and surrounded her eyes. Disapproval radiated from her imposing frame in waves.

She always looked at me like I was a bird-shit stain on her favorite Balenciaga bag.

"Nobody is expecting you to be a monk, darling. You just need to date women within your own tax bracket." Her words were playful, but the meaning wasn't. "We miss Emma. Why won't you talk to her? Emma would never sell you out like this."

I turned my face away. After the fall, everything had happened so quickly. Mother had been devastated. My head was a mess and I'd made a snap decision. Learning the truth about what I'd seen that night in Dad's office would have destroyed Mother. She'd loved Emma like a daughter.

"It's never going to happen with Emma."

A tiny line appeared at the top of Mother's nose. She looked disappointed, or maybe hungry. It was hard to tell with the Botox. Mother sauntered to the window. Claire hovered awkwardly by the couch. She eyed me with a wary expression. Why was this woman even here?

Mother sniffed a bunch of roses in the vase by the window and frowned. "These flowers aren't fresh."

"If you think that's bad, don't try the mushroom soup. I suspect it's from a tin. Was there anything else?"

She kept her gaze focused on the flowers. Her tone was velvet edged with steel. "I need you to keep out of the press. It's embarrassing. I'm spinning a lot of plates here. I have donors pulling out of the foundation. I'm selling off these awful sex clubs and cleaning up the Rivers name. It doesn't help when you're determined to follow in your father's footsteps. Reputation is everything, Gabe. Yours is . . . not good."

My stomach hardened. "So, we're back to the monastery?"

"The tabloids have been obsessed with you ever since your father . . ." She paused, twisting to pierce me with her stare. "Your behavior is giving the press precisely what they want. I don't know what to do with you. Is this because I didn't give you the team? You're punishing me?"

Of course it wasn't. Did she think I was that petty?

She cast her eyes downward. "You understand why I couldn't do it? Take on that team and everybody would scrutinize your every move. I am protecting you. Calverdale United was your father's baby. He didn't think you were ready."

Well done, Mother. Such a talent for stating the obvious. Dad had made it abundantly clear that he didn't want me to have his team. "Yes. I know."

She watched me with keenly observant eyes. "But a lot has happened since then. Maybe it's time . . ."

My chest lit with warmth. Time for what? Time to hand over the reins? I stumbled over the bedframe as I rushed to her side.

"Yes. I'm ready. I can do this. This is all I've wanted for so long."

"Fine. Fine. Don't get too excited, darling." Mother held up a hand to silence me and transferred her gaze to Claire. "That's why Claire is here. I'm going to give you the opportunity to prove yourself."

I searched her inscrutably smooth face for a hint of her latest scheme. "Fine? What do you mean, fine? I can have the team?"

She offered me a faint smile. Her eyes were full of half promises. "You can have *a* team."

Chapter 4

Gabe

My brogues sank into mud as I trailed over an endless soggy field with my mother and Claire. A fog-shrouded football pitch lay in the distance. Shouts and cheers from the game in progress drifted on the wind. This wasn't Calverdale United's training ground. It had to be an away game.

Mother groaned as she flicked a spot of dirt from her cashmere coat. "Why can't they do these things inside?"

Claire shot her a bemused look but kept her mouth shut. As we drew closer, I noticed the bobbing ponytails. Women. Why had Mother dragged me out of bed to watch women's football?

A frown pulled at my brow. "What's going on?"

"This is Claire's team. Claire is the manager of Calverdale Ladies."

Right. So what? Why the fuck did I care about this?

Mother shot me a sidelong glance. "You're their new director."

I froze a little way from the sidelines. The women's team? No way. This had to be a fucking joke.

A mischievous glint flashed in Mother's eyes. "You want a chance to prove you can direct a football team. What better way? You get to throw yourself in without all the pressure, and if you handle it well, then everybody will know that you're ready for a bigger challenge."

Ice laced my stomach. No. Mother was the devil incarnate, but she wouldn't screw me over this badly.

"I'm sure you're a little surprised, but this could be a fantastic opportunity."

"But I don't know anything about women's football."

"Careful, Gabe. Your misogyny is showing." Her mouth twisted wryly. "The funny thing is that it's exactly the same, except there are fewer penises."

I managed to reply through stiff lips. "This isn't about misogyny. It's about the fact that I should be directing the best team in England and you're giving me a shit team that nobody has heard of."

Claire Easterly coughed awkwardly. "If I may, my girls are incredible athletes. They are dedicated and hardworking. These women don't play for money and ego and fast cars. They play for the love of the game. This is real football. If you give us a chance, you'll see."

My brain reeled. Maybe this was a joke. The last I'd heard, the women were terrible. "But you're not even in a decent league, are you? These are part-timers. Your games aren't televised."

Claire kept her gaze fixed on the match in progress. "We are in the Championship League. It's only one league below the top. But we want to work. With investment, we have a brilliant chance of promotion to the Women's Super League. Then we'll be taken seriously as professionals."

Mother lowered her sunglasses and surveyed me. "The women don't get a fraction of the investment and time the men get. It's an injustice and I want to put it right. Your dad only wanted a women's team because he wanted to give the appearance of a modern organization. You could take this team and make something great."

A pulse pounded in my temples. This was unacceptable. "Calverdale United is the best team in the Premier League. I've waited my entire life to—"

"Or you could see this as a challenge, darling." Mother flapped a dismissive hand and turned her attention back to the pitch. "If you applied yourself to something useful the way you've applied yourself to chasing women this past year, you could achieve something incredible."

Anger burned my throat. Bull. Shit. This was utter bullshit. I'd been down this road with Dad, jumping through every hoop in the hopes he might finally relent and give me what I wanted. No. It was too much. Mother would string me along like Dad had.

I folded my arms. "No."

Mother's eyes narrowed in warning. "I'm throwing you a lifeline. You can't carry on like this. It's embarrassing. I'd hate to have to issue an ultimatum."

I snorted. Mother would love nothing more than to issue an ultimatum. "Dad did this to me. He made me promise after promise and then he kept moving the goalposts."

"I'm not like your father. Keep your name out of the papers. We'll get the best PR and clean up your image. No partying. No gold diggers. Show me that you can commit to a change, and I'll give you what you want. Or . . ." She transferred her gaze to the match.

"Or what?"

"I don't know, Gabe. What am I supposed to do with you? If you won't fall in line, then maybe it's time you learned the hard way. No more allowance. No more penthouse suite with every whim catered to. Maybe we've spoilt you too much. It hasn't done you any favors."

Mother was always threatening to "cut me off." Maybe she'd go through with it; maybe it was an empty threat. It wasn't worth the risk of testing her. Life was cushy living in a hotel. *My* hotel.

A roar of applause went up from the opposing sideline. A pretty, mud-splattered girl with a bouncing blonde ponytail had possession of the ball. She raced past two opposition players and danced past a third, then placed the ball with fluid grace past the keeper. It was a beautiful goal. Any idiot could swing a foot and bang the ball into the top corner, but it took skill to keep the ball at your feet. Another roar of celebration erupted from the opposing sideline. Claire winced.

Mother raised a questioning eyebrow. "What's happened? Was that good?"

"The other side scored. It's not good," Claire said dryly.

Nope. Nothing about the Calverdale Ladies team was good. It wasn't their fault if they hadn't had investment. In fact, it was a travesty. We had the best men's team in the country and our women's team was languishing in the amateur league.

The rest of the opposition players in red shirts piled on top of their goal-scoring number seven. A beaming smile lit her face. The ball came back into play and she got possession of it immediately. She dominated the pitch. She wasn't just fast, but an intelligent player, too. Number seven dashed the length of the pitch, but a much bigger Calverdale player barged her with a mean, dirty slide tackle. They both went down. The referee didn't blow her whistle. What the fuck? It was clearly a penalty.

I threw my hands in the air. "Ref!"

The blonde number seven didn't wait around. She was on her feet in a flash, regaining possession of the ball and scoring another effortless goal. The opposing sideline erupted with a jubilant celebration.

23

"Bloody Miri Forster," Claire muttered. "We should be winning this. The Swans are below us in the table. They are part-timers, but they have Miri Forster. She's head and shoulders above any player I've ever seen."

"Number seven?"

Claire nodded and patted her gloved hands together. "She's good enough to play for England."

"Why doesn't she?"

Claire shrugged. "I've tried to bring her on board. She won't hear of it."

A young man in a ball cap and leather jacket appeared. Another guy stood next to him, balancing a camera on his shoulder. My jaw tensed. How had the paparazzi tracked us down here?

Mother followed my gaze and smiled smoothly. "I invited them. We're making a documentary. The PR team suggested it would be good for your image."

My teeth gritted. Like hell I was making a documentary. "Nope."

Mother put a hand on my arm. "This is your perfect redemption arc. Gabriel Rivers taking over a women's football team. You smile and give them some nice sound bites. You won't notice them."

"Except I don't need a redemption arc, because I haven't done anything wrong."

"Well. Yes. Of course you haven't, darling. We all know that." A thin tight smile stretched her lips. "You know the tabloids love to make up their stories. Villains sell papers. We need to work on your brand. Your image needs some . . . rehabilitation."

The papers had chosen my brand. I'd stopped going on social media. I'd watched my own father die and then had to live through a bunch of wankers speculating on TikTok about whether I'd pushed him. My own fucking father. Some idiots had made a podcast about it. I'd inspired a million Reddit threads. At least the lawyers had managed to shut down the Netflix series.

There were serial killers with brands more redeemable than mine.

Mother gave me a placating smile, but her voice held a silken threat of warning. "It's not negotiable, Gabe. We discussed this. We need to clean up your image. It's going to take a miracle without a lot of work."

"I don't like the cameras."

"You need to take back control of the narrative. It's the only way to stop the lies."

I sighed and returned my attention to the blonde as she tackled an opposition player effortlessly and ran the length of the pitch with the ball at her feet as though she'd been born to do it. God, she was good. If Claire Easterly wanted her team to be the best, she needed a player like this. I'd been scouting talent for years. Some people were born with a gift. It was a spark that made no sense. This girl was a world-class player. She also looked like a goddess. She lifted her shirt to wipe her brow, revealing a flash of her white sports bra and a perfectly sculpted stomach. My mouth went dry. Those long, toned legs in those little red shorts were a nice image to store away for later when I got back to my suite.

A roar went up again as the blonde fired the ball straight into the back of the net. A triumphant smile lit her face, and she took off in a victory sprint. Her teammates rushed for her, but she sprinted too fast. She whipped off her T-shirt, flinging it round her head. Her tits bounced deliciously in her white sports bra. I fought to tear my gaze away from her tempting athletic physique. Maybe being involved with women's football wasn't the worst thing in the world if the players looked like this.

"How long do you expect me to do this before you give me the men's team?"

From the corner of my eye, I saw a smile pull at Mother's lips. She liked winning. Like mother, like son. "Get them promoted to the next league. Then you can have the men's team."

I whipped my head to study her face. Did she mean that? Calverdale United was all that mattered. I'd loved them ever since I could walk and kick a football. I'd lived the dream of every little kid who'd ever loved the game—I'd met my heroes and had drunken nights in the pub singing my heart out with football legends. I'd stood in the terraces, in rain or shine, chanting with the fans through countless victories and defeats.

Football was the only thing I'd excelled at as a kid. When I booted the ball into the back of the net, it always coaxed a smile from Dad. My best memories were the two of us at the stadium on match days. Calverdale United had been his baby. I'd assumed that one day he'd trust me enough with his pride and joy.

I could do this. I could get these women promoted, and get my hands on Calverdale United. If you threw enough money at something, you could do anything. With this girl on the team, it wouldn't take long.

I dusted my hands together. "Right. Fine. Let's get this done. Leave it to me."

Claire shot me a questioning look. "You've made a decision?"

"Yep. I'm all in. One hundred percent. Let's do this. First order of business, we get this number seven playing for us."

Claire took a deep breath and adjusted her smile. "It won't be that easy. I told you. I've been trying—"

"Leave it to me. If we need Mary Forster, then I'll get you Mary Forster."

"It's Miri," Claire said.

"Right. Mary. Miri. Whatever. I want this girl."

"Don't even think about it." Mother shot me a withering look. "Every woman is an employee. You can't lay a finger on any of them. If you do, it's got sexual harassment case written all over it. This is a new start for you. No more stories in the press."

"Of course. I'm capable of professional relationships. I want this girl for the team, that's all. I'm taking this seriously."

Lies. I wanted her bent over my desk. Technically, this woman wasn't my employee since she wasn't even on the team yet. I could do what I wanted until then. And what Mother didn't know couldn't hurt her. No reason I couldn't have her on my team. If I played it right, everything I wanted was within my grasp. I could get this woman on my team and in my bed and be directing the men's team within a couple of months. A smug smile curved my lips.

Maybe it was worth getting out of bed on a Sunday morning more often.

Chapter 5

Miri

"Miri? Can we have a word?"

An enormous camera appeared from nowhere. Claire Easterly stood awkwardly in front of me. We'd met a few times before when she'd been courting me for her team. A handsome chestnut-haired man towered next to Claire. Expensive-looking sunglasses shielded his gaze and a well-fitted suit hugged his lean frame deliciously. What idiot wore sunglasses in November?

Claire offered me a tentative smile. "Hi, Miri, great to see you again. I wanted to introduce you to some colleagues of mine. This is Joyce and Gabe Rivers."

The smartly dressed woman at Claire's side offered me her hand and spoke in a plummy tone. "Hello, darling. You don't mind if we film this, do you?"

Film what? And Gabe Rivers? As in *the* Gabe Rivers? What was a celebrity doing at a Sunday morning training session? Gabe perched his sunglasses on his perfectly tousled hair and his bright-green eyes met mine. I'd never spotted a celebrity in the wild. He was so much taller than he looked in the news. He had the kind of dazzling good looks that were best viewed through a pinhole camera like during an eclipse, in case the full force of him blinded you.

"Nice to meet you. We were watching you play. You're talented, Marie." His cool, clipped accent spoke of private schools, rowing clubs, and privilege.

I hated him already.

Claire coughed. "Miri," she whispered.

A muscle worked in Gabe's jaw. "Miri. I apologize. Is there somewhere we can talk in private?"

He shook my hand firmly. A warming spark crept up my wrist from his touch. My heart hammered, which only served to annoy me. If I was going to get starstruck by anyone, it should be a celebrity who was famous for something important, like curing cancer or hashing out some Middle East peace agreement—not for being so hot he could get away with murder. This guy might have been an A-list celebrity, but he was also a grade-A prick.

His glance was bemused. "Are you okay?"

I cleared my throat and tried to steady my racing heartbeat. "Fine."

"I'm taking you to lunch."

What? I glanced at my watch. No. Soon it would be visiting hours at the hospital. The guy holding the camera stepped closer. The back of my neck itched with embarrassment. Was this going to be on TV? I swiped my brow with the back of one hand and smoothed my ponytail with the other. Why were they filming me? I couldn't just stand around here feeling stupid. At this rate, I'd have to skip a shower and run to the hospital to see Mum.

I blurted the first words that came into my head. "I need to go to the hospital."

His dark brow rose a fraction. "Why? Are you unwell? Is something wrong?"

"No. Thank you . . . No . . . Not with me . . . No . . . Look. This has been . . ." *Awkward.* "But I have to go."

He stared back at me. He had extraordinary green eyes, flecked and ringed with gold. My pulse pounded. I set off, desperate to put some distance between us and to stop this sudden strange disconnect between my brain and my mouth. I didn't get flustered. I'd taken penalties that could win or lose the match in front of huge crowds. This wasn't me.

Gabe matched my strides. "I want you."

My neck heated. "What?"

"For the club. I'm the new director of Calverdale Ladies."

I froze. "You are? Since when?"

"Since about half an hour ago, and you thrashed us. I want you as our new striker. You're my first order of business."

Not this again. How many times did I have to tell Claire Easterly no? I wouldn't sign with Calverdale if it was the last club on earth. Claire and the cameraman caught up to us. Another guy held a microphone on a long stick, angling it right under my nose. A knot of nerves tightened in my stomach. Was I about to be in some crummy reality show? That's what this was. Gabe Rivers couldn't seriously care about women's football. It had to be a gimmick.

"I'm not interested," I said.

"Why not?"

I held Claire's gaze. *She* knew why. Everybody at that team turned a blind eye to Jerry Reynolds' behavior, but I couldn't. I had no time to go into it all now.

I threw my hands up with impatience. "Because . . . reasons."

A line appeared between Gabe's brows. He smiled blandly. "You have to give me a reason."

I couldn't help my incredulous snort. Do I, now?

"I want you on my team. Name your price."

"It's not about money."

"Everything is about money."

"Maybe for people like you."

30

There was a faint glint of humor in his eyes. Was he laughing at me?

"You need to give me something to work with. Tell me the problem."

A prickle of annoyance made me straighten my spine. He might have been hotter than hell, but entitlement and privilege oozed from every pore of this man's being. "I don't *need* to give you anything."

I kept walking. Gabe dodged in front of me, towering over me, blocking my path. His charming smile lit his handsome face. "We've got off on the wrong foot. Let me take you for lunch. We can talk about whatever the issue is."

"No. Thank you. I'm busy today."

"Then when?"

"I'm always busy."

I dodged around him, and the cameraman chased after me. My heart pounded too hard. I'd never liked being in the spotlight. I held a hand up to shield myself. "Can you get that thing out of my face, please?"

A guy in a ball cap and leather jacket stepped forward and shoved the microphone too close to my mouth. "What do you think of Gabe?"

I said the first thing that popped into my head. "I think he's a bit of a prick."

The guy in the ball cap frowned. "Cut!"

Gabe's dark chuckle chased me across the muddy field. "I'd say that went well."

Ice water stole my breath. Every muscle in my body screamed with pain. Gritting my teeth, I submerged myself deeper into the freezing tub. I took a deep breath, steeling myself not to make a sound. None of us wanted to do the ice baths; they were terrible. But we needed to keep injuries to a minimum if we were all going to get through this season in one piece. Phoebe dipped a toe in the other end of the bath and plunged in with a sharp cry. I drew my knees close to my chest to make room for both of us. She took deep breaths before she spoke, teeth chattering.

"What the hell was all that outside? Was that a camera crew? Verity said that Gabe Rivers is out there. *The* Gabe Rivers."

"He is. I called him a prick on TV."

Phoebe burst out laughing. "Why?"

I shrugged, annoyed with myself. "I don't know. There were cameras . . . It was all so surreal . . . and it slipped out."

Phoebe's grin was infectious. I couldn't help but chuckle along with her.

Shivering, I rested my chin on my knees. "He's the new director of Calverdale. He wants me for the team."

The laughter died on Phoebe's lips. "You're kidding?"

"I told him no, obviously."

Phoebe's gaze fixed on the row of lockers behind me. She wore a wounded, faraway expression. "You're not even going to think about it? This is your career. It's an incredible opportunity."

"It's a sham. He had a camera crew with him. I'm not getting involved in a circus like that. Besides, everything that happened with Jerry . . . It's the principle of it."

Phoebe's face dropped and I regretted even mentioning his name. She'd had it worse than me. Jerry worked as a talent scout for Calverdale United and had spent time with us when we were juniors in the Academy. He was a filthy old pervert, but he'd taken a special interest in Phoebe. She'd been so young—too young and inexperienced to recognize the manipulations of an older man.

Speaking out about Jerry had cost me everything. He'd made it his mission to block my progress to the professional league, and my career had faltered at every turn. Now, every day was a struggle to make ends meet, and it had gotten so much worse since Mum's stroke.

Phoebe shuddered with the cold and transferred her gaze back to me. "Talk to them, at least. They must be serious if they sent bloody Gabe Rivers down here. I can't believe it."

Of course it would be incredible if this was a serious offer. I'd get another shot at the dream I'd had to tuck away in a drawer a long time ago. I wouldn't have this constant cloud of worry about money hanging over my head. Money couldn't make you happy, but it could sure as hell make life easier. Still, I couldn't do it to Phoebe and all those women that Jerry had targeted and harassed. I wouldn't go anywhere near Jerry Reynolds—or a club that turned a blind eye to his behavior—even if it meant sabotaging my career.

"No." I grabbed her hand and squeezed it. "They can send Cristiano Ronaldo down here with a loofah to scrub my back in the shower and it's still a no."

Phoebe shot me a thoughtful look. "What was he like? The word on the street is that he inherited more than just his father's wealth, if you know what I mean." She raised a suggestive eyebrow.

"No. I don't know what you mean."

"Micky Rivers starred in all those dirty movies before he started making them. He was famous for his enormous—"

"Stop." I held up my hand. "I don't want to hear it."

Phoebe gripped the edge of the tub, raising herself up and taking deep shuddering breaths. "Have you heard anything from Jed?"

Jed. From enormous dicks to enormous dickheads. "It's over. We want different things. He wants to shag around behind my back, and I want a boyfriend that isn't a total bastard."

She flashed me a sympathetic smile. "His loss."

I sighed. I didn't want to talk about Jed. Ice water sloshed everywhere as I lifted out of the bath in one fluid motion. Pins and needles raced over my body at the sudden change in temperature. I dressed quickly and stuffed my dirty kit into my duffel bag. If I hurried, I'd still get the most out of visiting hours. I charged out of the changing rooms and straight into something solid.

"Watch where you're going, sweetheart."

A squat man with a beaky nose blocked the narrow corridor outside of the changing rooms. He regarded me with a mean twist of his thin lips.

"Excuse me." I stepped around him.

He moved back in front of me. "Miri, isn't it? I'm Deano, Jed's cousin."

He rubbed the back of his hand across his mouth and glanced over his shoulder. He flashed a cold, hard-eyed smile. "You owe me . . ."

"I know. I'm sorry. I can get it . . . Give me a couple of days."

His gaze drifted from my trainers and lingered on my chest. I pulled my team jacket tighter.

"Nah. That don't work for me. You've had enough time, but it's fine, the two of us can come up with an alternative arrangement."

He reached into the back pocket of his jeans and pulled out a business card with the words *Purple Leopard* embossed in gold on a black background. "I own a strip joint. A girl that looks like you would do well. You can work off the debt dancing."

I took the card from him, turning it over in my hands. "Me? No. I don't dance."

His lascivious gaze swept over me. "Just keep your trap shut with the customers. You look like a classy bird until you open your mouth and that voice comes out."

My lips thinned with anger. "Excuse me?"

"You're going to have to rein your accent in a bit."

34

My temper flared. I didn't let people intimidate me on the pitch. I wouldn't let them bully me off it, either. The only way to deal with bullies was to let them know you wouldn't stand for it. It wasn't a good idea to go toe to toe with a man that looked like this, but I'd have to put him in his place. He looked mean, but he was still just Jed's cousin. "And you might need to rein in your bullshit. I'm not dancing, and there's nothing wrong with my accent. I'll get your money my own way."

His laugh raked me. "Jed said you were a firecracker. No worries. The punters like a girl with a bit of spirit. It's not the girls with the best moves that earn the most. It's the girls with the best chat." He tipped his head in a nod. "I'll see you tonight at 7 p.m."

"Don't be ridiculous. You don't want me for this." I swung my arms out in exasperation. "Look at me. I don't even own a dress."

"We've got dresses. You'd better be there."

A little prickle crept up my spine. This was getting out of hand. "You'll be waiting all night. I'm not coming."

His mouth took on an unpleasant twist. "Has Jed told you much about me?"

"Just that you're his cousin. Listen, I know that—"

His vicious expression silenced me. "You don't want to piss me off, Miri. That's the last thing you want to do."

He couldn't really mean to make me go through with this, could he? Jed had been a lousy boyfriend, but he was harmless enough. He wouldn't put me in a dangerous situation. If Deano was anything like Jed, he was all talk. I could handle him. I just had to be firm. "I'll get the money, but I'm not dancing."

"Yes." He leaned in, tilting his face toward mine so close my nose filled with his smell of petrol and cigarettes. Malice filled his eyes. "You are, and if you don't show, there will be consequences."

"What consequences?"

His eyes were flat and hard. "Bad ones."

I opened my mouth and closed it again. This wasn't good. Maybe being firm wasn't the right approach, but what was? What answer could possibly make this situation better? There was no way I could do it. It's not like he could force me. He was menacing as hell, but this was still Jed's cousin. He wouldn't hurt me. He'd have to wait for his money, whether he liked it or not.

Deano gave me a brief nod and sauntered away. His cold words lingered in the air long after he'd left.

"Don't mess me about, Miri. I don't like being messed about."

Chapter 6

MIRI

My eyes burned with exhaustion. I hadn't slept after my conversation with Deano last night. He couldn't have actually been expecting me to show up on a Sunday night? A tense knot resided in my stomach and wouldn't let me relax. There was no way I could contemplate Deano's demands. Stripping was not an option. Getting up in front of people and dancing naked wasn't even something I could imagine. It just wasn't me.

I spent Monday morning in the gym trying to shift my foreboding with exercise. Later that afternoon, I lowered myself into an ice bath next to Phoebe after training. My teeth chattered and chills raced all over my skin. I sucked in breaths, trying to calm myself enough to tell Phoebe what was going on. She was my closest friend. The only person outside of my family that I trusted. I couldn't tell anyone else. They'd only worry.

Phoebe gave me a small smile. "So, hear me out . . . I have this friend. I've been wanting to set you up on a date—"

"Absolutely not." My body shuddered; I spoke through gritted teeth. "That's the last thing I need. There's something going on that I need to talk to you—"

"It's the best thing for a breakup. You need to get back out there. Nothing serious. Have some fun."

"No. Listen, Phoebe, I . . ."

I opened my mouth, battling to find the right words to explain what an absolute mess I'd made. Phoebe frowned and studied my face.

"Is it your mum? Is everything okay?"

"No. It's something else . . ."

My heart pounded. I'd have to tell her. She'd offer me the money, which would be embarrassing and awful, but still, better to owe Phoebe than a loose cannon like Deano.

"Phoebe, I've messed up. It's cost so much to get the house ready for Mum to come home, so I—"

My phone buzzed on the bench by the lockers. My nerves tensed. I eased out of the bath. Frankie's face flashed on the phone screen.

Mum.

I jumped out of the tub, wrapped a towel around myself, and answered the phone. Muffled conversations, beeping, and moaning filled my ears. My heart sank.

"Frankie? Is it Mum? What—"

"It's not Mum." Frankie's voice cracked with tears. "It's Reece. You need to come to the hospital."

I burst into the emergency room. Reece sat up in bed and Frankie hovered over him. Swelling and shining bruises marred my brother's face. Fresh blood splattered his crisp white shirt. Reece reached for a cup of water and it shook in his hands, spilling over the top. Blood crusted his knuckles.

A faint wry smile graced his lips when he caught the look of horror that must have been etched on my face. "You should see the state of the other guy."

"What happened?"

Reece sighed, his voice thin and tired. "I'm okay. It looks worse than it is. I can't go through it all again. Frankie, can you fill her in? And can someone get me a sandwich or something?"

"We'll be back in a minute." Frankie took my elbow and guided me out of the room and past the bays full of patients toward the foyer.

"I found him like that on the front step. He got jumped by some guys." Frankie shot me a sidelong glance and tongued at her lip ring. "Who the fuck is Deano?"

Noise and the greasy aroma of fries hit me as we entered the crowded cafeteria. My blood turned to ice. "What?"

"The guy said, 'Tell Miri this is a message from Deano.'" We slid into hard-backed plastic chairs. "So, who the fuck is Deano? And what the hell is going on?"

My stomach dropped to my knees. Oh God. No. It couldn't be. Deano had done this? This was my fault. My sensible, straitlaced brother had been beaten up because of me.

Frankie folded her arms and gave me a belligerent look. "Spit it out. You're hiding something. You've been shifty for weeks."

My throat ached with tears. I'd done this. I'd put my own brother in the hospital. Reece was such a gentle soul. He'd never even been in a fight before. How terrifying it must have been for him. Heat pressed behind my eyes. I cradled my head in trembling hands. There was no point in lying. This had escalated beyond anything I could handle. Deano had come for my family and not me. Oh God. This couldn't be happening.

Frankie's hand on my elbow made me jump. Her voice was softer than I deserved. "What's going on, Miri?"

39

I wiped my tears with the back of my hand. The words spilled out. "Deano is Jed's cousin. When I needed money, Jed told me that his cousin would lend it to me. I thought he was just a guy that loaned money. I didn't realize he was dodgy . . ."

Frankie frowned and fiddled with the silver ring in her nose. "A guy that does loans? What are you talking about? You know Jed's family is full of drug dealers and criminals. How much?"

I bit my lip until it throbbed like a pulse. "Ten grand . . . that's without the interest. It's twelve grand now."

Frankie paled. She slapped her palms down on the table and shook her head in utter disbelief. "Twelve grand?"

"I know. This is bad. I messed up. I couldn't tell anyone."

"I have some money from my student loan. Elliot will have some, too."

Elliot? Oh God. I couldn't drag my other brother into this too. A choked, desperate laugh escaped me. "No, this is my mess—"

"Not anymore. Now it's Reece's problem, and my problem." Frankie twisted a saltshaker frantically in her hand. "We need to get this paid off right now."

No one could make this money in a week. Oh God. We were screwed. Now I'd dragged everyone else into this. I was supposed to be sorting it out.

I held my tears in check. "Deano told me I can work it off dancing." It sounded ridiculous even as I spoke the words.

Frankie merely stared back at me.

"He owns a strip club. He wanted me to come in last night. I said no."

Frankie sat still, her expression grim. "Oh my God, Miri. You can't."

I leaned back in the chair and folded my arms. Heaviness centered in my chest as the reality settled over me. I had to do this, whether I wanted to or not. "He'll come back for us again. I've run out of time."

Frankie leaned across the table toward me, a glint of steel in her eyes. "I'll do it."

I could no longer hold back the tears. It was just like my younger sister to come to the rescue. I wouldn't allow it. "No. This is my responsibility."

"It could be dangerous. These places are seedy. They attract shitheads. There's no way I'm putting you in that situation."

"I can look after myself."

"But it's so not *you*."

Despite the dire situation, I couldn't help my dark chuckle. "What? You don't think I can be sexy?"

She flashed a smile, but it didn't reach her eyes. "It's the worst idea I've ever heard. You look like a newborn foal when you walk in heels."

"A sexy foal?"

"No. A foal walking over a very thin ice sheet." She offered me a tremulous smile.

Silence fell between us. The chatter from the canteen filled my ears.

"I have to do this, Frankie. I screwed up. I won't let anyone I care about get hurt. I have to get us out of this."

She reached across the table and gripped my hand. "I'm coming with you."

"No."

"I'm not letting you go alone."

I tried to swallow the lump that lingered in my throat. "I can't do it with you there. Please. I need to sort this out. Let me fix this."

"It's not up for debate. I'm waiting in the car outside for you. But will you do me a favor?" Frankie fiddled with her eyebrow ring, her tone laced with quiet emphasis. "Next time you even contemplate doing something so utterly, ridiculously, absolutely daft as borrowing money from Jed's shithead cousin, speak to me first."

Chapter 7

Gabe

Whisky seared its burning path down my throat. Three drinks still hadn't budged the heavy feeling that gripped me in Dad's mansion. We should have sold the place. Mother had insisted we keep it. She wanted to hold on to the memories of the good times. It didn't matter that it made me sick to my stomach anytime I glimpsed the staircase. I'd never left the ground floor since that night.

A firm grip on my elbow pulled me out of my reverie. Mother raised an expectant eyebrow and snatched the glass out of my hand. "You've had enough of those. Why aren't you mingling, darling?"

Because I can't be bothered. Because I'm sick of your demands. Yesterday she'd dragged me out of bed on a Sunday morning to watch women's football, and today it was a party I had no interest in. Mother smiled through thin lips and waved at a couple of men in suits. She lowered her voice to a hiss. "I hate those bastards. This party is a charm offensive. The foundation is falling apart. I need you on your best behavior."

I put a hand over my heart and spoke in a bland, innocent tone. "I'm doing my best. I've just been snorting coke off a stripper's arse in the cloakroom. I'm planning on setting fire to a few things later."

She raised an unimpressed eyebrow. "I don't like your jokes, Gabe."

"Yes. I understand you're not a fan of humor."

That's when I saw her. Emma swanned into the reception room swathed in an elegant jade dress, a glass of champagne in her hand. A wave of conflicting emotions passed over me. My throat burned with anger and disappointment.

Mother craned her neck and gave Emma an enthusiastic wave.

"What are you doing?" I hissed.

"I'm saying hello to Emma, darling."

"Why?"

"Because Emma and I got on like a house on fire. It's not my fault you break the heart of every woman unlucky enough to cross your path."

Emma sashayed around, greeting friends. She moved like a dancer, with grace and power. How had she had the audacity to come back here? Our paths hadn't crossed since *that night*. She raised her head and our eyes locked. She frowned and her gaze slipped away. Numbness smothered me.

Emma stopped to talk to a tall man in a tux. He slipped his arm around her waist, pulled her close, and kissed her.

Mother clucked her tongue in annoyance. "That one was a keeper, darling. You let yourself down when you let her go."

People began to dance. I watched Emma and her new man join in the fun. Despite everything, I hadn't wanted people's last memories of Dad to be jaded by that night. Everyone had assumed that I'd jilted Emma. All kinds of nasty rumors were flying round. Not only had I pushed my father down the stairs, I'd dumped the world's most beloved movie star. I downed the rest of my whisky. It only served to make my stomach twist with nausea. The raucous sounds of laughter and music filled the air.

Mother's face softened as much as it could. "Your father always liked a good party."

A grim, scratchy feeling filled my chest. He would have loved tonight. Yes. We were surrounded with all the things closest to Dad's heart—booze, revelry, and women.

Mother took a sip of her champagne and grimaced. "Are you still sulking about the team?"

I wouldn't give her the satisfaction of thinking she'd bothered me. "I don't sulk."

Mum peered over my shoulder as if looking for someone more interesting to talk to. The floor was packed with happy, smiling couples. For some reason, the hot blonde I'd seen playing football yesterday drifted through my mind. She'd been pink-cheeked and covered in mud and still she'd been mesmerizing. The things I could do to a woman with a body like that. Still, she was going to be a challenge to win over. She had the no-nonsense, flinty vibe of the locals around her, and she seemed like a woman who didn't take any bullshit. I'd have to find a new strategy to win her over. She'd want something, even if it wasn't money. I gave in to a small smile. I'd always enjoyed a challenge.

Loud music grated my ears. The smile dropped from my lips and a bead of sweat rolled down the back of my neck. I pulled the collar of my shirt, suddenly feeling too hot. I couldn't shift the ache that had settled in my chest since I'd watched Emma glide across the room as if she was on the red carpet. The booze had hit, but not in a good, happy way. I needed to get out of here. Nobody liked a depressing drunk.

"I'll go and do the rounds."

"Remember to smile, won't you?" Mother gave me one last unimpressed glance before she drifted off to mingle.

◆ ◆ ◆

Outside, a group of drivers was gathered near the gazebo.

A tall, slim man in a suit threw a cigarette to the ground and crushed it under his shoe when he saw me. He straightened his peaked chauffeur cap. "Mr. Rivers?"

"It's just Gabe, and you didn't have to throw that cigarette. Smoke if you want."

The driver's hand hovered around the pocket of his blazer, but he looked uncertain.

"I mean it. Have a cigarette if you want. I like the smell sometimes. It reminds me of Dad."

The driver flashed a faint smile, and produced a cigarette and lighter from his pocket. Shielding the flame from the wind, he lit the cigarette.

"What's your name?"

He took another drag. Smoke poured out of his nostrils. "It's Karl, Mr. Rivers."

"Are you having a good night, Karl?"

He rocked back on his heels. "Yes, sir. How about you?"

Cold night air wrapped around me, and I watched the party from a distance. Everyone in there was having fun, and I was standing out here. Why did I feel so shit? I should have been in there, mingling.

"Not really. Can you get me out of here?"

Karl nodded. "Of course. Back to the Beaufort?"

I sighed. No. An evening on my own in the Beaufort sounded even worse. "I want a drink in peace. Somewhere quiet and discreet where I won't be bothered. No paparazzi."

Karl scraped his beard and peered around the parking lot. "Not many places like that round here. I can only think of one."

"Is it discreet?"

Karl nodded. "Your dad used to own it."

45

In that case, it was perfect. Any place that Dad went to a lot would need to be discreet. I patted Karl on the back. "Fine. Let's go and have a drink."

Karl stiffened. "I don't drink while I'm on the job."

"Don't worry. I'll drink for both of us."

Chapter 8

Miri

The dressing room buzzed with chat and laughter. I rushed my makeup so I wouldn't have to linger on the girl that looked back at me in the brightly lit mirror. My fingers trembled as I positioned my electric-purple bob on my head. I tried to steady my hand to apply my liquid eyeliner.

The cloying scent of hair spray hung in the air so thickly I could taste it. I dusted another layer of powder around my eye, covering the bruise I'd got earlier in the day when Adele had elbowed me in the face during a bad tackle.

Deano stood in the corner watching us. My skin crawled to have him in there. None of the other women batted an eyelid. He leaned in to whisper. "You got my message, then?"

I glared back at his reflection in the mirror. This bastard had hurt my brother. I wouldn't let him lay another finger on anyone I cared about. "I'm here, aren't I? This is between me and you. Don't ever go near my family again."

He drew away with a bemused expression. "It takes a lot of confidence to take your clothes off in front of a room full of people." Deano shoved another clear shot into my trembling hand. "And when you don't have the confidence, it takes vodka."

The alcohol burned a path of fire down my throat. I wasn't a drinker, but there was no way I could do this stone-cold sober.

He gave me an appraising glance. "You ready?"

No. "How long do I have to do this for?"

"Until we're straight with your debt. If you dance good, it won't take long."

His dangerous gaze locked with mine in the mirror and he frowned. "What's up with your eye?"

"An elbow in the face."

"It doesn't look good." Deano nudged the woman applying her eyeliner next to me. "Make Miri pretty."

The woman measured me with a cool, appraising stare before she crossed to a dressing table on the other side of the room. She returned holding a decorative black-and-gold Venetian-style porcelain mask.

"A mask? Isn't this going to look weird?"

A bright mockery invaded Deano's stare. "Better to look like you've come here from a masquerade party than a boxing ring."

I secured the elastic around the back of my wig, fixing the mask in place. I tried to relax my face while the other dancer applied a thick coat of brick-red tint to my lips.

Deano looked me up and down with a critical squint. "Good enough."

"I don't want to do this. I don't know what I'm doing."

"You shake your tits about and grind in men's laps. It's not that difficult, sweetheart."

I squeezed my eyes shut and yanked down the gold fabric that clung to my body like liquid metal. It was backless—the flimsiest scrap of material in existence. Spaghetti straps scooped low enough to reveal my cleavage.

Think of Mum. Think of Reece. Frankie's in the car outside. It will be okay.

48

"No one's on the floor yet, so you can start with a private dance."

A shiver of panic rocked me. "Me? Are you sure you don't want someone else?"

He dusted his hands together. "Nope. Let's go."

Ice spread through my stomach. "Can I have another ten minutes? I haven't stretched."

Deano glared at me for a moment before bursting out laughing. "It's not a football match. You don't stretch. Just be sexy."

"I don't know how to be sexy."

He reached out and hauled me out of the chair. "Pretend that you do. No one will know the difference."

Chapter 9

Miri

We moved through a cloud of perfume and hair spray, past a couple of guys nursing Coronas at the bar, to the private suites at the back of the club. I'd hoped the place would be empty. Who comes to a strip club on a Monday night? Deano pushed me through a heavy red velvet curtain into a dimly lit room. Polished mirrors covered the walls and a disco ball refracted light in fleeting rainbows. A dark-haired man wearing a tux sat on a burgundy velvet couch. Another guy dressed in a suit sat next to him. It took me a moment to register that I was looking at Gabe Rivers. *The* Gabe Rivers.

What. The. Actual. Fuck?

I couldn't do this. Not for this man. I swiveled out of Deano's grip but he tightened his fingers around my wrist.

Blue light from Gabe's phone bathed his sharply angled face. He spoke without looking up. "I'm here for a drink."

Oh. Thank God. Relief flooded me. I'd got away with it. Gabe wouldn't know who I was under this wig and mask.

Deano cocked his head. "You're sure you wouldn't like some company?"

"I have company. Just another beer and a sparkling water for Karl. Maybe a couple of cigars if you—"

Gabe looked up and leaned back against the red velvet cushions. His full lips curved in a faint, curious smile, his eyes level under dark brows. My pulse pounded everywhere: my chest, my throat, my eyelids. Had he made the connection? Did he know?

A thick swath of chestnut hair fell across his forehead. Slowly, he undid the top button of his crisp white shirt before carefully rolling his sleeves to the elbows. I couldn't take my eyes from his long, elegant fingers and the dusting of dark hair on his muscular forearms.

He pocketed his phone and tilted his chin toward me. "What's your name?"

I opened my mouth, but I didn't dare say a word. He hadn't recognized me beneath a mask, but would my voice give me away?

Deano's gaze fell on my short purple wig. "She's Violet . . . Violet Delights."

My lips thinned. A stripper name seemed like something to be discussed in advance.

Amusement flickered in Gabe's eyes as they met mine. His voice was like silk. "Hello, Miss Delights. It's a pleasure to make your acquaintance." He spoke to the man next to him but didn't take his eyes off me. "You can go now, Karl."

The man at Gabe's side stood and brushed down his suit. "I'll be in the car when you're ready, Mr. Rivers."

The other man disappeared. Gabe's intense gaze made my breath quicken. He had no idea that he'd been talking to me yesterday. Oh God. There was no way out of this. Deano wouldn't allow me to run. He gave me a warning smile and disappeared behind the curtain.

Just the two of us. Me and Gabe Rivers. *The* Gabe Rivers. My ears filled with the music pouring from the speakers. "Work" by Rihanna. A voice inside my head screamed at me to move, but my feet were frozen in place. Gabe watched me from behind hooded eyes. My mouth went dry. A lap dance lasted two minutes. I'd have to pretend it was someone else and get through it. The concept of dancing in a "sexy" way was so silly it made my soul want to leave my body with cringe.

The low pulsing music sizzled over my bare skin and my arms broke out in goosebumps. Gabe's tongue darted out to trace the outline of his full lips, and I couldn't take my eyes from his mouth. I was supposed to be dancing, but nerves held me rooted to the spot. A bead of sweat ran down the back of my neck. What if I ran? What would Deano do? No. I couldn't. I had to see this through. Reece had already suffered because of me. This wasn't about me anymore. It was about the safety of my family.

Gabe frowned and shouted over the music. "Are you okay?"

My heart thrashed in my chest. I drew a shaky breath and nodded. My legs wouldn't move. I couldn't just stand here like a muppet.

He rubbed his eyebrow. "Are you sure you're okay?"

I nodded, even though my stomach churned as if I might throw up. Oh God. Was I going to throw up? Tears pressed at my eyes. I couldn't do this. My breath came so hot and sharp it burned my lungs. I'd have to dance because standing here in silence was even more awkward. What choice did I have? It didn't matter what it took. Family first.

I hooked a finger under the strap of my dress. My fingers shook so violently, I could barely lower it down my arm.

"Wait. No. Stop." Gabe frowned and held his hands up. "Keep your dress on." He put his beer on the table next to him. "Do you want to sit down?"

No. I had to dance. Still my legs wouldn't obey.

"It's fine. Please. Sit." He patted the couch next to him.

Sitting would be better than standing. My legs were about to collapse anyway, but nerves held me frozen. Gabe watched me with a frown, then rose fluidly from the chair.

"Here." With a large hand around my waist, he guided me to sit on the couch. His voice was a tender murmur. "It's okay. Sit down."

He dropped down next to me and shot me a sidelong glance. I smoothed my dress over my thighs with clammy palms. It only served to expose more of my cleavage. God. I had to get up. I had to dance or he'd tell Deano.

"I like your mask." He offered me a weak smile. "Sometimes I wish I had one of those. It must be nice to be anonymous."

I nodded. The music pulsed loud, engulfing us.

Panic rioted in my chest. This was a disaster. I had to stand. I had to dance. This wasn't me. I'd taken penalty kicks in the eighty-ninth minute.

"It's my first night. Please give me another chance."

"It's fine. I only came for a quiet drink."

I made to stand. "I want to dance for you."

A silken thread of authority weaved through his voice as he gestured to the cushion next to him again. "Sit."

I bit my lip; my gaze darted to the curtain. Was Deano behind there, listening?

I rested a trembling hand on Gabe's thigh, willing myself to calm. "Let me do this for you. I have to."

His gazed dropped to my hand on his thigh, and he frowned. "You have to?"

I swallowed and snapped my hand away. "No. I mean . . . I want to."

For a moment, he studied me with a curious intensity. "You'll get in trouble if you don't dance?"

I couldn't answer that. Not if there was a chance Deano was listening. "No. Let's try this again. I let my nerves get the better of me."

His expression stilled and grew serious. His voice was gentle and full of understanding. "I don't want a dance. I want to chat. You're still going to earn your money. You don't have to worry."

A sudden relief made my shoulders loosen. He sank lower into the red velvet cushions. "Do you know who I am?"

Of course. Everyone in England knew. But he wanted the anonymity. I could grant him his own mask.

"No," I lied.

A smile tipped his lips. "Really?"

"Really."

"Oh." He smoothed his hands over his trousers. "I have a reputation, you see. Not a good one. Terrible, actually." He gave a bleak, tight-lipped smile. "People say all kinds of things about me. If you listen to everything you hear, then I'm a very bad boy."

"Are you a bad boy?"

"Sometimes." A shadow passed over his face. "Not all the time."

The vodka was hitting, numbing my senses. A pleasant glow spread through my chest. Gabe Rivers was surprisingly easy to talk to. It was almost possible to forget he was famous. "You know what's better than a bad boy?"

He raised a questioning eyebrow.

"A grown-arse man with his shit together."

He regarded me with amusement. "Is that the kind of man you're looking for, Violet?"

"I'm not looking for a man."

"A woman?"

"I'm not looking for anyone."

"Why not?"

My chest tightened. "It doesn't matter."

His eyes roved over me. "Because you've been hurt?"

"Something like that."

He nodded thoughtfully. "I'm supposed to be at a party tonight, but I escaped. It was full of smug couples and I got stuck talking to my mother, who was in fine form, as always. Then I saw my ex-girlfriend, and she looked incredible . . . and happy, which I find inconsiderate." He raised a rueful eyebrow. "She could have had the decency to look miserable without me."

His elegant tapered fingers caressed the neck of his beer bottle. Sadness lingered around his beautiful jade eyes. A pang pulled at my heart. This Gabe Rivers was so different from the man I'd met at the match yesterday. A million miles from the arrogant playboy the tabloids made him out to be. What was he doing in a strip club? He could walk into any bar and take anyone home he wanted. Was Gabe Rivers lonely? *The* Gabe Rivers?

"So, about this person who broke your heart. What did they do?" he asked.

My mind drifted to Jed. Some part of me had known what kind of man he was. I'd been an idiot. "I didn't say I had a broken heart."

"You didn't need to. It takes one to know one." He pointed his beer bottle at me for emphasis. "Take it as a lesson learned. Never let your guard down. That's when you're most vulnerable."

Gabe frowned and peered around the mirrored room. Music rushed in to fill the silence between us. He twisted his gold watch. It glinted in the light from the disco ball overhead. His voice softened. "How did you end up here, Violet?"

I pressed my lips together. I had sense enough to know Deano wouldn't be happy with me telling the truth. I should have been grinding in Gabe's lap by now. He studied my face and I was glad of the mask to cover my shame. He surveyed me kindly, with a bland smile, but stayed silent.

"Are you sure you don't want me to dance?"

"No. You shouldn't have to do something you don't want to do. Besides, I enjoyed talking to you." He reached inside his jacket, pulled out a huge wad of notes. "For your troubles."

"That's too much. I didn't do anything."

He pressed the money into my hands. "Nonsense. You're better than my therapist, and he charges ten times as much."

"Please. I can't take it—"

"I want you to have it, but I'd get another job if I were you. Life is short. Don't waste your time doing things you're not passionate about."

He lifted my hand to his lips and kissed the back of it. His pretty green eyes found mine and he winked. Heat flooded my body.

"Goodnight, Miss Delights."

Chapter 10

MIRI

I hardly slept a wink in my old bed at Mum's house. In the morning, I found Reece in his pajamas at the breakfast bar. The bruises on his face had faded a little, but my sensible, straitlaced brother still looked like a human punching bag. Guilt prickled the back of my neck.

My fault.

"How are you feeling?"

He cricked his neck. "I'm on the mend."

I poured myself a coffee, searching for the right words. "Look, Reece. I don't even know where to start. I'm so sorry that this happened—"

"Frankie told me what you were doing last night."

Boiling coffee sloshed on the counter as I missed the cup. I'd asked her to keep it to herself. I should have known better. Frankie and Reece had always been tight.

"What do you think you're doing, Miri?" he said softly.

A barb speared my chest. This was typical Reece. He'd been beaten up because of me, but he could still look at me with empathy as if I deserved it. I didn't.

A pulse thudded at my temple. "I have to get the money."

"Not like that."

"Then how?"

His eyes dropped to the chipped mug in his hands.

"I have to make this right. I'm so sorry that Deano came for you. If I'd known . . ."

He watched me in his quiet, thoughtful way before he slipped off his glasses and cleaned them with his little cloth.

"The club is perfectly nice. Everyone is friendly. The women there are trying to make extra cash . . . students . . . single mothers. It was fine."

"This isn't you. You're not going to feel comfortable. It's not . . . feminist. We need to find another way to get the money."

I took a sip of too-hot coffee and cringed. "Thank you for mansplaining feminism to me. A woman making her own choices is feminist. I'm choosing to do this."

"No you're not," he muttered uneasily. "You're doing it because we're in trouble. You're not choosing it. I don't like the thought of you in that environment. There will be drugs and booze. Men in these situations can be violent. I'm worried for your safety."

The irony was I'd felt safer in that club with Gabe Rivers than I had walking around in the area that surrounded it. He'd been so . . . nice. So different from when we'd met the first time.

I swallowed hard, trying to manage a feeble answer. "I'm *choosing* to do this to solve the mess I made. Frankie's outside in the car if I need her."

"What use is she outside?"

The scent of coffee in the kitchen overwhelmed me, and nausea gripped my stomach. A thin chill hung on the edge of my words. "Are you this judgmental with your therapy patients or just with your family?"

"I have no issue with what goes on between consenting adults behind closed doors, but this isn't true consent. You're doing this for us, and I won't have it. We'll find a way to make this money."

I drew a calming breath. I had to be nice to my brother. He'd been beaten up because of me. Still, his unflappably calm manner never failed to wind me up. He was always so serene it was like arguing with Buddha. "It won't take me long in this club. I made a grand last night."

"A grand?" He rubbed the bridge of his nose and his eyes slipped away. "It's just dancing, isn't it, Miri? You're not . . ."

"No . . . it's not . . . *that*. They aren't allowed to touch me."

I took another deep breath and tried to relax my shoulders. I'd known this wouldn't be palatable, but I'd hoped Reece might be more open-minded. "I'll take my clothes off every night of the week if it means you don't get the shit kicked out of you again. This is my mess. I'm going to sort it."

A loud knock sounded on the front door. Reece blew out an audible breath and lowered his fork to his plate with a gentle click. A prickle lifted the hair on the back of my neck. He turned to me with a taut, serious expression and pushed me toward the back door. "Get out of the house. Go next door."

"I'm not leaving you."

Another knock sounded.

He shoved me lightly. "Go, Miri. I'll handle this. It could be those guys again."

"And if it is, then they deal with me. Not you."

I dashed down the hall to the front door, but still Reece got there first. He held me at arm's length and peeped through the tiny glass spyhole. He frowned. Confusion swam on his face. Then he moved to peer through the hole again.

"What is it?" His bewildered silence set my nerves jangling. I pulled out my phone. "I'm calling the police."

He waved a hand to still me. "No. It's . . ." His frown deepened. "I think it's . . . Is that who I think it is?"

I nudged him out of the way and pressed my eye to the spy-hole. Gabe Rivers stood on the doorstep. A nervous swoop made my stomach lurch. What was Gabe doing here? Was this about last night? Had he tracked me down?

Oh God. Why come here? Was he angry? I pulled at the over-sized lilac striped T-shirt and pajama shorts I wore. My hair was unwashed and tangled. I looked a mess. What did it matter? How did he even know where I lived? There was no way I could answer the door. Hopefully he'd think I wasn't in, get fed up, and leave.

He hammered his fist against the door again. Nope.

Reece moved to open the door and I grabbed his arm.

"What the hell are you doing?" I hissed.

Reece shot me a bewildered look. "Opening the door?"

"Well. Don't. Obviously."

"How is that obvious?"

"I know you're in there. I can hear you. Open up." Gabe's muffled voice traveled through the wood.

Reece swung the door open. Oh God. Gabe stood tall and imposing in another well-fitted suit. Sunlight illuminated that impossibly handsome face. A sunbeam struck his hair, making it gleam like polished chestnuts. How the hell did anyone look this good after such a late night?

Gabe lowered his sunglasses and his gaze transferred from Reece to me. "Ah, there you are. Can I come in?"

I pushed my brother down the narrow hallway and shoved him into the kitchen. How had Gabe even figured out it was me last night? Was he trying to out me to my family? Maybe he was going to use this as a bargaining chip to blackmail me into joining his team. Was he capable of that? If the tabloids were to be believed, he was capable of much worse.

"You don't have to worry. I'm alone. I ditched the cameras." He peered down the hallway past me. "I like your house. It's very . . . cozy."

"What do you want?" My voice came out more impatient than I'd intended, but if he'd come here to embarrass me then I had no time for it. How had he guessed? Deano must have let something slip when I'd handed over the cash.

Gabe smoothed a hand through his perfectly tousled hair. "I've come for an apology."

"What for?"

"You called me a prick."

"I did?"

Humor lit his jade eyes. "Sunday morning?"

"Oh, right. *Right*. It was an accident. Sorry. I'm not used to the cameras."

He flashed an easy smile. "It doesn't matter. I've been called worse, and most of the time I am a prick. Can I come in?"

He peered down the hallway again. Any normal person would have taken his coat and offered him a drink by now, but I needed him out of here. My neck heated at the memory of last night. His gaze drifted down my pajamas to my slippers.

"Now isn't a great time. What can I help you with?"

"I told you. You're my new striker. I need to know what it's going to take to get you on my team. I'm on a mission to woo you."

"This isn't about last night?"

He shot me a puzzled glance. "Last night? What about last night?"

He doesn't know. Oh, thank God. He doesn't know.

I'd gotten away with it. I stiffened my spine to stop my shoulders from slumping with relief.

He peered past me again. "It won't take long."

"Fine." I stepped inside and ushered him toward the living room.

He stopped at the door and peered into the adjacent dining room with undisguised interest, his attention caught by the wheelchair, the commode, and the bed with rails we'd set up ready for Mum downstairs. We were hoping to get her back into her own room upstairs at some point, and bring the dining table back, but this would have to do for now. He followed me into the living room, crossed to the window and propped a finger in the blind, pulling it down to look outside at the surrounding red-brick terraced houses.

"I'm investing in Calverdale Ladies and I want you for the team. This time next year you could be in the Women's Super League. With the right coaching, you could be playing for England in the World Cup. I'm offering you the dream. I need to know why you don't want it. Whatever the problem is, I will solve it."

Not this again. Gabe Rivers showing up to give me an answer to all my problems on a silver platter. It would be so easy to say yes. This wasn't even just about achieving my dreams. Things had gotten desperate. I'd never needed money more. My family were in danger because of my stupidity in taking that loan.

Still, I had to stick to my principles. Jerry had screwed me and my friends over so badly. That team was rotten. Jerry Reynolds was an open secret, and nobody had done anything about him. Besides, I was handling the situation with Deano. If I just carried on at the club, all of this would be resolved.

I folded my arms. "Maybe there isn't a problem. Maybe I'm happy where I am."

He leaned casually against the window frame. "No. You're not. No athlete is happy with mediocrity. Go and bring your boyfriend in here. See if he can talk some sense into you."

"My boyfriend?"

"The man in the glasses. He looks like he irons his underpants."

I pulled a face. "Reece? That's my brother."

"You live with your brother?"

"Yes, and my mum."

"All three of you in this one house?"

"Five of us, actually. My younger brother and sister are at university."

His voice was casual, but his green eyes held a gleam of interest. "No boyfriend? . . . Girlfriend?"

"I don't see how that's any of your concern."

A wry grin ghosted his lips. He sauntered to the mantelpiece and picked up a snow globe. He looked at it curiously as he shook it. "I want you. Give me a reason why you're so resistant and I'll leave you in peace. You won't get me out of here until you tell me."

Bloody hell. The man didn't give up. "Fine. The problem is Jerry Reynolds."

He spun to face me. His burning eyes held me still. "Jerry? The development officer?" He slid gracefully into an armchair. "What's wrong with Jerry?"

"He's a pervert and a bully. He scouts women for the Junior Academy, but his behavior is inappropriate. He stalked one of my friends . . . texting her . . . turning up at her workplace. When she complained, the club turned a blind eye. They'd rather cover for him than listen to the women he harassed. When she complained, she was told he'd be investigated, but nothing changed. We were all supposed to ignore him like a pervy old uncle at Christmas dinner. It's unacceptable."

He watched me, cold and businesslike. A million miles away from the relaxed, open Gabe from last night. He didn't have a clue that it had been me in that room with him. He didn't have the same hungry, interested gleam in his eyes as he appraised me now. This Gabe was a shark out for blood, and I was an un-fuckable woman standing in the way of something he needed. A target to manipulate. A prickle of anger made me stiffen my spine. He had another think coming if he thought I'd roll over like a puppy.

He sat still, his eyes narrow. "If Jerry is a problem, then he's gone."

I held his gaze. It wasn't enough. Jerry needed to be shamed and prosecuted. Not sent off to retire with a golden handshake. It was the principle of the matter.

"I complained about him, and I was dismissed from the junior coaching program. I was blacklisted. I couldn't get a spot on any decent coaching program. The only way I can play is in the part-time leagues. We were told that an investigation was being conducted." I glanced away. "It wasn't. He ruined my career before it had begun, and countless other girls', too."

He leaned back in the armchair, studying me with curious intensity. Silence fell between us. Tingling lit the pit of my stomach.

"That's why you don't play at a higher level?" he asked quietly.

"Yes."

"Then he's gone. I'll deal with him personally."

"I don't want him gone. I want him brought to justice."

Gabe dusted his hands together. "Fine. Then we'll do that. Whatever you want."

I scoffed. "I'll believe it when I see it."

He smoothed his tie and rose in one fluid movement. "Leave this with me. I'll deal with Jerry, and you can come across this afternoon and sign with us."

"It's not that simple. I have other things to think about—"

He looked at me intently, then strode toward me, closing the gap between us. I took a sharp breath at his nearness. His fingers fluttered around my cheek before he drew his hand away. His voice was as soft as a kiss. "What happened to your eye?"

64

My hand flew to cover my bruised cheek. "Nothing. An elbow to the face."

His extraordinary eyes clung to mine. "You're good enough to play for England. You have more talent in your little toe than most players. You can throw as many reasons at me as you want, but in the end you'll realize . . ."

"Realize what?" My voice was barely above a whisper.

"That I always get what I want, and I want you. Don't drag this out longer than it needs to be. We both know you want this too. You're an athlete. Winning is all that matters to people like us. Stick with me, and I'll take you all the way to the top." He arched a dark brow, his low voice like silk draped around my bare skin. "Wouldn't you like to be on top, Forster?"

My whole body spiked with heat. I couldn't tear my eyes from his full lips. What were we talking about? He was standing so close; his beautiful mouth hovered inches from mine. His eyes fell to my lips. My heart pounded. Oh God. Why had I let myself get so close to him?

Even if he got rid of Jerry, I couldn't walk away from the Swans. Those girls were my best friends. I owed them loyalty. Besides, I had no time to go up the league. Training was already becoming inconvenient with visiting Mum, and when she got out of hospital it would only get worse. My caregiving responsibilities would take precedence. My job was looking after Mum and my family. Not football.

Try again, Rivers.

"Winning isn't anywhere near the top of my priority list."

His brows set in a straight line. "Then what is?"

I took a breath and stepped away. "You wouldn't understand. If you'll excuse me, you're making me late for the team I actually play for."

Chapter 11

GABE

I reclined in the leather chair in my new office, testing the bounce. Outside, women in white kits ran laps around the sprawling expanse of rough training pitches. These grounds were tiny compared to the men's facilities. Ruby, my PA, sat in the corner making calls that sounded important and scrolling her phone.

"Why are we here, Ruby?"

She covered her phone's mouthpiece and cocked her head. "Here? You have a meeting with Jerry. That's followed by PR, and then after that—"

"No. I mean, why is the women's team training over here? The men's team has the best facilities in the country. State-of-the-art turf, gym, sauna, personal trainers. What are we doing over here? We could be sharing those facilities."

Ruby shrugged. "It's the way your dad set things up."

"If we want the best team, we need to give them everything they need to be the best. Find out the schedule for the men's team and fit our sessions around that. I want our women in the gym over there, using the men's facilities."

Ruby's brow wrinkled in confusion. "The men's team won't be happy about that."

"Tough luck. They need to learn to share."

Ruby peered through the glass office door. "It looks like Jerry's here. I'll leave you to it."

"Wait." I watched Jerry through the glass and kept my voice low. "Have you ever heard any . . . rumors about Jerry?"

"Rumors? What rumors?" She cleared her throat and kept her voice low. "I'm not a gossip."

"Let me ask you a question, and I expect an honest answer. Would you leave your teenage daughter alone in a room with Jerry?"

Ruby swallowed and met my gaze. "Hell. No."

Dad and Jerry went way back. They'd been friends since they were kids. Awful to think of Dad turning a blind eye to bad behavior, but not as surprising as it should have been. Jerry had worked as a talent scout for years. He'd been dealing with women hungry to play football with a professional club. Young women. My hand ached around the stress ball I'd been squeezing too tightly.

Miri had been forced to endure his bullshit. The thought of it made me sick. Jerry had held back such an exceptional talent. I hadn't been able to go all the way with football, but if I'd had the skill and Jerry had killed my career, I would have been fuming.

Miri and all those women must have felt so powerless. I knew what that was like. People had been trying to control me my whole life. My father had used the promise of the team as a way to manipulate me, and now my mother had happily taken over the mantle. It was an absolute injustice. If there was a chance to put it right, then I had to. I'd deal with Jerry, and I'd see this woman go all the way.

"Thanks. That's all I wanted to know."

I dialed Miri Forster's number. She answered after the third ring.

"Gabe?"

"Put your phone on mute. You're going to want to listen to this."

I opened my desk drawer and set the phone inside so Miri would be able to hear. The door buzzed and Ruby brought Jerry in. He was a sweaty, porky man with a bald head and button nose. I'd always thought he was harmless enough. He'd got away with it in plain sight.

"Take a seat, Jerry."

Ignoring me, Jerry pulled me into a bear hug and thumped my back. "I heard you'd got the team." He bellowed with laughter. "Shame it's the women's, eh? Although it isn't all bad, coaching women."

I held my tongue. Better to let him talk. With a man like Jerry, you only needed to hand him a bit of rope and he'd hang himself. He slouched into a chair at the other side of the desk, his belly visible in patches where his shirt strained against his trousers.

"I'm all for equal opportunities, but it's all gone too far, hasn't it? Though you've got to make the most of a bad hand. I wouldn't mind scouting for the women again. It was always more fun." He gave me a wink and raised a suggestive eyebrow. "Fresh meat."

I linked my hands over my chest and rocked back in my chair. "I've had some complaints, Jerry. I'm afraid we're going to have to let you go while we investigate."

A bead of sweat rolled down his porky face. "What?"

"Effective immediately."

"I've worked at this club for forty years."

"Right. Maybe we're ready for some . . . *fresh meat*. We'll be conducting a thorough investigation. An outside contractor. No stone left unturned. I'm not sure I trust our internal processes. As director of the women's team, I take any complaints seriously."

"Your dad wouldn't want this."

Somehow, I kept my voice level. "Dad's not here."

68

Jerry's mouth spread in a thin-lipped smile. "No. He's not."

He wanted to say more.

Go on. Say it. I fucking dare you.

The silence stretched between us.

"Anyway, if you'll excuse me. I have another appointment."

Jerry mopped his brow with a handkerchief. "Don't let them hang me out to dry, Gabe. Your dad wouldn't have wanted that."

I needed to deal with him properly or he'd go straight to another club to continue his bullshit. But I needed him distanced from the club before I took him down, so it didn't drag us all into the mud with him.

I forced my lips into a smile. "If you have nothing to hide, then you have nothing to worry about."

"Come on, Gabe. Please."

I held up a hand to silence him and pointed toward the door.

Bye, Jerry. Fuck off, Jerry. Don't come back, Jerry.

He left, slamming the door behind him.

I picked up the phone.

"Did you hear that?"

"I heard." Miri's voice held a smile.

"I'm sending a car."

Chapter 12

GABE

I met Miri at Calverdale Stadium. Leggings clung to her perfectly toned legs and a snug orange team hoodie hugged her athletic physique. I had to work hard to keep my gaze from dropping to travel over the exquisite curve of her peachy backside. The wind kicked at her golden ponytail. Her body was so athletic and powerful, but her delicate feminine features were wholesome and innocent. A perfect recipe for corruption.

Miri twisted in a circle on the spot, gazing awestruck around the empty seats. "I can't believe I'm in the stadium. I used to come here all the time when I was a kid." She dragged her sneaker lightly over the ground. "This feels incredible. So springy."

"Polypropylene fibers. It's the latest technology in turf. Artificial fibers are injected into natural grass approximately every inch across the pitch. It gives a more durable and even surface."

A chuckle escaped her. "I didn't take you for a grass nerd."

"I want my team to have the best. In fact, I'm moving the women over to the men's training pitches. Dad kept the facilities separate, but it makes no sense. The men have a superior gym, steam rooms, hydrotherapy, physiotherapists, and dietitians. The men train from 8 a.m. until 1 p.m. and then the place is dead. It's a waste."

Surprise touched her pale face. "Impressive."

"I told you I'm serious about this team, Forster. Anything the men have, we'll have. I'm investing." I ticked off on my fingers. "New kits, gym equipment, coaching . . ."

A strange silence echoed from the empty stands. The delicious scent of freshly cut turf filled my nose. I'd loved this stadium on match nights when fans packed every inch, chanting. I'd always dreamed of playing my first match here, back when I still thought I had a chance of making it as a professional player.

Miri flashed a glance at the camera crew that trailed my every move, and squirmed. I gave Curtis, the producer, a polite nod. "Excuse us for a second."

I took Miri by the elbow, guided her out of earshot of the cameras, and dropped my voice low. "I'm not a fan of the cameras either, but the documentary is to raise awareness. I want to pull in sponsorship money. The community needs to know what we're doing here. The more we get local supporters behind us, the better the atmosphere. It will be great for morale."

A slight smile of defiance curved her lips. "You're certainly saying all the right things."

Why was this woman so resistant? She should have been biting my hand off to sign this contract by now. I'd got rid of Jerry and offered her a chance to train in world-class facilities. The best facilities in the country. What more did she want?"

She folded her arms. "So, this is real? It's not a gimmick. You're serious about women's football?"

"I'm giving this everything I've got. I'm moving this team up to the Women's Super League. I'm going to see it through. Look, Forster, I know your stats for the season. You've scored a lot of goals, but it's only a fraction of what you should be scoring. I'm willing to bet you're getting balls that the others can't even read. You're too good for the girls you're playing with. If you had better players around you, you'd get more chances on goals."

She stiffened her spine. Her eyes flashed with fire. "I'm playing with my best friends. We've won together and we've lost together. I love playing with the Swans."

I smoothed my tie. Okay. She was loyal. Wrong angle. "Your loyalty is admirable, but this is your career, not summer camp. My job is to uncover potential. You need the right environment and support, and you could go all the way. We're talking about playing in stadiums like this . . . playing for England. Your friends would want to see you reach your potential."

She opened her mouth and closed it again. I'd got her on the back foot with that. Time to go for the jugular. I kept my voice casual. "It's not standard, but I'm willing to negotiate a signing-on fee."

"How much?"

"Name your price."

She swallowed and kept her eyes fixed on the grass. Uncertainty crept into her expression. "Twelve thousand?"

It was a lot for a new signing to the women's team, but much less than we'd offer the men.

"Fine," I said.

Her eyes snapped to mine. "Fine?"

"Yes."

She pulled at the strings of her hoodie and turned her face away. "How quickly would I get the money?"

"It will need to go through accounts. A couple of days. You'll get an additional ten thousand when you complete your probation period."

She paled and drifted to the goalpost. She ran her hand over the frame, and I noticed her fingers trembled. This was it. A little nudge and I'd have her. I planted myself next to her. "You came to speak to me. You could have said no. Some part of you is interested in a transfer."

A rueful smile pulled at her lips. "I'm not going to turn down a chance to stand on this pitch. This is Calverdale bloody United."

I chuckled. I liked her bluntness. It was refreshing. "You're a fan?"

"I grew up with this team. My dad was Calverdale mad. No one else in my family is bothered about football, so it was something that was just for us. He used to bring me all the time when I was little . . . as much as we could afford, anyway. I used to love it, not just because of the football, but because it was the only time I had Dad all to myself."

"I know that feeling. This team was everything to my dad. We used to come to matches together. He was so busy all the time with work, but he'd always take time for this."

She scanned the pitch, looking up at the executive area. "I take it you were up there in the posh bit."

"Not if I could get out of it. I'd much rather watch from the terrace. I'm here for the atmosphere. The buzz on match days."

"So you slummed it with the rest of us?"

She flashed a teasing smile that caught me off guard. Chatting about football had loosened her up. Me too. She seemed as passionate about this team as I was.

I matched her smile. "It was never slumming. I'd take the terraces any day."

A stray ball sat at our feet by the goal. I passed it to her. She caught it under her foot.

"Come on," I said, moving into the goal. "Take a shot. Score a goal in Calverdale Stadium. Unless you think you can't get one past me."

A bemused glint appeared in her eyes. "Have you ever kicked a ball before, Rivers?"

"Once or twice."

I took off my suit jacket and passed it to one of the camera guys. Carefully, I rolled my sleeves up. Her guilty eyes dropped to my forearms before she quickly averted her gaze. I'd be useless in slippery brogues, but I needed to give her a taste of what she could have here. A little temptation wouldn't hurt.

Miri blasted a ball at me. I sidestepped to save it, but I had no chance without diving, and I didn't much fancy covering an Armani suit in mud. Miri's face lit with a smug smile and she patted her hands together.

"You got lucky," I shouted.

Her laugh was full-hearted. "Don't confuse skill for luck."

I toed the ball back to her and she blasted it straight into the top corner. This girl had raw talent. That strange spark that some people are born with. I'd trained hard, but I'd never had this quality. I'd wanted it so badly, but I couldn't quite cut it. Miri blasted another ball at me. I jumped, but it soared over my head. There was so much power behind the shot. Nobody would stand a chance.

"You don't get your hands dirty often, do you, Rivers?"

"I'm just warming up."

I rolled the ball back toward her.

A goading smirk crept onto her face. "Are we going to have some fun, then, Rivers? You want to see if you can get the ball off me, or do you need more time to warm up?"

I snorted. "Why don't you show me what you've got? Or do you just want to talk about it?"

I ran at her for a tackle. She dodged and weaved, dancing away from my every attempt to get to the ball. She held me at bay effortlessly. She was too good. By some miracle, I kicked the ball out and got free of her. She tore after me, hooking her foot to get to the

74

ball. She moved in front of me and my foot connected with hers. I tripped, landing hard on my knees. Pain shot through my shin.

She stood over me, concern flashing in her eyes. "God. Sorry. Are you okay?"

Pain radiated through my knee, but I kept my face level and gave her a reassuring nod. "Fine. I have an old injury from when I used to play. It gives me trouble sometimes."

She extended a hand to pull me up. "You used to play?"

Her palm was smooth against mine as she pulled me to my feet. "I played for the Junior Academy, but I broke my leg. I thought I could get back there with rehab, but it's never been the same."

She pressed her lips together and frowned. "I'm sorry."

I forced a smile. "It's one of those things. Everybody talks about the success stories . . . the kids that have been playing since they were four and make it all the way. Nobody talks about the failures. The kids that gave their heart and soul to a junior team but were never quite good enough to make it as a professional. Football was everything. All I ever wanted was to play for Calverdale. When I knew I wasn't going to make it as a player, I started working as a talent scout, but it's not the same. Being on the pitch, being part of a team like that, the exhilaration of a match. It's a feeling you can't find anywhere else."

Her eyes clung to mine, gentle and understanding. "It makes you feel alive."

"Exactly."

Miri watched me with a thoughtful expression, rolling the ball underfoot. I cleared my throat. "You look good on this pitch, Forster, like you were born to play here."

A small smile graced her lips. She scooped up the ball, stashed it in the crook of her elbow, and gazed around the stadium.

"When Dad couldn't afford tickets, we'd listen to the radio on match days. Sometimes, we'd stand outside the front door, and if the wind was right, you'd hear the chanting on the breeze. Those are some of my happiest memories, before he got sick . . ." Her eyes shone and she turned her face away. "We lost him ten years ago. Sometimes it hits me. Being back here . . . it's strange . . ."

"I get it. Of all the things Dad owned, this club was the most meaningful to him."

My happiest childhood memories were those with my dad and this team, too. We might have come from different backgrounds, but this was something we shared.

Silence fell between us. I'd dated models and Hollywood stars who wouldn't leave the house until a team had spent hours getting them ready, yet Miri Forster had mud on her face and a cocky smirk and I couldn't keep my eyes off her. She was so natural and unselfconscious. I had to stop this nonsense. If she was signing with us, then it needed to be a professional relationship.

"What more can I do to convince you?"

She chewed her lip. "It's not an easy decision. It's a big move. I'll need to speak to my family. I have . . . commitments. My mum isn't well. She's coming out of the hospital soon. I need to make sure this doesn't interfere with my responsibilities at home . . ."

"It won't. We'll make sure it doesn't. Whatever you need, you ask me and you can have it."

A sensuous energy wound between us. Did she feel that too? A tinge of pink flushed her cheeks. She drew a breath and took a step away from me.

"The team is having a get-together tomorrow night," I said. "Come along and meet the other girls and the coaching staff. You have no obligations. Come and have fun."

She spun on the spot, gazing around the stadium in awe. I couldn't help but study her delicate profile. She smoothed her pony-tail. "You really think you can move this team up to the WSL?"

"I know I can."

"Fine. I'll come to your party." She flicked the ball toward me and a wicked grin lit her face. "But only if you can score a goal past me."

Her goading smile made my heart beat harder. What was more attractive than a woman this confident? I'd almost gotten her to sign. A couple more little nudges and we'd get this deal over the lines. Frustration made a muscle quiver in my jaw. I couldn't have Miri Forster, but after all this sexual chemistry, I needed to get laid. I never had to work for it. I couldn't call one of my regular fucks, since I didn't trust anyone to be discreet anymore. Ironically, the last time I'd had this much fun talking to a woman like this was in a strip club. Maybe I could go back again tonight. Not for sex. I couldn't risk being front-page news tomorrow. But we could talk. Violet Delights had been a good listener.

Miri rolled the ball under her football boot and cocked her head. "Ready, Rivers?"

"If you think you can handle me, Forster."

Chapter 13

Miri

The speakers blasted out "Milkshake" by Kelis. The loud bass vibrated in a pulse like fingers stroking over my bare skin. I took a breath and wrapped my hand around the pole above my head. The chill against my bare back sent shivers racing across my shoulder blades.

Every second that dragged by in this club was too long, but Deano wouldn't take me at my word that I'd have his money any day now. I couldn't get my hands on it quick enough. I'd had to do my best to look normal and not scream and leap for joy when Gabe had agreed to the signing-on fee. He'd been so casual, as though twelve grand was small change you'd find behind the sofa cushions and not the answer to all my prayers.

The trouble was, Deano wouldn't be satisfied until he had the cash in his grimy hands, and even then I had this horrible sense that he'd find a way to drag this out. The man was the worst kind of creep. He was always lurking around in the dressing room, or standing too close when I found myself unlucky enough to have to talk to him. Until the money came through, I was stuck here whether I liked it or not.

With my eyes closed, I tuned into the music and invited it under my skin. Even if I had no rhythm, I had strength and flexibility on my side. A rush of nerves set my blood alight, but I imagined myself in front of the net, about to take a penalty. Everything depending on one moment. I had to rise above the noise inside my head and focus.

Then I saw *him.*

Gabe Rivers leaned casually against the bar, watching me. My heart almost exploded with panic, but I still had the mask and the wig. He wasn't watching Miri Forster. He was watching Violet Delights. An expensive-looking charcoal suit hugged his muscular frame. His commanding presence couldn't be contained in one room. No matter the environment, he looked masterful and imposing, as if he owned the place. Probably because, more often than not, he *did* own the place.

He was so handsome, but in an unusual way, with his chestnut hair and face full of sharp angles. His tantalizing eyes met mine and my body flooded with warmth. And somehow it was easier to dance for him in this room full of people than it had been when it was just the two of us. Maybe it was the adrenaline or the vodka kicking in, but the voice that had whispered in my head before about how silly I looked had vanished. In its place, a powerful confidence and sensuality thrummed through me. The dance had been for me, but I wanted to invite him into it. From behind my mask, I kept my eyes fixed on him as though nobody mattered but us. Everything faded and sharpened at the same time. The music dimmed to a faint buzz and my skin tingled with heat. His intense gaze locked with mine as I ran my hands over myself, imagining all the places I'd want him to touch me if things were different between us.

The beat vibrated in the soles of my feet, in my eyelids, pounding with my heartbeat, in my inner thighs. My lips tingled with vodka. In the mirror, I caught a glimpse of skin and twirling white silk under the flash of the disco ball. The club transformed into a velvety night full of silver stars. And it was beautiful. I was beautiful under his intense gaze. People could watch if they wanted, but this dance was about me and Gabe Rivers. My soft lilac bob caressed my shoulders, and I savored the strength in my muscles honed through endless hours of football training. The music guided my limbs. I surrendered to it. A euphoric rush washed over me.

Gabe had chipped at all my reasons not to join his team. He'd shown me his commitment to fair play, he'd offered me more money than I could refuse, he'd shown me what I could achieve and that they understood I had commitments outside of work. Still, something held me back. He thought I could go all the way to the top, but what if I couldn't? What if I wasn't good enough?

I twisted the other way around the pole, but when I spun back round Gabe Rivers was gone. My heart sank. After I'd had his undivided attention, it was hard to let it go. But it was for the best if I did. Gabe Rivers was bad news. A playboy, and not just any playboy—one of England's most notorious playboys. He'd spent a lifetime getting what he wanted, and I'd be an idiot to fall for his charms. If I wanted to join his team, then I had to do it because it was right for me, not just because it was what he wanted. I couldn't trust him not to manipulate me; but then, that wasn't the Gabe I'd met in this club. He'd been open and kind. What if that was the real Gabe Rivers? I moved swiftly to the dressing room.

Deano grabbed hold of my wrist. "Let's go. Gabe Rivers wants you."

Chapter 14

MIRI

A faint smile played on Gabe's lips. "Miss Delights. I see you've overcome your nerves. You were incredible."

The back of my neck heated. Deano disappeared behind the curtain. Silence fell. Did Gabe want to talk again? A little spark of warmth flared in my chest, but it was quickly followed by a twisting knot of guilt. It was wrong to pretend to be someone different when I'd been speaking to him only this afternoon. What the hell was I doing? This was a fantasy. I spent my life covered in mud. No man had ever looked at me in the lustful, hungry way Gabe was looking at me now. It was intoxicating.

He tapped his forefinger to his lips. Music pulsed into the tiny, mirrored room. Had he brought me here to talk or to dance? Was it weird that this time I wanted to dance? The nerves that had frozen me to the spot and made my legs shake last time had disappeared. I'd gotten to know him, and I understood now that he wasn't a man to fear. He'd treated Violet Delights with respect and kindness. Underneath his arrogant playboy exterior, Gabe Rivers was quite . . . nice. If anything, he seemed a little lonely. Could a man that had everything in the world be lonely?

It irked me to admit that I'd warmed to him so much. I couldn't deny how much I'd enjoyed his eyes on me while I worked on the pole. I couldn't deny how much it had turned me on.

"Do you want me to dance for you?" I blurted the words without thinking about them. The anonymity made me bold.

"No. I like talking to you."

An odd disappointment stirred in my chest. The thought of stripping in front of him when he was fully dressed in a smart suit made me hot and excited.

"What if I want to dance for you?"

"Do you?"

I swallowed and nodded. "I owe you a dance."

"I don't pay women to give me attention."

"I *want* to give you my attention."

He bit his bottom lip and his gaze dropped guiltily from my lips to my thighs. A smug sense of power surged through me. That greedy glimmer in his eyes was for me. A wonderful, excited awkwardness wound between us, like the moment before a kiss. I drew a breath and twisted my body. I slid my hands over my silk dress, grazing my thighs and stomach. In my real life, I could never be with Gabe Rivers like this. If I was serious about signing with the team, then he was my boss. Well, actually, my boss's boss's boss's boss. He was off limits, and he wouldn't be interested in me anyway. Miri Forster was a muddy tomboy, but Violet Delights was the kind of woman that Gabe was attracted to.

The vodka was hitting hard. My insecurities were dissolving, leaving a daring confidence and pleasure in their wake. I danced in a way to show off my flexibility, my strength and power. I danced to show him the possibilities, winding my hips in a figure eight, like an ancient princess bewitching her prince into forgetting about the rest of his harem. I'd never have believed this could be enjoyable, but seeing a man like this practically drooling over me made my body vibrate with a warm, sensuous energy.

My heart hammered. Was I really about to get naked for Gabe Rivers?

"I didn't come here for this, honestly. You don't have to—"

I hooked a finger under my dress strap and lowered it slowly down my arm. Gabe's mouth snapped shut. His throat bobbed as he swallowed, and his eyes guiltily traced the movement. My fingers only trembled a little, and not with nerves but with anticipation. I couldn't wait to see the expression on his face. I took a breath and worked the other strap down. I unhooked my bra at the back and held it out to the side, letting it drop to the floor.

He didn't speak, but his hooded gaze travelled over my breasts. A ripple of pleasure raced up my spine at his obvious approval. The silk dress pooled at my stilettos and I stepped out of it. Wearing only a skimpy white G-string, I made sure to bend slowly, straight-legged and graceful, angling myself to give him a good view as I scooped the scrap of material from the floor and tossed it out of the way.

The low pulse of the music sizzled over my bare skin. My nipples firmed into hard pebbles under his hungry gaze. His tongue darted out to trace the outline of his full bottom lip. I would have done anything to feel it flick over my breasts.

I drew a breath. This was supposed to be a lap dance. The thought of grinding against him made my stomach drop, but a strange thrill shot through my nerves. I turned around; backing up and hovering over his lap, I ran my hands over myself. Every urge screamed at me to sit in his lap and savor the friction of his body.

He groaned as I ground my backside against him. The stiff fabric of his suit was cold against my bare back as I rested my head on his shoulder while I rocked my hips and squirmed in his lap. I caressed my stomach, sliding my hands over my breasts and down into my waistband, teasing him as if I might slip my G-string off at any minute.

His expensive cologne filled my nose and his stubble grazed my cheek. His words were a hot whisper against my earlobe. "You don't have to do this for me."

"But do you like it?"

"Yes. I like it. I just don't want to make you feel uncomfortable."

His clipped, crisp voice made everything tighten in my core. My body flooded with heat. I turned around and put my hands around his neck, straddling him, my thighs wrapped around his. I ground against him, arching my spine so that my nipples hovered close enough to graze his face. The press of his impressive, hard length made me quiver. So, not all the rumors about Gabe Rivers were false.

"I apologize." He shifted his position in the chair. "It's been a while."

He was hard for me. I rode him, wearing only a G-string. My confidence spiraled upward, and a warm tingling glow made my heart pound. I'd never been so turned on. So beyond intimidation. So free.

I'm in control.

I have the great Gabe Rivers powerless and under my spell.

My G-string was so wet I was probably ruining his expensive trousers. Good. So what? None of this was about him. He'd spent a lifetime getting what he wanted. Now, I'd get what I wanted. I rose up and the rough stubble of his jaw and his soft lips brushed my nipple. He let out a groan, his breath hot against my skin. The sensation shot straight downward, causing heat to tingle between my thighs. I couldn't contain my moan. My head fell back on my neck. The unbearable ache of impending climax grew. I bit down on my lip so I wouldn't make another sound.

His lips grazed my ear. "I'm serious, you don't need to do this for me. We can just talk if you—"

My nipple grazed his lips again and he snapped his mouth shut and turned his face away. It was almost impossible to hold back the shaking release that threatened to wrack every inch of me. Sweat prickled my top lip. I sucked in breaths, shuddering and trying to come back to myself. This wasn't me. I never acted like this. Oh God. I didn't want him to know the effect this was having on me, but I couldn't stand another minute without him touching me. It had never been like this with Jed.

I grabbed his hands and put them firmly on my hips, encouraging him to explore. He snapped his arms away, pressing them down to his sides.

"I'm trying to be a gentleman here, but you're making this very hard for me." His tantalizing eyes met mine and he raised a dark brow. "Excuse the pun."

"It's okay. I want you to touch me," I whispered in his ear.

I guided his palms back to my breasts, giving him permission. He brushed his thumb lightly against my nipple before snapping his hands away. My fingers dug into his soft hair and I gripped his broad shoulder with my other hand.

He swallowed. "I'm trying to be restrained here, but you're killing me—"

"It's okay. I want to be touched . . . Please . . . I need it . . ."

He raised his hand tentatively. His featherlike graze of my nipple wasn't enough. It was too late to stop what had been put in motion. I guided his hand down to where I ached for his touch, directing him in smooth circles and then firm, hard strokes.

He watched me before dipping a finger slowly into my wet heat. A moan escaped my lips.

"Is this okay?" His words were a hot whisper against my neck.
"Yes."

He slipped in a second finger, filling me, his thumb still rubbing torturously slow circles. His lips grazed my ear, his voice a soft whisper. "Take off the mask. I want to see your face when you come undone."

"No."

His fingers froze. He held perfectly still. He'd left me dangling on a precipice. My breath came in sharp gasps.

A whimper escaped me. "I'm so close. Please."

"Take off the mask, and I'll give you what you need."

No. I was in control. Not Gabe Rivers. If he wouldn't give me what I wanted, I'd take it. Spicy cologne filled my nose as I pressed my face into his neck and rode his fingers, grinding, using him shamelessly.

"Oh. It's like that, is it?" His lips were hot against my ear. "You're a bad girl. You don't do as you're told."

His dark chuckle filled my ears. An agonized series of gasps escaped my lips. Climax hit me, sudden and intense. Everything narrowed to the feeling of my body contracting around his fingers, gripping and tightening in intense waves of ecstasy. He tilted his chin to watch my face.

Music filled my ears again over the roaring white noise. I sagged against him, still straddling his lap, my bare breasts crushed against his chest. I sucked in breaths, spent from the most incredible orgasm of my life.

Lazily, he withdrew his fingers. Oh my God. Reality hit me like a football boot to the face. What the hell had I done? I grabbed my dress from the floor, tugged it over myself and ran.

◆ ◆ ◆

Deano's hand caught my elbow, his voice a low hiss in my ear. "Where's the money?"

"I didn't get any."

"Don't lie. You danced for Gabe Rivers." His vodka-laced breath turned my stomach. "He gave you a grand last time."

"I'm not lying." I yanked my arm free.

My heart pounded. I needed to get to the dressing room. Everything had happened so fast, I hadn't even picked up my bra from the floor. Deano recaptured my arm and threw me into a dimly lit private room, closing the heavy curtain behind us.

He pulled me in tight by my elbow, his voice a harsh whisper in my ear. "After what the two of you got up to in there, he should be giving you more than a grand."

My blood turned to ice. "What do you mean?"

"I heard you, sweetheart. They heard you down on Queen Street."

Bile hit my throat. He shoved me toward the white leather couch.

"Sit," he barked.

I hovered at the curtain. Adrenaline coursed through me at the menacing look in his eyes. His shirt was misbuttoned and cheap white trainers poked out from under his crumpled trousers. The strobe light from the disco ball overhead glinted on his sweating brow. His glassy eyes roamed over me as though he was appraising his purchase, examining me like a piece of flat-pack furniture he was deciding how to screw together.

Music blasted in the room. He frowned and his eyes roved over me. "You gonna take off the mask?"

I fingered the smooth porcelain mask. "No."

"How did a prick like Jed get a girl that looks like you?"

The greasy scent of fries from the bar clung to the air, making me want to throw up. My legs weakened.

His lips pulled into a tight smile. The hairs at the back of my neck lifted at his sinister expression. "Now, this isn't normally the place for this, but if you're willing." He glanced down at his lap and raised his eyebrow suggestively. "You can get this debt paid off quicker."

I sucked in a steadying breath and resisted the urge to fly out of the room.

"No. I have a plan to get your money. It's going to take me a couple of days."

"You don't mind if it's Gabe Rivers." He pouted and gave me a wounded-little-boy look. "Isn't this easier? You may as well if you're here anyway."

"I'm dancing, that's all. This isn't prostitution."

I backed away. He lurched. His fingers wrapped around my wrist and my gut filled with panic. He pulled me into him. A scream left my mouth. No one else was around. Nobody would hear us above the pound of the music.

The vodka on his breath filled my nose. He yanked me, trying to pull me down onto his lap. I struggled, managing to free myself and dash to the curtain. He grabbed my wrist and jerked me back again. My heart pounded. White noise pushed every thought from my head. I balled my hand into a fist and aimed for his face.

Chapter 15

GABE

I drained my beer and called Karl to meet me out the back. I needed to find Violet and give her a tip. I'd come here for some company to relieve my frustrations, not make them ten times worse. What the hell had I done? I'd tried to be a gentleman, tried not to encourage it, but the chemistry was undeniable. She'd destroyed any attempts I had at self-restraint the moment she'd dragged my hand down so desperately between her thighs.

Guilt made my stomach sour. Men who paid for sex sickened me. Normally, I wouldn't be so weak, but I hadn't been able to resist once I'd realized how much she wanted me to touch her. One story in the press and my dreams of the men's team were over. Still. It had been worth it. The little whimpers she made had almost been enough to push me over the edge with her. It had been so long, and this woman had a body to die for.

I wasn't the kind of seedy shit that would take advantage of a woman in a difficult situation. I'd come here trying to get another woman out of my system. When the girl in the mask had been riding me, my mind wouldn't stop drifting to Miri Forster. Miri Forster with her muddy knees and her bruised face. Miri Forster with her hair that smelled of earth and wet turf. What noises would Miri Forster make, grinding over me like that?

An odd sound like a scream broke through the low pulse of music. I stepped outside the private room. Violet stood in the narrow hallway. Shock was etched into her features, and she cradled one hand in the other.

"Are you okay?"

She pointed a trembling finger at the red curtain in front of her. A man lunged out from behind the curtain. She leaped out of his way. I intercepted, shielding her behind me. The man planted himself in front of me, poking gingerly at his bloody nose. His eyes passed over me and he forced a tight smile onto his lips.

"Excuse me, Mr. Rivers. I've got some business with this woman."

He looked around my shoulder, and he beckoned the girl, who stood behind me with a curled finger. "That's enough. Come with me. Let's go."

Violet's labored breathing was audible at my back. "I don't want to."

"If you know what's good for you, then you'll come with me."

I pulled out my phone. "I'm calling the police."

Violet's hand curled around my arm. "Wait. No. No police. This is my fault. I owe him money." Her fingers trembled as she smoothed her purple bob.

The guy's menacing gaze tracked over her and a sneer twisted his face. Anger made my jaw tense. That made sense. I'd thought something was up the first time Violet had showed up in that private room, shaking like a leaf. But she'd seemed so different just now. So confident and in control. Shit. Had I gotten it wrong with that lap dance? It had been so hot, she'd begged me to touch her, but this woman was being exploited here. I didn't want to be just another sleazebag taking advantage of a woman. No way did this man get to intimidate her like this.

"How much money does she owe?"

The man gave me an appraising glance. "Twenty grand."

"Eleven! I already paid you a grand, and I only borrowed ten. You can't keep adding more interest," she cried.

"It's twenty. Your sugar daddy looks like he can afford it."

"If I pay you now, will you leave this woman alone?"

Violet stood next to me. "You don't have to do that."

I patted down my jacket. Not that I'd have that cash on me. I unfastened my watch and put it in the man's hand. "Here. Take this."

He ran a finger over the ridged gold metal and read the writing on the face. "A Rolex?"

A grim feeling weighed heavy in my chest. It had been Dad's. I plastered a casual smile onto my face. "I know. It's awful, isn't it? It's so gaudy. I got it in a goodie bag at some award ceremony. Not my style."

The man's eyes lit with greed. "How much is it worth?"

"More than twenty grand."

More like a hundred.

"It's too much. You don't have to do that." Violet's voice was soft.

The man pulled out his phone and tapped the keys. Blue light lit his mean features as he scrolled.

Violet shook her head. "I can't let you do this . . . I don't know what to say. It's too much. I'll pay you back."

"It's fine. I hate that watch."

Her shoulders slumped with relief. "Are you sure?"

The man transferred his gaze from his phone to the girl in the mask. "We're square."

No shit. At least he wasn't as stupid as he looked.

She swallowed. "Really? It's over?"

"Yup." He slipped the watch onto his wrist and held it out to admire it. "You were right about one thing. You're not a dancer. I'd stick to the foot—"

"Great," she blurted. She took my arm and pulled me away. "Thank you. Why don't you go and get a drink at the bar."

"No. I'm done. Let's get you home. My driver will take you."

Her eyes widened. "No." Her voice rose an octave. "I don't want that."

I held my hands up. "I need to make sure you get home safely. I'm not hitting on you."

She shook her head. "I have someone waiting for me outside. Thank you again. You don't know how much this means to me."

She adjusted her mask and fled.

Chapter 16

MIRI

"It tickles. Are you done yet?"

Frankie tutted in annoyance and dragged the kohl pencil over my eyelid, finishing her precise flicks. She tilted my chin with her finger and squinted at her handiwork, her voice a terse whisper. "Shut up and keep still. Perfection takes time."

I hadn't worried at all about what to wear to Gabe's party until Frankie found me pulling a pair of jeans out of my wardrobe and insisted that she save me. She'd been wanting to give me a makeover and relive some 1990s teen makeover montage fantasy her whole life, and she'd grabbed her opportunity in both hands.

She blotted a smudge on my cheek and beamed. "All done. You look incredible."

I tugged the neckline of the black cocktail dress in the mirror. It was backless. I'd never had much up top, but what I did have was barely contained. It was a beautiful dress, and about as revealing as the one I'd worn last night in the strip club. Frankie had always had expensive taste. I felt like a kid playing dress-up. I may as well have been wearing a tutu and slippers.

"It's too over the top. This is not me."

Frankie curled my last lock of hair, and it fell hot from the curling iron onto my bare shoulder. "Of course it's not you, that's why it's good."

A laugh escaped me. "Thanks."

She watched me. "You're in a good mood."

"I am."

Of course I was. The crippling guilt of owing the money had been lifted off my shoulders. Gabe Rivers had given me the most intense orgasm of my life and then solved all my financial woes in one night. The man was my savior. It was like emerging from a cool river, cleansed of my sins. A Gabe river. Not that he knew he'd done any of that for me.

"Look, anyone who is anyone in football is going to be at this party. There could be some super-hot football guy ready to sweep you off your feet. This is your chance, Miri. You need to meet someone new and move on from Jed. You have to look the part."

"This is not a hookup opportunity. I'm going to meet the other girls on the team."

"That's loser talk. This is absolutely a hookup opportunity. You can do both. Have you never heard of multitasking?" She threw her lipstick in her makeup bag and slapped my nails away from my mouth to stop me biting them. "Stop worrying. You look amazing. You can't spend your life in sweatpants. Hold out your wrists."

I presented my arms and she sprayed me with a cool vanilla mist. "Make sure you talk to people. Don't sneak off to pet a dog."

"I'm sure Gabe won't let me do that. He won't leave me alone until he's got what he wants."

Frankie raised an amused eyebrow and put her hand to her head. "Oh, how terrible to be wanted by a billionaire. What's he like, anyway?"

I grabbed a cardigan from my wardrobe and pulled it over the revealing dress. "He's quite . . . he's not like what you read in the news. And he doesn't *want me* want me. Not in the way your dirty mind works. He needs a new player for his team. He's very . . . nice."

She smothered a smile. "Nice?"

I shrugged. "Nicer than you'd expect."

"You mean you don't think he's a murderer?"

"He's not a murderer. You do know that's all ridiculous lies, don't you?"

Frankie pulled the shoulder of my cardigan, trying to take it off me.

"Hey! What are you doing? I need this."

She tugged the cardigan sleeves. "I didn't make you this hot for you to transform yourself into a grandma."

I gripped the cardigan in place. "I'm not taking it off."

She stood back and shook her head. "Nope. It looks terrible."

"It's fine."

She sighed. "Do you want to get laid or do you want to wear a cardigan?"

I couldn't help my laugh. "Are those my only two options?"

Her eyes dropped over me and she nodded woodenly. "Yes, if that's the cardigan then those are your two options."

"Fine, I'll take the cardigan."

She swatted my arm. "You're a lost cause, Miri Forster. I give up." Her soft makeup brush tickled my cheek as she swept on pink blush. "Do you like him, then?"

"Who?"

She kept her tone light, but her bright eyes gleamed with interest. "Don't play innocent. Do you like Gabe Rivers?"

What did it matter? Gabe was a celebrity. A porn baron's billionaire playboy son who spent his evenings giving women in strip clubs amazing orgasms. No doubt he always had a different girl on his arm. I'd had one boyfriend before. Never any casual hookups. I wasn't about to get my heart broken by a womanizer.

I looked up to find Frankie watching me. "He's a beautiful man. It wouldn't hurt to have a bit of fun, Miri. You don't always have to take life so seriously."

Things like this came easy to Frankie. She was cool and popular, an extrovert who took parties in her stride. I didn't like to play dress-up and mingle. I liked to be in shorts and football boots, not dresses and heels.

"If you like Gabe Rivers so much, I can introduce you."

She laughed and wrinkled her nose. "Nope. He's far too pretty for me. You know I like them rough and ready."

"He's a womanizer."

"So? If you know that up front, what's the problem? Don't get too invested. Have a bit of fun and get out with your heart intact."

"If I join his team, he's going to be my boss."

"Exactly. That's hot."

"It's not hot. It's messy."

"He will be your boss's boss's boss. You'll hardly see him. Don't overthink everything all the time."

I laughed. "I can't believe you're encouraging me in this."

She grabbed me by the shoulders and swiveled me to face her. Her face was lit with amusement. "Can't you?"

I laughed. Actually, I could totally believe it. Of course Frankie would be encouraging me in this.

She tried to drag the cardigan off me again. "You're under orders to have fun."

I pushed her away and wrapped my arms around my middle. "This is a professional meeting that happens to be at a party."

"Fine. Enjoy your professional party and your cardigan." She twisted me and shoved me out the door. "Good luck. Somebody might have got laid in a cardigan at least once in history."

Chapter 17

GABE

I sipped my water and turned my back on the rows of bright bottles at the bar. I needed to keep a clear mind tonight, and that meant no booze. This was a full-out charm offensive to get Miri Forster to sign on the dotted line. It had been dragging on for too long. Tonight was about temptation. I had to show her what she could be part of. I'd spent time with the women's team and they were a great bunch. Miri would fit right in.

Music and chatter filled my ears. I greeted a group of players and squeezed through to the kitchen. Some old Motown tune drifted from the speakers, wrapping around my heart. A sudden grief stabbed my chest. Dad had loved the house when it was full like this. Parties had brought him to life. Mother should have sold this place, but it had been in her family for so long she couldn't part with it.

Dad hadn't been around much growing up, and he'd betrayed me and Mother more times than I could count. He'd cheated on me with my own girlfriend. But still my chest hurt. Some stupid part of me ached for him. Whatever he'd done, he was still my dad. Heat pressed behind my eyes. Jesus. I needed to get myself together. This was what nobody told you about grief. Everything would be fine, then some stupid song would come on the radio and destroy you.

I needed some air. Weaving through crowds of guests, I left the party and found a spot on the smooth stone steps that led from the kitchen. Music pulsed faintly behind me, but it was quiet out here. I took in the dark expanse of grounds. A tiny light in the bushes caught my eye. Bloody paparazzi. How low could these bastards go to get a shot? Anger made my jaw clench. Fuck that. We'd already had a press conference after the match today. They'd had the opportunity to ask all their stupid questions.

"I can see you. You may as well come out," I called.

The hedge parted and a blonde girl tottered out. Long pale-golden waves cascaded down her back. She wore a plum-colored cardigan and, underneath, a revealing black dress clung to her exquisite physique. It took me a moment before it hit me. Miri Forster. My pulse beat harder. It shouldn't have been possible for this woman to be more beautiful, but here she stood, radiating like a divine being. I'd suspected she had a banging body under that football kit, but Miri Forster scrubbed up better than even my dirty mind could imagine.

Nope. Professional. This all had to be professional.

I kept my voice casual despite the effect she had on my pulse. "I didn't realize we'd hired a new gardener. You know you don't have to get inside the hedge to trim it."

"Funny." She smoothed her hands down her sides and strode toward me.

"What are you doing in the hedge?"

"This place is so big. I was trying to avoid all the cameras at the front door and then I got . . . lost." Her eyes met mine. "This is embarrassing."

"It could be worse."

"Could it?"

98

I shrugged. "You could have been pissing in there."

She burst out laughing. I couldn't help the smile that pulled at my lips. Somehow, when she laughed it was with her whole face. It was hard to look away from. She peered through the kitchen window to the party inside before smoothing her dress over her thighs and sinking down to sit neatly on the step beside me. I leaned across and pulled a twig from her hair and swooped a stray curl behind her ear. Even in the moonlight I caught the blush that stained her cheeks.

She shot me a look. "Is something wrong?"

"Why would it be?"

"You're sitting in the freezing cold and everyone else is in there."

"I needed a break. Every time there is a party in this house, it reminds me of Dad."

She pulled her dress over her thighs and drew her knees to her chest. She flashed me a glance. "It hasn't been that long, has it?" She cleared her throat, awkwardly. "I heard something on the news . . ."

Of course she had. The press had fixated on Dad's passing. The most awful time in my life and nobody could leave us alone for a second. "Just over a year."

A wrinkle appeared between her eyebrows. "I get it. Dad had a chair in the kitchen he always sat in to read. For a while, I couldn't even bring myself to look at it. These things take time."

She brushed her golden hair over her shoulder. I let my gaze drift over her. The skimpy dress clung perfectly to her taut stomach and slim hips. She had the body of an athlete, strong and toned, with a feminine and wholesome beauty. My fingers itched to trace the freckles dotted in cinnamon constellations over her milky skin.

It was a terrible idea, but I couldn't help thinking the sight of Miri Forster riding me could do something about this ache in my chest. I moved closer, inhaling her vanilla scent. She looked incredible in that dress. She'd look better without it.

She opened her mouth as if she might say more and closed it again. She chewed her pillowy lips and shot me another nervous glance. I leaned closer, watching her throat bob as she swallowed. I needed to keep this professional, but what mattered more than getting this woman in my bed tonight? Fuck it.

"I want to kiss you," I said.

Her bright blue eyes widened. "I'm sorry?"

A jolt of amusement went through me at her look of surprise, but somehow I kept a straight face. "I want to kiss you. It's all I can think about."

"I thought you wanted me to join your team."

"I do."

"Kissing does not mix with professional relationships. It's a terrible idea."

"You're right. It's an awful idea." I couldn't drag my eyes away from her lips. "But I still think we should."

Her lip twitched as though she was trying not to laugh. "I don't."

"Are you sure? We could get the camera crew over. Let's give them something worth filming."

She chuckled. "No."

"You have the most beautiful laugh."

"You say that to all the girls."

"I do, but it doesn't make it less true. You don't want to kiss me?"

"It doesn't matter if it's a good idea or not. We can't kiss if I'm going to play for your team."

"Why not?"

She threw her hands up, but the smile hadn't dropped from her lips. At least I was amusing her. "If you're serious about the team, this can't happen between us. You don't always get what you want."

"You don't know much about me, do you? I always get what I want. What do you want me to do? You want me to seduce you?

100

I can do all that if you want it. You want to be wined and dined? Flowers? Dates? I'll take you for dinner in Paris tonight."

She snorted. "No."

"Rome?"

"No."

"Kuala Lumpur?"

"It doesn't matter where. It's all a means to an end." A faint smile twisted her lips. "Aren't you a sex addict? I shouldn't be propping up your addiction."

"I'm not a sex addict. That's bullshit the papers say. I don't get cold sweats if I don't fuck. It's been ages for me anyway. I've resisted a lot of temptation lately. A lot."

She frowned and patted my knee. "Well done. You managed not to have sex for a while. Have a cookie."

"How long has it been for you?"

She chewed her lip and picked at the stone step. "Aren't we going to go inside? You wanted me to meet the team."

She stood and I grabbed her wrist, stilling her. "Tell me. How long?"

She shook her wrist from my grip and lowered herself back down. "It's been a while. I had a bad breakup. Let's just say I'm fine without men."

"Well, I know what a bad breakup feels like."

Her eyes met mine. My throat closed up. The last thing I wanted to talk about was Emma or what had happened at this house.

I leaned in, lowering my voice. "You know the best way to get over a bad breakup? Mind-blowing sex with someone new. I don't mind helping you out. It's my duty. Nobody with a body like yours should be going without."

She chewed her lip. "And what will people think if I hook up with the director of the team and then I get a spot to play?"

"I don't live my life by what other people think of me."

"How wonderful that you have that privilege. The rest of us have to pay attention."

I frowned. "Privilege? I have cameras following my every step. I have papers writing bullshit about me every day. If I cared about other people's judgment, I'd never leave the house. It's a survival strategy, not a privilege."

"I thought you brought me here to introduce me to the team. Or do you only want me to play if I'm sleeping with you?"

A pulse beat in my temple. This conversation was not going well. "Of course not. I want you for the team regardless." I held my hands up in surrender. "There is no pressure. No strings. You don't have to turn it into something sordid."

"But that's what it is. That's what people will think."

A rough hand clamped on my shoulder. "There you are, Gabe."

Lana and Sophie, two of the midfielders, lurked behind me. They were both pink-cheeked and shiny eyed. Between them, they dragged me to my feet.

"What are you doing? I want you to meet my friend, Miri. She's the striker I've been telling you about."

Sophie flashed Miri a wave and a smile. "Hi."

"We've wrestled the microphone from Mel. You're on next." Sophie shoved me forward into the house. "It's tradition."

My eyes narrowed. "What tradition?"

"Every new signing has to sing karaoke."

"I'm not a new signing."

"But you're new to the club, so . . ."

Miri smothered a smile. "You'd better do it, Gabe. You want to make a good impression on me or not? I'm not joining your team unless I know you're on board with the team's needs."

Fucking hell. Karaoke? No man had ever worked so tirelessly to get a woman to sign a piece of paper.

I shook my head. "I'll get you back for this, Forster."

Chapter 18

Miri

Guests crammed every inch of the enormous mansion. Most of the girls I recognized from the team. We'd played Calverdale plenty of times. I followed the girls, who pushed Gabe through the mansion. They shoved him to the front of the opulent sitting room. An enormous sound system and flat screen dominated the wall.

Gabe held his hands up to protest, but the Calverdale goalkeeper forced a microphone into his palm. An awkward silence wrapped around us. Would he walk off? The music kicked in and the lyrics began to roll on the screen. Gabe swallowed, lifted his chin, and boldly looked me in the eye. He smirked and plunged carelessly into a rendition of "We Don't Talk About Bruno." The team roared with laughter. I couldn't help but laugh along. He'd taken it with good humor at least.

Gabe Rivers was an enigma. The press made out that he was a ruthless bastard who had pushed his own father down the stairs. He had his faults, but he wasn't deserving of his reputation. With the team he was relaxed and fun, and in the strip club he'd been charm personified. Not to mention talented with his fingers. The rumors of his arrogance might have been exaggerated, but I was certain he was still a womanizer. If I let my guard down even a fraction, he'd get everything he wanted from me, and when he was done he'd walk away. That's what men did. They hurt you.

"He's a good sport." Claire Easterly passed me a glass of champagne and smiled.

I couldn't help my laugh. "Oh God. Please make it stop."

Claire laughed. She flashed me a glance. "You're still thinking of joining us?"

"I'm thinking."

She watched Gabe and smiled. "I thought it was a gimmick when Joyce Rivers told me about her plan, but Gabe has surprised me. He's sincere. He's taken the role seriously. Micky didn't care about the women's team. He wanted to tick the boxes. But Gabe is different. He's working to move us into the men's facilities. He's interested in what we've been doing. He's studying the replays from the past season, and he has so many fresh ideas. I don't doubt his commitment to this. With his enthusiasm and investment, we could go all the way."

"It's a big move for me."

She sipped her drink thoughtfully. "It is, and you shouldn't be rushed, but if you're in any doubt as to whether this man is genuine, then let me assure you he is."

A group of women charged the stage and threw their arms around Gabe, cheering him on and singing with him. His handsome face lit with a smile. Clearly, the team was taking him on board as one of them.

I looked up to find Claire watching me. She twisted her wineglass in her hands. "I heard Jerry's been given the boot. That son of a bitch won't be back."

"Did you know what he was up to?"

"There were rumors. He was Micky's best friend. Untouchable."

"So you turned a blind eye?"

"I complained. Of course I did. Nobody listened. I should have done more, but I didn't want to lose my job, Miri. This is a man's world. We know that better than anyone. Micky would always protect his own."

My shoulders tightened. Claire wasn't off the hook in my book, but she wasn't responsible for Jerry. His behavior lay with him and the boss that had shielded him.

She shook her head and pressed her lips flat. "Gabe will have removed every obstacle he can, so what does that leave?"

Me. It leaves me. What if I'm not good enough?

Claire regarded me for a moment before she shifted her attention back to Gabe and his terrible singing. "I was there the moment he saw you play for the first time. You mesmerized him. He couldn't take his eyes off you. I wish I could bottle up whatever you have and give it to every woman on this team. Even the best of us doubt ourselves sometimes, but you don't need to. Gabe sees what everybody else sees. You're a star. Join this team and we'll make sure you get everything you need. I want to see you get called up for England."

I'd shelved my dreams to play professionally such a long time ago that playing for England was something I'd never even allowed myself to imagine. Gabe thought I could do it, and now Claire was saying the same thing. I hardly dared reach for something so out of my grasp, but maybe there was a chance. A giddy pleasure rushed through my veins. Maybe such an incredible achievement wasn't as impossible as I'd always believed.

I slid Claire a sidelong glance. I'd never particularly liked this woman. She hadn't done enough about Jerry Reynolds. But life wasn't black and white, and she was a woman in a man's world too. I knew what that was like. "Thank you, Claire."

She inclined her head in a nod. "Don't mention it."

The song ended and a woman pulled Gabe, laughing, into the gathered crowd. Ignoring his good-natured protests, the team lifted him up on their shoulders and paraded him around the room.

"Come on." Claire put an arm around my shoulders. "They won't let him go for a while. Let me introduce you to the girls. They're going to love you."

Chapter 19

Miri

Claire paraded me around the house until my jaw ached from smiling. I'd met most of these girls before, but they'd always been my rivals. I'd never taken the time to get to know them. We met in battle on the muddy pitch and then we went back to our lives. But I had to admit that I liked them. I liked them a lot. I sat on the kitchen counter, legs dangling over the edge, chatting with Lana. I'd only ever known her as a badass bitch infamous for her mean tackles; now I knew we shared an undying love for Taylor Swift.

My body had filled with a strange restless energy after the conversation with Gabe. I'd almost kissed him. It had been torturous to walk away, but I couldn't go there. We had to keep things professional. It had been fun to speak to everyone, and they couldn't have been more welcoming, but I'd reached the stage of the party where I wanted to go home and curl up in bed with a hot chocolate.

"Ah, here she is. Can I steal Miri for a moment?"

Claire inclined her head in a nod and I let Gabe lead me away. His hand rested lightly at the small of my back as he shepherded me into the hallway. He paused at the bottom of a winding flight of marble steps. For a moment, he stood and stared upward.

"Is everything okay?"

He forced a smile. "Do you want to get a drink?"

I held up my champagne glass. "I have one."

He raised a brow. "A better one?"

"Okay."

I followed him in silence up the marble steps before we got to an endless landing. I'd have guessed Gabe's house would be big, but I couldn't imagine something like this. It was more like a city.

"Your house is huge."

"I live at the Beaufort. We're holding the party here."

"You live in a hotel?"

His lip twitched with a smile. "It's not *a* hotel. It's *my* hotel."

"Oh."

He opened one of the doors on the endless landing and flicked a switch. Light flooded a luxurious study. Bookcases heaving with old tomes lined the walls and a huge pool table dominated the living space. A walnut desk sat in the corner by a bay window that looked out onto a starless night.

Gabe hesitated for a moment, drew a breath, and stepped inside. He crossed to the desk and reached into a drawer at the bottom. He took out a bottle and tumblers and poured us drinks.

"Here." He passed me a heavy tumbler of amber liquid.

"What are we drinking to?"

He cocked his head and raised a questioning brow. "Well, that depends on you."

He wanted my decision. I'd been on the fence until the conversation with Claire, but she was right. I had to believe in myself. I'd overcome so many hurdles to play football. This could be the greatest career move of my life. Time to stop holding myself back. Gabe gazed at me expectantly. I could have put him out of his misery, but I liked him like this, pretty and eager to please. It wouldn't hurt to keep him on his toes a little longer.

"Well." I tapped my finger against my lips, pretending to ponder. "It was going to be a yes to joining the team, but then I heard your singing . . ."

His lip twitched. "That's fair."

I held my glass up. "To karaoke and the wonderful singing career that awaits you."

Amusement crept onto his face and he chinked his glass against mine. "To karaoke."

The whisky burned my throat on the way down. He took a sip and studied the glass, twisting it in his hands. The sight of him in a well-fitted suit, bathed in soft lighting, took my breath away.

He smoothed a hand over the polished walnut desk. "They've kept everything how it was." He drifted to the window and peered out into the darkness. "It's as if he never left."

"Your dad?"

His voice sounded tired and distant. "I keep thinking he might poke his head around the corner. It will never happen, but sometimes the heart doesn't listen to the mind. I haven't been up here since . . ."

His beautiful lips were downturned and shadows haunted his eyes. His expression was miles from the joyous karaoke performance. An ache speared my chest. I moved to the window to stand next to him. His slender, masculine physique exuded power and confidence.

"Why come up tonight?"

"I don't know. Maybe you make me brave, Forster." He lifted his glass to rest against his lips and I couldn't take my eyes from his exquisite mouth. "Tell me something about you that no one else knows."

"Why?"

He took another sip of whisky. "Because I need to take my mind off the way it feels when I'm in this room."

My heart sank. Should I tell him? What would he think if he knew it was me who had been grinding over him in a strip club? It was a betrayal. I knew about an intimate moment that we'd shared, and he didn't. What if my admission jeopardized my spot on the team?

I swallowed. "Okay. I'll tell you something, but it's bad."

He raised an eyebrow, set his glass down and rubbed his hands together. "I think I'm going to like this."

I opened my mouth and closed it again. Shit. No. I couldn't do it. Not now. After tonight, meeting the girls and talking to Claire, I'd never wanted to join this team more.

"I don't have anything interesting. I'm quite boring."

"There must be something."

"Fine. I kissed three boys in one night once."

His eyes widened. "What?"

"It was at Laura Mayhew's party. We were doing truth or dare, and I kept getting dared. I was thirteen. I have no regrets. It was an incredible night."

He put his hand on his heart, his smile bemused. "Nope. I want something juicier."

"More juicy than kissing three people at one party?"

He shrugged and raised an impish eyebrow. "That sounds like a typical Saturday night."

I laughed. "Maybe for Gabe Rivers."

Silence fell between us. He chewed his lip and tousled his perfect hair. "You want to know my darkest secret?"

"Yes."

"Are you sure?"

"Certain."

He set his whisky on the desk. "My dad died because of me."

Holy shit. What? Was it true? He'd pushed his dad? It couldn't be.

110

"We were arguing, and he grabbed his chest . . . then he fell. It was the stress . . . it must have brought on the heart attack." The animation left his face and his voice cracked. "I tried to grab him, but I couldn't . . ."

What a terrible burden of guilt to carry around. "It's not your fault, Gabe. If his heart was weak then it could have been anything that brought that on."

A look of tired sadness passed over his handsome features. "But it wasn't anything. It was me."

His eyes slipped away. I cupped his face with my hands and forced him to look at me. "It wasn't your fault."

"Everyone thinks it is. There's a whole podcast about it, for fuck's sake."

"Those people are idiots."

He studied my face, analyzing my reaction, seeking permission. He brushed a strand of my hair behind my ear. No doubt he'd pulled that move a thousand times with a thousand other girls, and still it set off wild swirls in my stomach.

He traced the line of my jaw with his thumb. "All I can think about is kissing you."

A thousand birds took flight in my chest. He tilted my chin with his knuckle, forcing me to look into his beautiful eyes.

"I want you, Forster."

"We just had this conversation outside."

"I know. I still want you."

Oh God. I wasn't going to do this, was I? I couldn't. My heart hammered. I stiffened my spine, trying for some resolve. The silence thickened. He stepped closer. My back hit the desk. He positioned himself between my thighs.

"I want to keep things professional . . ." The sentiment sounded half-hearted even to me.

Slowly, he lowered his face. His lips brushed mine. "Me too."

"I don't want to do this with you."

"Me neither."

My insides jangled with excitement. "We can't do this if I'm going to join your team."

I watched his throat bob as he swallowed. "We really can't. Do you want to join my team?"

He'd worn down my defenses. I had no reasons left. "Yes."

His warm breath fanned my face, and his lips touched mine again, soft and sweet. "Then we absolutely can't kiss."

"I know. We can't."

He whispered against my lips, "You should tell me to stop."

Even if I'd wanted to stop, my mouth wouldn't form the word. I held my breath. His lips covered mine, and he pulled me roughly toward him. Blood pounded in my ears. Muscles deep within me tightened, longing to be filled. I wanted to forget myself in this tangle of tongues and teeth. It was only the need that mattered. Every part of me was too tense, begging for release like a violin string pulled too taut.

His mouth seared a path over my neck and he pulled my cardigan down, kissing the hollow of my throat and across my shoulder. His warm lips found mine again, firm and masterful. My senses filled with spicy cologne and expensive whisky. Instinctively, my body arched against him, and his finger traced a path over my collarbones and the bare skin of my shoulders, sending currents of desire through me. An electrifying heat bloomed over every patch of skin his fingers brushed. Oh God. I'd wanted this. This was a kiss to escape into, to get lost in, to drown in. I couldn't stop it. Not now. If this was my chance with Gabe Rivers, then I'd take it.

He tugged off my cardigan and tossed it on the desk. At least Frankie would be happy it was finally banished. My head fell back, a moan escaping, and he chuckled into my neck. His large hands traced the bumps up my spine and pleasure raced through me. He lifted me onto the desk. His hands skimmed my thigh, bunching my dress.

I rested my forehead against his, my breathing labored. "We should get back to the party."

His lips trailed across my throat. "I'm enjoying our party up here."

I didn't want to stop kissing him, but things were getting too hot and heavy too fast. I couldn't believe I'd let my guard down. What on earth was I thinking? This wasn't me. I was way more sensible than this. I couldn't get involved with this man. He was a professional heartbreaker.

"People will wonder where we are."

"So?"

"So, you have a new striker. Don't you want to make your announcement?"

He frowned and studied my face, feature by feature. "You mean it? You're joining my team?"

"We'll need to discuss the terms, but yes."

A huge smile lit his face. "What made you change your mind?" His incredible eyes sparkled with mirth. "The singing?"

"Yes. The singing. That's what swung it."

Before I had the chance to make a sound, he lifted me in the air by my waist and spun me around.

A breathless laugh escaped me. "What are you doing? Put me down."

"You won't regret it. I swear it. We're going to the top, Miri Forster. You and me. All the way to the top."

He set me on my feet. My lips felt swollen from his kiss. A sudden awkwardness came over me. What the hell was I doing? I couldn't be kissing him if I was serious about this job. This had to stop before it got out of hand. We'd both been drinking. We could put it down to a moment of madness.

I walked to the door. He grabbed my wrist, pulling me back to him. "Where are you going? I'm not done with you."

"Don't you want to tell people the news?"

"They can wait."

I pulled my wrist free from his grip. "This stops now. If I'm joining your team, then let's do things right. I don't want people to think I got this job based on anything other than my talent."

He frowned. "It is based on your talent."

I straightened my dress. "But what will it look like? I need to make a good impression. I don't want to be gossiped about straight off the bat. We keep things professional."

His mouth tightened. "Is that what you want? Nothing more?"

No. I wanted to feel his lips on mine again. I wanted him to lift me back onto the desk and take me right here in this office, but that was a terrible decision, and I'd always been sensible. I had to continue to be sensible no matter how much this man made my heart pound.

I pasted a smile onto my face. "Yes. We keep things professional. That's what I want."

Chapter 20

GABE

Four weeks passed in a blur of fitness tests and training sessions. I watched Miri from the sidelines. The team had welcomed her with open arms. This was a boost for all of us. It was a bright Saturday morning in mid-December when she played her first match for us. Even Mother came to watch the occasion.

"You got the player you wanted?" Mother cast an unimpressed eye over the pitch.

"Yes."

I hadn't taken my eyes off Miri Forster for the entire match. Ever since we'd kissed, I couldn't get her out of my head.

Mother frowned. "Ruby tells me you've been doing a good job. Has the team moved up yet to the women's special league . . . ?"

"The Women's Super League, and no. This is their first match with Miri."

"It all takes a long time, doesn't it?" A little wrinkle appeared under her eye. "I'm hearing some positive things about you, and I'm also hearing some not-so-positive things, darling."

"Oh?"

"Apparently, you've formed a . . . friendship with a stripper."

My shoulders tensed, but I made no reply. How could she know I'd been to that strip club? Wonderful. Someone had ratted me out to my mother.

"Don't you think the tabloids would love a story like that?"

"I just wanted a quiet drink somewhere. It's one of Dad's old clubs."

She pressed her lips together. I turned my attention back to the match. One of the opposition players tripped Miri over, sending her flying.

I flew to the sideline. "Penalty!"

Miri lay curled on the grass. The medics darted across the pitch. I made to go over when Mother grabbed my wrist. "Let them deal with it, darling. You don't need to get involved." She flashed me a cool look. "I'm going to spend Christmas in Dubai with the girls . . ."

I couldn't care less about Dubai. Mother's voice became an annoying drone in my ear. I couldn't take my eyes from Miri. A terrible tenseness gripped me. Why hadn't she gotten back on her feet? The medics worked on her ankle and she stood tentatively, stretching her arms above her head. Thank God. My shoulders relaxed down from my ears.

Mother's drone sharpened back into focus. ". . . I can't bear the cold at Christmas. I can't believe I've lasted here as long as I have." Mother shook her head. "Strippers and alcohol. This is explicitly what I warned you about. You're giving the tabloids everything they want."

A pulse pounded in my temple. This conversation was giving me a headache.

Mother drew a breath. "Also, you can't fire Jerry. Jerry was your father's oldest friend. He's not going anywhere."

I turned to glare at my mother. "Jerry is a disgrace. He's sexually harassing young women."

She scoffed. "You shouldn't believe everything you hear. Jerry likes a little flirt. If you tell him no, then he'll stop. It's harmless. Everyone is so sensitive these days. Football is a man's world. If the female players can't handle it, then they can go back to netball or hockey."

I gave her a cold smile. "Careful, Mother. Your misogyny is showing. Jerry is disgusting. He doesn't respect women. He's gone. The only way we can get Miri Forster is if Jerry is gone. If he doesn't go it's a deal breaker. Besides, if he hasn't done anything wrong, then you needn't worry."

Mother flexed her fingers and examined her perfect manicure. "I don't want to hear about you associating with strippers anymore. Your image needs to be squeaky clean." She sighed. "We miss Emma. Everybody loves you with Emma."

Not going to happen, Mother. "I'm never getting back together with Emma."

Miri blasted a goal into the top corner. She whipped off her top and did a victory lap. Her breasts bounced in her white sports bra as she raced in a circle before her teammates dive-bombed on top of her. A delicious shudder heated my blood at the sight. Fuck it. I had to have this woman. Whatever it cost me. One night. I needed to get her out of my system so I could concentrate on my fucking job. I didn't chase women, they came to me; but how could I get anything done around here with this constant distraction?

"Whatever you did to Emma, you can fix it. You need to grovel, and you can win her back."

"I don't want Emma back."

Mother sighed. "You need a woman like Emma, with her own money. How else can you know you're not with a gold digger?"

"Because I have good judgment."

Mother rolled her eyes and rested a cool palm on my cheek. "My darling boy. You've always been so naive. It's like your dad always used to say. You have no experience of the real world."

I flinched and pulled her away. "I live in the real world."

"I have every faith in you, Gabe. You're going to behave yourself now we've had this little talk. Call Jerry and make your peace and keep out of the papers." Mother watched Miri and wrinkled her nose. "One day you'll have the men's team and these women won't be your problem anyway."

Chapter 21

Miri

It's funny how life can change so dramatically in such a short space of time. Finally, the hospital discharged Mum and our lives transformed overnight. The bonus was no more running back and forth to the ward; the downside was trying to figure out with Reece how we were going to do this. We had backup from the caregivers who visited the house, but it was down to me and Reece to manage the rest of the time. The first week went better than we could have expected. Reece was a natural and I muddled along, following his lead. The hardest adjustment was us all living back together under one roof, getting under each other's feet. At least at the training pitches I could breathe.

I towel-dried my hair, pulled it into a ponytail, and left the changing rooms.

"Miri?"

Gabe's low voice made me jump. He leaned casually in the doorframe. His arresting good looks knocked all thought from my head. We hadn't spoken since the transfer, but I often felt his intense, watchful presence on the sidelines. He had dropped in on the contract negotiations and he observed every training session, but we hadn't had any time alone together since the kiss at his party.

He flashed an easy smile full of white teeth and pushed off the wall. "My office. I need to talk to you."

"About what?"

He glanced at my teammates filtering out of the changing room behind me. "We need to finalize some points in your contract."

"We do?"

He nodded confidently and strode away down the corridor. I followed him to his office.

"How are you settling in?" He closed the door and sat behind his desk.

"Good. Thank you."

He leaned back in his chair, watching me. "You had a great game out there."

"Thanks."

He gestured to the chair opposite his desk. "Aren't you going to sit down?"

I hesitated for a moment. It was dangerous being alone for too long in a room with him. His charming smile made me lose all sense of reason.

I slipped into the chair. "What about the contract?"

He pressed his lips together. "This isn't working for me."

"What do you mean?"

"You running around that pitch in those shorts, looking like that."

Confusion pulled at my brow. "I don't understand."

"I can't stop thinking about you. It's distracting. I can't do my job."

What? I expected him to shoot me a wry smile, but his expression was one of pained tolerance. He wasn't joking? My heart pounded. "I don't see how that's my fault."

He sat still, looking at me intently. "Well, it's not my fault."

Silence fell between us. My breath quickened under his intense gaze.

He leaned back, sizing me up. "Come to my place tonight. I'm cooking you dinner."

"You cook?"

"I cook."

"You're full of surprises."

A smug smile curved his full, sensual lips, but his eyes sparkled with teasing. "You have no idea."

This was too much. I couldn't get involved with him, no matter how wildly my heart hammered. Besides, I was deceiving him. He'd already given me the best orgasm of my life, and he didn't even know. How could I get into anything with him, knowing I had a secret like that?

"No. If you want to discuss work, then we can discuss it now."

"It's not work. It's dinner. I need to get you out of my system, Forster. Spend the night with me. One night. We both need it. Then we can both get on and do our jobs."

He spoke in a casual tone, as if he was asking to borrow a pen, not arranging sex. Christ. The arrogance. I couldn't stop my incredulous snort. "Who said I need that?"

"Don't you?"

Yes. Of course I did. I drew a breath. He'd never looked hotter. Or smugger. He knew I wanted him. When had anyone not? But not just for one night. I folded my arms across my chest. "We said we were going to keep things professional. I don't think 'getting me out of your system' qualifies as professional."

"I want you."

"You got me." I threw my arms up. "I'm on your team."

"And now I want you in my bed. One night, Forster. That's all," he said matter-of-factly. "My driver will come for you at 8 p.m."

My face heated at his bluntness. This wasn't the Gabe I was used to. He'd been so restrained and respectful when I'd been grinding in his lap in the strip club. Never pushy. "Your driver is going to have a wasted journey, because this isn't happening. You're still my boss, Gabe, and honestly you're coming on way too strong. What's gotten into you?" I tried to maintain my composure, even though he was looking at me like the Big Bad Wolf about to eat me alive. "When a girl says no, she should only have to say it once. This is sexual harassment."

His expression grew serious. "Are you accusing me of sexual harassment?"

That wasn't entirely fair. I wanted him, but one of us had to be sensible. This couldn't happen. "You're making an indecent proposal. What if I say no? Are you going to fire me?"

"Of course I'm not going to fire you. Why would you even say that?" His usually calm voice held the faintest edge of exasperation. He dragged a hand over his face. A rare crack in his usual poised confidence. "This is all new to me, Forster. I don't chase. I don't ask women to spend the night with me. Women come to me. If I'm messing this up, then it's because I don't know how to handle a situation like this. I don't know what I'm supposed to do."

I smothered my smile at his frown. Poor little rich boy. He was so used to women throwing themselves underneath him, he'd never had to work for it.

He ran his tongue over his lips and held his hands up. "Fine. You're right."

"About what?"

He got up and walked toward me, planting himself in front of me. He looked incredible in his dark suit and polished brogues. I stiffened my spine even though I wanted to melt into a puddle on the floor.

"Look me in the eyes and tell me you don't find me attractive," he said.

My heart pounded so hard he could probably hear it. I opened my mouth to lie and snapped it shut. "It doesn't matter. We can fight our urges."

With his powerful hands, he hauled me to my feet. He traced his thumb along my jaw; heat tingled in its wake. "Why would I fight my urges when I can indulge them?"

"Because we're not children and actions have consequences."

He chewed his bottom lip. He took out his phone and showed me the screen as he scrolled to a voice recorder app. I watched him press the red circle for record.

"Do you find me attractive?" He put the phone face up on the desk.

I swallowed. "What are you doing? Are you recording this conversation? Why?"

He came closer, looking down at me intensely. The desk pressed at my back. "Do you know my full name?"

"What?"

"It's Gabriel Hamilton Broderick Rivers. Tonight, I'm going to kiss every inch of your body. You're going to spread your legs for me, and I'm going to sign my name between your thighs with my tongue over and over. I'm going to make you come so hard you see stars."

A hot swoop of desire pooled in my lower belly. I opened my mouth and closed it again, at a total loss for words. No man had ever spoken to me so brazenly. Jed's pillow talk had been about who needed to empty the dishwasher.

"You have a filthy mouth," I said.

"You have no idea." He smirked and it should have been annoying, but it was irresistible. "If you're going to accuse me of sexual harassment, then let's make sure there's no doubt in your mind about what I want from you. I want to fuck you. I want to make you beg me not to stop. I want my name to be on your lips when you come."

His gaze froze on my lips. "Give me one night. If you don't want me to fuck you, then this conversation is harassment. You can have this recording because you should definitely report me. You can say no if you want, and I won't ever bother you about it again. If you do want me, then this conversation isn't harassment." He returned to his chair, his eyes fixed on mine, and his elegant fingers made a steeple over his lips. "It's foreplay."

I swallowed. I had no idea how to reply to something so direct.

"If you want me to stop pursuing you, then tell me now and this ends. You have my word. I don't want to make you feel uncomfortable, but I have the sense that you feel this thing between us too. Give me one night to worship you. You won't regret it."

My whole body bloomed with feverish heat. Gabe Rivers was the devil in an Armani suit, and I'd never been more ready to go to hell. "Eight p.m. it is."

Chapter 22

MIRI

I'd walked past the Beaufort Hotel hundreds of times but never once set foot inside. Its soaring red-brick facade was iconic. The most expensive hotel in the city. The immaculately presented doorman's eyes flashed over me, but he didn't bat an eyelid as Gabe's driver escorted me through the back door. My neck heated. I knew what this looked like. Gabe probably brought a different woman here every night.

My boots clicked on the polished marble floor. An awkward silence fell between me and Gabe's driver in the lift, and I did my best not to fiddle with the buttons on my coat. I'd had no idea what to wear, but standing in the opulent lift, I realized it had been a mistake to dress so casually. The driver punched a code in the PIN pad on the wall. The ascent filled me with trepidation. We went up and up. Maybe we'd keep going until we burst out of the ceiling.

"How much higher?"

"Right to the top."

Gabe's words from my living room echoed in my mind. *Wouldn't you like to be on top, Forster?* Heat stole into my face.

A *ping* rang out as the doors opened, revealing a long corridor with thick cream carpets. A sweet floral scent like sun-warmed roses hit my nose. I followed the driver to the door at the end before he smiled politely and left me there. Nerves filled me and I had the strangest urge to run back to the lift, because I didn't want to be alone with Gabe Rivers. Things beyond my control happened when the two of us were alone.

My heart hammered, but I gathered my courage and knocked on the door to the suite. Gabe opened the door and smiled, giving a glimpse of his beautiful straight white teeth. He was dressed more casually than usual in a dark sweater and jeans. It looked simple enough, but if I knew Gabe, that one outfit cost more than my entire wardrobe. At the sight of him, the words fell out of my head. His sleeves were pulled up to his elbows, and I worked to keep my attention on his face instead of getting caught up on his muscular forearms.

Sadness lingered around his eyes. Gabe Rivers was something unreal. A billionaire. A celebrity in a magazine. A fantasy. It was easy to get carried away with that circus. Easy to forget that he was a human being. That somebody so rich and pretty could have any problems. That they could be messed up and get hurt like the rest of us. But I'd seen a different side of him. I'd seen him breaking in his dad's office.

I stepped inside his sumptuous suite and my breath caught. The suite was arranged in a circular configuration. I wandered to the window. The city skyline shone in the black night in an endless, glittering panorama. "Wow, what a view."

Gabe stood next to me. His spicy cologne drifted to my nose. "Beautiful, isn't it?"

I didn't have the energy to fight my desire for him tonight. I edged away instead, creating a distance so I could breathe.

"You live here, then? In a hotel?"

He nodded.

"Wouldn't you prefer a house?"

126

"Why? Everything I need is here."

"Isn't it a bit . . . lonely?"

He flashed a smile, but his green eyes became as flat and unreadable as stone. "I don't get lonely, Forster. I have everything I could ever want."

I wandered around the suite, taking in the opulent furniture. A huge four-poster bed occupied the farthest room. There was even a gym in one of the adjoining rooms. Gabe tipped his head to a golden velvet chaise longue by the floor-to-ceiling window. I perched on the seat, feeling suddenly strange and awkward. What the hell was I doing here? I wanted him, but it was a terrible idea. We'd have one night together and then he'd kick me out the door.

After Jed, I'd sworn I wouldn't let my heart get trampled again. In theory, it was easy. I just had to keep my heart out of it. None of this had to mean anything. It was only deep if I let it get deep, but that meant denying the truth. Casual sex wasn't me. I threw my heart into everything I did, and this was about to break it. I was already too attached to Gabe. But if one night was all I could have, then I didn't want to let it slip through my fingers.

He sat next to me, and a sudden rush of nerves made my heart pound. I jumped up from the chaise. "Shall we have a cup of tea?"

"A cup of tea?"

"Yes. Wouldn't that be nice? Maybe we should chat first . . ."

He hesitated, measuring me for a moment, then eased into a smile. "Sure. I'll make some tea."

He moved to the kitchen area and put the kettle on. I took my first proper full breath since I'd entered the suite. It was too hard to think straight when he was so close. I leaned with a hip against the sprawling marble island.

"Do you know how to make tea? Don't you have people to do that for you?"

He chuckled darkly. "Of course I can make tea. I can cook and I can make tea."

"I never imagine you doing normal stuff."

"I do normal stuff. I'm a normal guy." He raised a wry eyebrow. "I just happen to be incredibly rich and good-looking."

I couldn't help my laugh. "But not modest."

A bemused smile touched his lips. "No. Not modest."

He made us tea and passed me a mug. It was easy with him. How could it be this easy with someone like him? This is how he'd been at the strip club. Relaxed and down-to-earth. Funny and charming. How could the media have gotten this man so wrong?

"How is it?" he said, watching me carefully.

"It's a cup of tea, Gabe. You did well."

He beamed and leaned against the counter. "Thanks. I thought so, too."

I sipped my tea and wandered over to the window. The suite was beautiful, but I could imagine him being bored in here. What did he even do all day? I'd read stories about him online. The tabloids claimed he was addicted to every drug going.

"Do you do drugs?"

I regretted the question as soon as it had left my mouth.

"Well, that escalated. I thought you wanted tea?" He smiled, but it didn't reach his eyes. "And no. I don't do drugs."

"Me neither. I just wondered." I blew steam from my tea and took a sip. "There are a lot of stories about you . . ."

He held up his hands in mock surrender. "I'm afraid it's all exaggerated. I don't do drugs. I'm cleaning up my act. No booze. No sex. I'm on a sex ban." He raised a bemused eyebrow. "The PR team insists."

"A sex ban? How's that working out for you?"

"Not great. I propositioned my new striker." His gaze dropped to my lips. His voice was silk. "I want to change, but you're making it difficult for me."

My back hit the pool table. Somehow, our bodies found a way back to being close to each other like magnets, even when I created a distance between us. A swoop of desire made my stomach clench. His lips were so close to mine now, I'd only have to make the smallest step to kiss him. I wanted to kiss him.

"About this sex ban. What counts as sex? Is it just penetration?"

He chuckled darkly. "Say that again."

"Say what again?"

"Penetration. It sounds funny. It makes you blush."

My cheeks warmed under his gaze. "It doesn't."

He raised a brow; a smile twitched his lip. "I didn't clarify the details."

"Maybe you should have read the fine print." I tried to keep my breathing level, but my voice came out a whisper.

His eyes dropped back to my lips. "Maybe I should have."

I held still. My pulse pounded at his lazy appraisal and the smoldering look in his jade eyes. A faint tremble ran through me. What the hell was I doing? This was Gabe Rivers. He'd toss me aside tomorrow, and then I'd have to see him every day at the football club knowing that I couldn't have him. I could stop this now and spare myself the heartache.

I swallowed, thinking of a way to buy myself time. "More tea?"

His incredible eyes came to study my face, analyzing me. "Is something wrong, Forster? You're not nervous, are you?"

"A little." I tried to keep a breezy smile on my lips, despite my thundering heart. "I don't do this kind of thing . . ."

"What thing?"

My words escaped me in a rambling stream. "Casual. Hookups. I've only had one boyfriend before . . . It didn't end well . . ."

"What happened?"

I bit my lip. I wasn't ready to talk about that. "We drifted apart."

His teasing expression grew serious. "I want you. I can't deny that. I've wanted you since the first moment I saw you annihilating your opposition on that pitch, but I'm not a sleazebag like Jerry Reynolds. Nothing that happens between us will ever affect your position with the team. If I haven't made you feel safe or comfortable, then I apologize. I can't not go after what I want, but if this needs to stop right now, you can walk out of here and we won't speak of it again—"

"No. It's not that. I feel safe with you."

Gabe had been respectful at the strip club. In public, there was a maddening hint of arrogance about him, but in private he was like this—charming, sincere, and unpretentious.

"This is just . . ."

His compelling gold-green eyes riveted me to the spot. My sister's words rang in my head. Maybe I *did* take everything too seriously. This was one night. I could just enjoy it for what it was. It wasn't as though I wanted a relationship after how Jed had treated me.

"This is just . . . different for me."

"Different good?"

"Yes. Different good." I cleared my throat.

His smile relaxed measurably. "We don't have to do anything you don't want. We can just talk or watch a movie. If you don't want to do more than that—"

"No. I want to." My voice was thick and unsteady. "I came here to be with you. I didn't come to drink tea."

He peered at me intently. His finger traced the line of my jaw. A rush of delight gripped me.

"I'm thinking about kissing you again, Forster. Lately, it's all I think about." His voice was tender, almost a murmur. "Would you like that?"

I nodded, barely able to find my voice. Heat rose in my cheeks. He took the tea out of my hand and put it on the side. Slowly, his mouth descended to meet mine. His kiss was surprisingly gentle. I slid my tongue against his, devouring his warmth and tenderness.

His lips left mine, and he whispered against my ear. "You don't have to worry about anything with me. I'm going to look after you. If you want to slow down or stop, just say the word."

His velvet voice made my body flood with heat. He recaptured my lips, more demanding this time, and pulled me against him. The heady sensation of his kiss made my knees weak. Gently, I helped him peel off my T-shirt. His hungry gaze dropped from my eyes to my shoulders to my black lacy bra. It was the same way he'd looked at me in the strip club. This time, I had no mask to hide behind, but I wanted him under my spell again.

I unfastened my bra and tossed it aside. His eyes riveted on my face, before they moved slowly down to my breasts. He drew a sharp breath. Tingling lit the pit of my stomach at his obvious approval.

"Beautiful," he said.

He bowed his head and took each rosy nipple in his mouth, sucking hard. My senses reeled as if short-circuited. I couldn't help the groan that escaped my lips.

"Good?"

"Yes." I arched against him, burying my hands in his soft hair.

He showered my breasts with hot kisses, tantalizing and teasing my nipples, which were swollen to their fullest. All the while, his cool hands explored my body, sliding over my stomach and curling over my hips.

My heart turned over when his hands moved lower. He worked the button on my jeans and slid them down my thighs. He caressed the back of my legs with cool palms before he dropped to his knees, kissing his way up. His lips trailed at my ankles, my calves, the backs of my thighs, making me weak. Jed had never bothered to touch or kiss me in those places before, but Gabe didn't leave an inch of me unexplored.

He helped me out of my jeans and stood in front of me, still fully dressed. It reminded me of the strip club. The memories of how hard he'd made me come on his lap filled my mind. My skin prickled with anticipation.

His lips found mine again, and I succumbed to his kiss. It wasn't tender anymore, but a demanding, lustful crash of teeth and tongue that left me breathless. His cool finger traveled under the waistband of my knickers, parting me and resting so lightly where I ached for him. His touch was so gentle and exquisite it was almost like not being touched at all.

His words were a hot whisper against my throat. "Do you like it when I touch you here?"

"Yes."

He moved his mouth to mine, and my moans died under his punishing kiss. Another gasp left my lips at the press of his finger, slipping into my wet heat, stretching me. He curled his finger, hitting a spot that made me groan.

"Still okay?"

"Yes."

He pulled me roughly to him and lifted me onto the pool table.

"Lie back," he said, his voice rough and dripping with authority.

I did as he commanded. Cool fabric pressed at my back. He slid my knickers off and buried his dark head between my thighs. The hot press of his mouth made me cry out. Jed had hardly ever gone down on me. I loved the sensation, but Jed had never focused on my pleasure. I'd always suspected it had been a power play on his part. He didn't want to give me what I craved. Gabe had no such reservations. He swirled his tongue against my sensitive bundle of nerves. A hot swoop of desire tightened everything in my lower

132

belly. He started slow, sucking and probing, savoring me. I couldn't stop my agonized gasps.

"Yeah? Like that?" I could hear the grin in his voice.

I could only moan in response.

He lapped at me, and a divine pleasure gripped me. My thighs clenched around his head and he chuckled and pushed them apart, spreading me wide, on the pool table, so he could continue his feasting. Oh God. Was he doing the thing he'd said, spelling his name?

I dug my fingers into his hair, stilling him. "Do you have a condom?"

"Patience, Forster." He dragged his tongue slowly at my center and his eyes lifted to meet mine. "First I need to feel you come undone on my tongue."

His whispered words against my clit had me arching up with need. Heat flushed through my veins. The world disappeared to nothing but him—the warmth of his firm, probing tongue, the indecent groans he gave that broadcast his enjoyment as he worked, the aching need between my thighs. A desperate tension made me arch and my thighs contract around him. It felt so incredible, but it wasn't enough. My body ached to be full of him. Gently, I pushed his head away and reached for his waistband. I worked to undress him while his lips recaptured mine, forcing me to taste myself on his tongue.

His commanding voice was rough against my ear. "The bedroom. Now."

No. The bedroom was too far. I couldn't wait. I turned around and braced my hands on the pool table. My heartbeat throbbed in my ears. This is how I wanted him to take me. Deep and hard. If we only had one night together, then there was no point being shy. This wasn't about romance. Gabe had made it clear he only wanted sex.

His tongue traced out over his full lips. "Here?"

"Yes."

He nudged my legs apart with his knee and pressed me flat with a large palm at the base of my spine. I had to ask him about protection, but my head was spinning. I threw a glance over my shoulder. He slid his trousers and boxers down. I gulped. The rumors were true. Gabe Rivers had inherited more than his porn star dad's money. His eyes met mine, and he raised a bemused eyebrow. No surprise that he knew how impressive that was.

His fingers fumbled to open the condom packet. I hadn't even seen where it had come from. This was all so practiced for him. So mundane. Or was it? His fingers were trembling and he was breathing hard. I'd never seen him lose his cool or do anything in a hurry. Usually every movement was precise and measured, but whatever this crazy tension was between us, he'd lost his patience. It gave me a smug sense of satisfaction to know that this was unraveling him too.

He pulled me into position, his bare skin warm against the back of my thighs. Then his cool hands were everywhere, exploring the soft hollows of my back, caressing my hips.

"Tell me you want this. I need to hear you say it." His voice broke with huskiness.

"I want you."

He took a firm grip of my hips. I waited. Cold air caressed my sensitive exposed flesh. My body throbbed with need. I tossed my head to peer over my shoulder. He stood frozen, his gaze trained on my lower back. He traced a finger at the base of my spine then he pushed into me. The stretching burn was sharper than I'd expected. I was ready for him, but goddamn, he was big. I spread my palms flat on the pool table.

Gripping my hips tightly, he pushed deeper, stretching and filling every inch of me. I took a hard breath. He wrapped his hand around my ponytail, tugging it back lightly, making me arch for him. I moaned, biting my lip so I wouldn't cry out.

"Look at me."

I twisted as much as I could with my hair still in his hand. My fingers dug into the pool-table cloth as I braced myself to take more of him.

His eyes were full of concern. "Am I hurting you?"

"No."

I clung to the table as every snap of his hips brought me a punishing pleasure. I threw another glance over my shoulder. Maybe he didn't play football anymore, but he still had the body and stamina of an athlete. His delicious abs contracted and rolled as he worked, thrusting in steady, even strokes. His fingers dug into my hip hard enough to bruise. He fisted his hand tighter into my hair, making me arch. My neck flashed hot. He pulled my back against him, every intense thrust leaving me desperate for a release just beyond my grasp. His breath was harsh and uneven as his strokes became wilder and more erratic.

A series of rough cries and gasps left my lips. Noises I didn't even know I was capable of. Raw pleasure exploded in a shuddering release where our bodies joined and rushed in waves through me. Gabe's final quick, uneven strokes left me breathless, as he found his own release. His heavy weight pressed me flat before he straightened.

Gently, he twisted me and hauled me into his arms. I curled into his hard chest. The tantalizing scent of his sweat filled my nose.

"Fuck, Forster." An astonished grin overtook his handsome features. "That was . . . Fuck . . . I don't even know what that was . . ."

I couldn't help my laugh. I didn't know what it was, either. Sex had never felt like that with Jed. Gabe made me feel safe, but empowered and sexy, the same way I'd felt with him at the strip club.

He frowned. His concerned gaze traveled over me. "Was it good for you?"

Warmth lit my chest. "Better than good."

His brow relaxed and he eased into a teasing smile. "I'm just glad you could keep up with me, Forster."

Chapter 23

GABE

Miri had laughed at the idea of eating in the bath, but I'd convinced her. Trays piled high with sandwiches, charcuterie, and intricate cakes filled the bathroom, alongside bowls spilling over with fruit. She sat at one end of the Jacuzzi tub drinking her cup of tea, and I sat at the other.

She smiled. "Tea and cake in a bath bigger than my house. It doesn't get better."

The scent of rose and eucalyptus wrapped around me. I couldn't stop my eyes from dropping to her beautiful tits, barely covered with soapy bubbles. To stop myself from staring, I transferred my gaze to her elegant fingers as they twirled circles in the silky water.

She shot me a shy glance. "Were you doing the thing you said? With your tongue?"

"You liked that?"

A rush of pink stained her cheeks. "Yes. You don't mind being down there? Doing that?"

"Mind? What do you mean?"

She put her tea down on the side and scooted toward me. "My ex . . . Jed . . . He didn't like to do stuff like that."

"Jed sounds like a prick."

She laughed. "Yeah."

"And he's missing out. I could spend all day doing *stuff like that*."

She chuckled. "Be serious."

I turned her around and pulled her into my arms. The milky soft skin of her back was hot against my face.

"I am being serious." My lips brushed her earlobe. I kept my voice low. "It's the truth. I could spend all day between your thighs. You taste divine."

She gave another embarrassed chuckle, but I felt the quiver that ran through her. Pressing my ear between her slippery shoulder blades, I listened to her thrumming heart. Warmth bloomed in my chest. It hadn't been like this since Emma. In the beginning, anyway, when things were good, before she'd screwed me over.

I didn't want to fall for this woman. I couldn't let anyone have that power over me again. I wouldn't do it. I had to have more resolve. This was just sex. Amazing sex. One night. But what would it hurt to ask her to stay? How could I let her walk out of here after that? It would break my rules to have a woman stay over, but I needed more time.

"Stay with me tonight."

"I thought we were doing this once." Her voice was sleepy.

"We agreed one night. We didn't specify how many times."

"I can't."

"Why not?"

"I have responsibilities."

"What responsibilities?"

She stiffened slightly in my arms. "What time is it? I should get going."

I pulled her back to me. "It's still early. You don't have to rush."

She lay back against my chest, but her muscles were tense. Her perfect rosy nipples poked through foamy bubbles and I couldn't stop myself from brushing a thumb around the outline. Her soft hands slid all over my body to lather me with soap. She plunged a jug into the water.

"Close your eyes," she said.

"I give orders, Forster. I don't take them."

She laughed indignantly. "Maybe it's time you started. Close your eyes. I'll make it worth your while."

Well, in that case . . .

I did as she instructed and she poured water over my hair. With gentle fingers, she washed my hair, massaging my head carefully. I couldn't help the groan that escaped my lips at the perfect pressure on my scalp as she worked the soap in. My nose filled with the scent of roses. Water cascaded down my back as she emptied the contents of the jug over my head to wash away the soap. I slipped down low into the water, letting the heat soothe away all my tension.

Her hands slipped under the water. I hissed and gripped the side of the bathtub as her fingertips brushed along my shaft. I pulled her toward me so that she straddled me. I took hold of her hand and guided it up and down, from root to tip, showing her how to please me.

I rested my head back on my hands and watched her as she bit her lip and pumped her hand up and down.

"Faster," I said.

She slowed her strokes. "Don't tell me what to do, Rivers. It will only make it worse for you." She laughed her beautiful, unself-conscious laugh. The water sloshed out over the top of the tub as she picked up her pace.

"Do you like that?" she said breathlessly.

"Mm-hmm."

She moaned and I closed my eyes because the sight of her wet and flushed with pleasure and her perfect breasts bouncing was enough to send me over the edge, and I didn't want it to be over so soon.

"You're beautiful. You know that, don't you?"

She laughed. "You're just saying that because I've got my hand wrapped around you."

"That's a factor, but it's also the truth."

Her lips covered mine and our tongues wound together in a filthy kiss full of lust and need. This woman was going to kill me. She picked up her pace. My fingers tightened around the edges of the tub. Oh God. This was too good. The last time I'd let a woman into my world, everything had come crashing down on my head.

The water lapped up the sides of the tub as I tried to pull her down onto me.

"No. Not without a condom. Just relax."

I rested my head back against the tub while she worked. Heat and intense pleasure engulfed me, and I couldn't help my groan. Who was I kidding? One night wasn't enough. I couldn't fuck this woman out of my system. I could only make this longing in my chest for her worse.

Miri Forster had me completely fucking done for.

Chapter 24

MIRI

The next morning, I found Reece and Mum in the kitchen. Reece was kneeling next to Mum's wheelchair, the two of them whispering.

Reece stood and Mum flashed me a glance. "You were back late last night."

The back of my neck itched at the lie, but I didn't need them prying. "I was with Phoebe. We opened a bottle of wine . . . I lost track of time."

"Did Phoebe get a new job?" Mum asked.

"No. Why do you ask?"

Mum kept her tone light and innocent. "Oh, I thought she must have had a salary increase since she dropped you home in a Lamborghini." She sniggered. Reece flashed her a glance and raised a bemused eyebrow.

"You are both so nosy and so juvenile. Aren't you above this kind of thing? You're worse than Frankie. This is why I don't tell you anything."

Reece lifted his hands in mock surrender and raised a sardonic eyebrow. "I'm just happy for Phoebe. It's wonderful that she's doing so well."

The two of them shared a look and laughed.

Mum clucked her tongue. "You don't have to lie to us about your boyfriends, Miri. It's been so long since Jed. Whoever he is, you should invite him round for dinner."

I couldn't stop my incredulous laugh. I could imagine my family trying to play it cool with Gabe Rivers in the house. I'd die of embarrassment. It was a stupid chain of thought anyway. Gabe didn't want a girlfriend. He'd wanted *one* night. God only knew how awkward it would be when I saw him again after Christmas.

The sound of a key in the door and excited chatter drifted from the hallway. Frankie burst into the kitchen, followed by her twin, Elliot. Frankie dropped her bag and ran to hug Mum first before pulling me into a hug. Elliot hung back, waving a greeting.

Frankie smoothed a hand over her dark-green-tipped hair. It had been blue when she'd left for university. "We would have got here sooner but I had to drag this knucklehead out of the gym." She thumbed in the direction of Elliot, who stood tall and imposing in the corner. He towered over all of us by at least a foot, even Reece.

Mum smiled. "Well, I'm so glad you're both back. Now we have everyone home for Christmas."

Frankie raced to Mum and dropped down to hug her again. "And we have *you* home. I can't believe we're all together in this house again. It's so weird."

Reece shook his head. "I haven't bought enough food. I'm going to have to go shopping. I've planned the menu this week."

Frankie smiled. "No worries. I'll come and give you a hand."

A brief grimace flashed across Reece's face. He wouldn't welcome help. He had his own fastidious systems for doing everything, and Frankie was the embodiment of chaos.

Frankie smiled. "And Miri can tell us all about her celebrity boyfriend, Gabe Rivers."

I'd have to shut down this nonsense. "He's not my boyfriend."

141

Mum's eyebrows flew up. "Is that who's been giving you rides in a Lamborghini?"

Frankie reached across me and grabbed a mince pie. "He's been giving her more than that."

My cheeks flamed and I covered my ears. "Stop. Gabe Rivers is not my boyfriend. He's my boss."

Frankie laughed. "Oh my God, you're as red as a beetroot. You're in love with Gabe Rivers, aren't you? *The* Gabe Rivers."

"I am not in love with Gabe Rivers. *The* Gabe Rivers. He's the director of the club I play for. It's a professional relationship."

"Yeah. Yeah. Of course it is." Frankie clapped her hands together in excitement. "Right. Reece, hurry up with that tea. I need to catch up with Miri." Frankie pushed me out of the kitchen. She leaned in low to whisper in my ear. "The word on the street is that the man has the meat. How big are we talking? I need you to confirm the facts, and don't spare me a single detail."

Chapter 25

GABE

I sat in the enormous lounge, waiting for Mother to meet me for brunch. Bright December sun streamed in through the tall windows, and the gentle clicks of the ancient grandfather clock pierced the silence. Portraits of dead relatives stared down at me from the walls above a crackling fire. Unlike my dad, Mother was "old money." The house had been passed down through generations dating back to the eighteenth century. Her side of the family were all crusty old aristocrats. If enough people died, she'd even have a claim to the throne, and God help us all if that ever happened.

Perhaps she'd invited me over to discuss plans for Christmas. I didn't fancy spending a day here, but it was better than being alone in the Beaufort.

I drummed my fingers on the coffee table before I pulled out my phone.

My fingers hovered over the screen. Screw it. I didn't text my casual fucks. They texted me. I didn't chase. I was supposed to be behaving myself. But why play games? I could check in after last night. It didn't mean anything. It was basic politeness. I sent a text.

Last night was fun.

Little dots appeared then disappeared.

I stared at the screen. I managed to wait an entire minute before I typed another message.

What are you doing today?

The dots appeared again. About to get in the shower after training.

Heat seared through me. Miri Forster naked was a sight to behold. Are you naked right now?

Not yet.

Send a picture when you are.

No.

You don't get to tell me you're about to be naked and not send me a photo.

We said one night.

It's one photo.

I waited for her reply. Nothing. My heart pounded. What was I doing? Texting a woman after sex. A woman that I almost begged to stay the night. That was two of my rules smashed in less than twenty-four hours. The memory of her desperate whimpers and her taste forced their way into my mind. I positioned a cushion strategically over my lap.

Mother breezed in with three fluffy white Pomeranians trailing at her high heels. My assistant, Ruby, scurried behind her, carrying a clipboard.

"Darling." She pouted and air-kissed both my cheeks. "How lovely to see you."

She smoothed her skirt and sat next to me. Ruby pressed her clipboard to her chest, her face grim. Why was she even here? Wasn't she supposed to be *my* assistant?

My phone buzzed in my pocket and my fingers itched to grab it. For fuck's sake. That could be a photo of Miri Forster's tits and I had to sit here and make small talk with my mother. I smoothed a smile onto my face. Whatever this was, I needed to get it wrapped up ASAP.

"I'm disappointed, Gabe."

"What have I done now?"

Ruby dropped her gaze to her knees.

"What have you told her, Ruby?"

Ruby spread her arms regretfully. "The truth, Gabe. I'm sorry. I have to be honest with Joyce. Karl said he brought a girl to you last night. One of the players . . ."

My teeth gritted. So, not just Karl. Ruby was ratting me out as well.

"I thought you brought me here to talk about Christmas dinner?"

Mother's eyes flashed with confusion. "Christmas dinner? I'm flying to Dubai this afternoon to spend Christmas with the girls. Didn't I tell you, darling?"

Only about a hundred times. "You might have mentioned it."

Mother pouted and patted my leg. "You know I'm never happy in England at Christmas. No, I came to talk about your future." Mother shook her head. "You're up to your old tricks again. We want the best for you. You told me you'd behave, and already you've been photographed in a strip club and now you're associating with a girl you employ. How do you think this looks?"

"I don't care how it looks."

Mother sighed. "We miss Emma. The two of you looked so perfect together. Everybody loves you with Emma."

"Give it a rest, Mother. I'm never getting back together with Emma."

She patted my knee. "Well, I believe that you're trying. I have every faith in you, darling. You want the men's team, so you must behave yourself now we've had this little talk."

My blood went cold. "This is ridiculous."

"Happy Christmas, darling. Let's see some better behavior in the New Year."

My phone buzzed again in my pocket. Fuck it. I couldn't wait anymore. I pulled it out and opened an image of Miri's face. Her golden hair hung damp around her slim oval face. A teasing smile twisted her pretty lips and her jaw was set at a stubborn angle. It's how she'd looked last night when we'd finally gotten out of that bath, and she'd let me dry her with a towel. Fresh-faced and relaxed. Not a scrap of makeup, but so wildly beautiful it took my breath away.

It was all so effortless and natural with this woman. Her eyes sparkled with vitality, and her lips were so soft and inviting. Of course she wouldn't do as I'd asked. This was her playful side. Miri didn't take herself too seriously. I couldn't remember laughing as much as I had last night, when she'd told me some of the stories about her family.

Her sense of humor was one of the things about her that was so endearing—one of the many things. This wasn't the photo I wanted, but there was something more intimate in that teasing smile than a nude shot. It was dangerous. It made me feel off-guard and undone. This wasn't meant to be deep. I was supposed to be appreciating Miri Forster's tits right now, not her charm and sense of humor. Fuck that. I wasn't supposed to be texting this woman at all. This was sex. Ridiculously addictive sex. Nothing more. If I hadn't made that clear, I'd have to double down so she understood.

I sent off a quick text. I want you naked.

You don't always get what you want.

You don't know me very well, Forster.

She might be smirking now, but she wasn't smirking when I made her come three times in a row last night, and she wouldn't be smirking when I did it again.

Mother watched me with an unimpressed expression. "Keep out of the papers. I mean it."

I held my hands up. "I'm on my best behavior."

"Make good choices. Actions have consequences."

Chapter 26

Miri

A knock sounded on Mum's front door. I opened it to find Gabe on the doorstep. My stomach swooped and I stepped onto the doorstep, pulling the door behind me.

"What are you doing? Why don't you ever ring before you show up? Do all rich people turn up on each other's doorsteps like this or just you?"

He smiled. "It's urgent. I'm waiting for my picture."

"Picture?"

"After your shower."

What? Did he expect me to sext him? "I sent you a picture."

"That's not the picture I want."

I leaned in, keeping my voice low. "What are you doing, Gabe? You can't turn up like this. I thought you wanted to get me out of your system. We had our night together."

"Right. The problem is, it's made things worse." He leaned in and whispered in my ear. "Now I've had a taste of you. I need more."

His confident voice made me hot and excited. I stepped away. We were on my doorstep. My family was inside the house. This wasn't the time or the place for getting swept away by Gabe Rivers.

I couldn't let myself fall for this man. He'd drop me like a hot brick as soon as he'd had enough. We'd said one night. It wasn't enough for me either, but better stop now before I got in too deep.

I folded my arms. "This sounds like a 'you' problem, not a 'me' problem."

A hint of amusement danced in his expression. "Is that so?" He swept a thumb along my jawline and my heart pounded. "You enjoyed yourself last night. What's changed?"

"We said one night."

"I know, and now I've changed my mind. I need to fuck you again tonight."

My face warmed. I peered down the empty street. This village was full of curtain-twitchers eager to gossip. "Keep your voice down."

Shouting and laughter blasted down the hallway behind us. Gabe tried to peer behind me through the crack in the door. "Aren't you going to invite me in?"

"It's not a good time. The twins are back from university. The house is chaos."

"We're fucking again tonight. My driver will come for you at eight p.m."

He twisted his cufflinks. The memory of when he'd given away a Rolex to help out a virtual stranger drifted to mind. Guilt prickled the back of my neck. I wanted to, but I couldn't go there with him. Not after Jed. I had to protect my heart.

"I'm sorry. I have plans tonight."

"Cancel them."

"I can't."

"What are you doing?"

I couldn't help my incredulous snort. What was going on here? "I'm going to the ballet. My brother has a show."

"Fine. I'll come with you and we can fuck afterward," he said matter-of-factly.

"Keep your voice down," I hissed again. "You're not coming. My whole family is going."

"So?"

I threw my hands up in exasperation. "So, you said one night and now you want to come and watch ballet with my entire family?"

"No. I hate ballet. I want to fuck you again tonight, and if I have to watch ballet with your family, then I will, because that's how much I want to fuck you again."

I opened my mouth and then closed it again. "Absolutely no way."

"Is that Gabe Rivers?" Frankie's excited voice boomed from behind. A groan left my lips. My sister pulled the door open at my back. She nudged me out of the way to get onto the doorstep.

Her mouth fell open. "Oh my God. It is." She turned around and cupped her hands over her mouth to shout down the hall into the house. "It *is* Gabe Rivers. I told you!"

My neck heated. I could have sunk into the drain and disappeared. Why did I have to have the most embarrassing human being in existence as a sister?

I rolled my eyes. "This is my sister, Frankie."

A small smile ghosted Gabe's lips. "A pleasure."

Frankie grabbed Gabe by the hand and pulled him past me inside. "Come on. We've been dying to meet you. It's Gabe Rivers." Her voice was sing-songy and gleeful. "*The* Gabe Rivers."

Oh God. My stomach dropped out of me with embarrassment. She flashed me a glance and her wink told me she knew exactly what she was doing. I tried to squeeze past them to block their progress to the kitchen, but I couldn't.

"Gabe doesn't have time for this," I said.

"Nonsense," Frankie said, releasing Gabe's hand. "It will just be a minute."

The chatter in the kitchen fell silent as we walked in. Reece and Elliot's heads shot up simultaneously to study Gabe like he was an exotic exhibit in a zoo.

Frankie grinned and clapped her hands together with excitement. "This is Gabe Rivers, everybody. It's Gabe Rivers in our kitchen."

I maneuvered Frankie out of the way. "These are my brothers, Reece and Elliot."

Gabe crossed the room to shake Elliot's hand and then Reece's. Thankfully, Mum was still asleep in the other room. At least it wasn't my entire family in one fell swoop. Reece donned his oven gloves and pulled a tray of mince pies out of the oven and deposited them on the island. The delicious pastry-and-cinnamon aroma filled the kitchen.

Elliot moved to grab a mince pie and Reece knocked his hand away. "Too hot."

Reece turned his smile on Gabe. "Tea and a mince pie? They'll cool down soon."

Not soon enough.

"Gabe doesn't have time for all that." I tried to push him toward the door, but he held firm against my shove.

I gave him a withering look but he smiled blandly back. What the hell was he doing? This was mortifying. My family were the most embarrassing humans alive. They had no concept of playing it cool. Why was he even here? Didn't he have better things to do, like run his empire from his personal luxury hotel? He'd had his face buried between my thighs less than twenty-four hours ago and now he was here in my kitchen. It was just sex. This shouldn't be happening.

"Miri's right. I should get back, but it's a pleasure to meet you all."

Relief made my shoulders drop as Gabe headed to the door. He paused and turned back to look between my brothers. "Which one of you is the dancer?"

A wry smile twisted Reece's lips. "That would be Elliot. People would pay me to stop dancing, but I'm taking it as a compliment that you had to ask."

Gabe smiled and turned his attention to Elliot. "You're performing tonight?"

Elliot inclined his head in a nod.

"Which theater?"

Elliot's intense gaze met Gabe's. "The Grand."

Gabe kept his voice casual, but his eyes sparkled with mischief. "My family has a private box at the Grand. You can all use it if you'd like."

Frankie beamed and clapped her hands together. "Fantastic. It would be nice to get out of the cheap seats for a change."

Gabe flashed an easy smile. "No problem."

"We already have tickets. You don't need to do that," I said.

Gabe brushed off my protest with a wave of his hand. "It's fine. It's empty. Free champagne and the best view in the house. Why let it go to waste?"

"That's good of you, Gabe. Thanks." Reece's shrewd eyes flashed from Gabe to me and I knew he wasn't missing a minute of this unfolding. "But only if it's not a problem."

Gabe shook his head. "It isn't. I haven't seen a show in a while." He turned on his heel. "I'll see you all there later."

What? No. Had he invited himself to the ballet?

I chased Gabe down the hall to the front door.

I grabbed his elbow, stilling him. "What are you doing?"

He raised an eyebrow. "Going back to work."

"No. I mean about tonight. You're seriously coming to watch ballet?"

"Yes."

"Why?"

He stepped close, blocking me in against the wall. He gave me a bold, raking gaze. "When I ask for a naked picture, you'd better send it straight away next time. I want you in my bed tonight, Forster, and if I have to sit through an evening of pirouettes and your brother in tights, then so be it."

Heat stole into my cheeks. I opened my mouth and closed it again. A half smile crossed his face before he turned on his heel and strode to the door.

Chapter 27

GABE

I sat on a bench in the park near Calverdale Station. For a moment, I shut my eyes and let the chatter of the birds fill my ears. I had work to do this afternoon, but Miri Forster's pretty face wouldn't be removed from my mind. A glow of amusement lit my chest just thinking about the horrified look she'd worn when I'd met her family. It was going to be fun at the ballet tonight. I liked making Miri Forster squirm. She was so easy to tease. I just had to get through one evening of ballet and I'd have her to myself again. She was a drug and I couldn't wait for my next hit.

A woman in a caramel trench coat with dark hair in a neat bun dropped down on the bench next to me.

"Mr. Rivers. A pleasure to meet you." The woman gave me a tight smile.

I shook her hand. "The trench coat is a nice touch. Is that an essential for a private investigator? Like part of the uniform?"

She kept her face flat. Right. No sense of humor. I supposed that wasn't an essential for the job.

I took a deep breath. "I've heard you're the best."

She inclined her head. "If there's dirt on Mr. Reynolds, I'll find it."

"Oh, there's dirt, but I need enough evidence for the police to prosecute."

She smoothed her pencil skirt over her knees. "I'll do everything I can."

A blast of noise wrapped around us as a group of children skipped past. I lowered my voice. "It should go without saying that this needs to stay confidential. I can't trust anyone within my organization. You will have to do some digging, but discretion is the key. My dad tried to bury issues raised in the past. I want hard evidence—no expense spared."

The PI flashed me a glance as though she wanted to ask a question, but looked away again.

I twisted my new Rolex on my wrist. "What is it?"

"You have a lot of skin in the game. If evidence of harassment comes to light, it's not going to look good for Calverdale United."

"I know."

She shot me a glance. "And you're okay with that?"

I nodded. "I want to do the right thing. Men like Jerry can't be allowed to get away without being held accountable. This is the right thing to do, regardless of the effect on the club."

She shot me an incredulous look. A grim kind of amusement rose up in me. "Is it so hard to believe I want to do the right thing?"

She hesitated, choosing her words carefully. "Not hard . . . a pleasant surprise, maybe. You have a certain reputation, Mr. Rivers . . ."

Don't I know it. I held my hands up in surrender. "You got me. I'm not a pure altruist. This is also about a girl. I made her a promise. I want to see it through. Jerry's clearly a piece of shit that needs to be dealt with, but I wouldn't have known if it hadn't been brought to my attention. Now I know. I won't turn a blind eye."

Mother would be furious when she found out about this, but I couldn't rest knowing what Jerry had been up to. Anger prickled the length of my spine. It was disgusting. The thought of this man even being in the same room as Miri made me feel nauseous. Jerry had been in a position of authority and harassed women who trusted him to do the best by them. He'd ruined people's careers. He'd almost succeeded in ruining Miri's career. It must have been so awful to feel so powerless and vulnerable. I hadn't been able to protect her then, but I'd do everything within my power now. I couldn't change the past, but I could make sure Jerry was held accountable for his actions. I wouldn't let him anywhere near Miri again.

"Good for you. I don't judge people on their reputations anyway. Only their actions." The PI raised an approving eyebrow and stood. "I'll be in touch."

Chapter 28

Miri

Spotlights followed the elegant twirling figures as they pirouetted and leaped in front of the elaborate set. Gabe sat next to me in the private box, his thigh so close to mine it was almost touching. Dressed in a smart tux, he was nothing but charm personified. It was hard to say who out of my mum and Frankie was swooning harder. Either way, they were both embarrassing the life out of me. What game was he playing? We'd said one night. I couldn't have anticipated he'd want more. Did he want more? How long until he got bored? Two nights? A week? This was a dangerous game. Gabe was getting under my skin, and I'd promised to myself I wouldn't let this happen. I'd been such a fool to let Jed treat me the way he did. I couldn't do this to myself again.

A brush of warmth against my thigh made my heart contract. Gabe inched his hand to his side, his thumb touching my little finger. It was the smallest of contacts, but I couldn't concentrate on a single second of the performance because of it.

The lights went up for the intermission and Frankie groaned and flicked through the program on her lap. "What the hell is happening in this one? It's even more bonkers than *The Nutcracker*."

I couldn't help but chuckle. We'd all come to watch Elliot in the previous show and Frankie had been less than impressed.

Gabe leaned across me to address my sister. "What part don't you understand? It's about a prince that falls in love with a swan."

Frankie blew out her lips. "That doesn't make sense." She folded her arms and slumped in her chair. "I'm not going to understand any of this, am I?"

Mum shook her head. "It doesn't matter. We're here to support Elliot. He appreciates it."

I wasn't so sure. Elliot had always been impossible to read. I got the impression he'd rather we all left him alone.

Gabe inclined his head in Frankie's direction. "Prince Siegfried's mother is sick of his playboy behavior and wants him to marry a member of the nobility. He's annoyed he can't marry for love. He goes to a lake and sees a flock of swans. He's about to shoot one when one of the swans turns into the most beautiful woman he's ever seen, Odette. She's a victim of a spell cast by an evil sorcerer, Rothbart. By day she is a swan, and she can only take human form at night by the lake."

Frankie frowned. "You got all that from watching this?"

He shrugged. "I dated a prima ballerina once."

I bet he had. Dancers. Models. Actresses. Gabe had a revolving door of beautiful women. What did he want with me? I couldn't be his usual type. Maybe that's what this was. I was a novelty for him. A footballer to add to his collection, like a new charm on a bracelet.

Gabe cleared his throat and continued. "Siegfried falls in love with the Swan Queen. In order to break the curse, he must publicly declare his undying love, but Rothbart tricks him with a fake version of Odette. Siegfried asks for the fake Odette's hand in marriage, so now the curse can't be broken. Odette is devastated by his betrayal and chooses death by jumping in the lake rather than remaining a swan. Siegfried is heartbroken and jumps into the lake after her."

Frankie frowned. "They both die? That sucks, and also you could have given me a spoiler warning."

Gabe smothered a smile. "In some versions they have a happy ending. They both ascend to heaven together."

I frowned. "If they're both dead then that's not a happy ending. Romance fans expect an HEA."

Gabe flashed me a quizzical glance and scratched his head in confusion. "HEA?"

Frankie rummaged through the handbag on her lap. "Happily ever after, of course."

My sister nonchalantly pulled out an enormous bag of popcorn, and my heart almost stopped beating.

"Nope," I ground out through gritted teeth.

Her eyes widened. "What?"

"I swear to God, Frankie. If you're about to start munching popcorn in here—"

"What's the big deal? You love it at the cinema."

My voice was a terse whisper. "This is not the cinema."

I dared a glance at Gabe. He kept his eyes on the stage, but I couldn't miss the faint twitch of his lips.

Reece returned with a tray laden with small tubs of ice cream. When he spied the bag of popcorn on Frankie's lap, he grimaced and shook his head. "Popcorn at the ballet?" He turned around to head back out of the box. "I'm off to find a different family to join. It's been nice knowing you all."

"Good luck with that. Like any other family is going to put up with you." Frankie shoved the popcorn back in her bag, and reached for a tub of ice cream. "You all need to loosen up."

Mercifully, the lights dimmed and the dancers took to the stage before Frankie pulled anything else out of her handbag.

Gabe kept his eyes fixed on the stage. A light brush of his thumb on the side of my finger sent electricity through my wrist.

He leaned in to whisper in my ear. "I want you to stay with me tonight, Little Swan."

Little Swan. Those words in his velvet voice made my heart pound.

"I never ask women to stay over. It's against my rules." He traced his thumb around his full lips but kept his eyes on the stage. "But I'm here watching ballet with your family because I'm so desperate to touch you again. It's fair to say the rules don't apply anymore."

Gabe's warm hand wrapped around mine and he held my hand lightly on my knee. My heart pounded. Beautiful music wrapped around us and I didn't dare move a muscle. We'd spent a night learning each other's bodies and yet holding hands like this, still and quiet in the darkness, felt like one of the most intimate moments we'd shared. Did he feel the same as me right now? Was his heart beating out of his chest and every nerve in his body on fire just from the touch of hands? What was this madness?

I couldn't go with him tonight. My family was too nosy and there would be too many questions to answer. Besides, it was Christmas Eve. I couldn't wake up in a different place on Christmas morning. I'd moved back home to support Mum. I needed to be in the house in case anything happened.

I pulled my hand away. "Not tonight."

Disappointment shadowed his face. "When?"

I glanced over my shoulder at Mum. Tears misted her eyes as she watched Elliot's impressive leaps.

"I can't stay over. I have responsibilities."

He frowned. "Then I'll stay at yours."

"No. You won't."

"Stop muttering," Frankie said, angling her champagne flute at me. "This is the best bit."

"What do you care?" I hissed. "I thought you didn't understand it."

She raised a wry eyebrow. "It's a swan and a pampered playboy falling in love, isn't it? This is the part where the swan is having to do some shifts at a strip club, because she—"

"Shut up." I glared at Frankie in warning, and she smiled back sweetly.

Gabe raised a wry eyebrow. "What?"

"Ignore her." I patted his knee. "The only way to get along with my family is to immediately disregard everything they say."

After the show, we waited for Elliot in the noisy bar.

"What are you doing for Christmas, Gabe?" Mum asked.

Gabe bent to Mum's wheelchair to be heard over the chaos. "Nothing much. My mother's gone to Dubai, but I didn't fancy it. They'll do a nice dinner at the Beaufort."

Mum's face dropped. "You're having dinner alone?"

He shrugged. "It's fine. I do it every year. Christmas isn't a big thing to me."

Mum's mouth dropped open. "No. You're not spending it alone. You'll come to us. We'd love to have you."

Alarm went through me. No way did I want to extend this awkwardness with Gabe and my family. "Mum, Gabe doesn't want that. Imagine what Christmas dinner is like at the Beaufort compared to what Reece is going to put together."

Reece threw me a narrow, glinting glance. "I've been planning the menu for weeks."

161

Frankie patted his shoulder. "Ignore her. Nobody does brandy butter like yours." Frankie whispered behind her hand at Gabe. "If you come to ours, can I take your place at the Beaufort?"

Gabe chuckled darkly and smoothed his tie. "Thank you, but I can't put you out like that. Christmas is a time for family."

Mum clucked her tongue. "Nonsense. You are welcome to come for dinner, Gabe. The more the merrier. If you want to, of course . . ."

Frankie drained her champagne. It had to be her fourth glass at least. "You're going to love it. We have dinner, then I thrash Reece so hard at Monopoly I make him cry, then we argue over what film to watch."

Reece laughed. "You wish. You're the worst Monopoly player in the world. Who buys every square they land on?"

Frankie shrugged. "It's a great strategy." She shot Gabe a ponderous look. "In fact, I can't wait to play Monopoly with a member of the one percent. Maybe Gabe will be willing to donate real money?"

Gabe smiled and held his hands up. "I'm more of a Clue man."

Frankie smirked. "That figures. Murder in posh gazebos. I love that for you."

I couldn't help but cringe. My sister had no filter. "Frankie! You can't say that."

Gabe smoothed his tie and held his dazzling smile in place. If he was bothered, he didn't show it, but maybe that's just the way he'd had to adapt. All kinds of nasty rumors followed this man around. It shouldn't have been something that anyone had to get used to, especially someone like Gabe. Everything that the media said about him was so wrong.

Mum smiled. "Yes. Join the fun, Gabe. You can stay over if you like. Then you can have a drink with us in the evening. The boys can share a room. We can make up the spare."

I couldn't help my incredulous laugh. "Mum, don't be ridiculous. Gabe has a driver. You don't have to be worried about him drinking. Besides, he has the penthouse at the Beaufort. He doesn't want to stay in our spare room."

Gabe coughed and shot me a questioning look, seeking permission. "It does sound fun. Although I wouldn't want to put you out . . ."

Gabe turned his mega-watt charming smile on Mum.

I'd never seen my mother blush, but pink tinged her cheeks. "Of course not. Our home is your home. We'd love to have you round."

Well, that was that. We'd gone from "one night" to Christmas dinner with my family in less than twenty-four hours. I might have been breaking Gabe's rules, but he'd detonated a nuclear bomb on mine.

Chapter 29

Miri

Reece put the sliced turkey on the food-laden table. The tempting aroma of the hot roast dinner made my mouth water. Everybody slid into their seats. Silence fell as we looked around at each other.

"Gabe isn't here yet," Frankie said.

An odd twinge of disappointment made my heart sink. I hadn't wanted him to come, but this wasn't just letting me down. It was letting my family down. Mum had wanted him to come so much.

I sighed. "Let's eat. It's getting cold."

A knock sounded on the door.

I jumped up to answer it. I flung the door open to see Gabe standing in the doorway. Snow clung to his chestnut hair and laced his dark peacoat. He stepped inside the hallway and the cold wrapped around me.

"I'm sorry I'm late. A story in the press. I've had to have an emergency meeting with PR. Some nonsense to do with Taylor."

"Taylor?"

"Taylor Swift."

My mouth dropped open. "*The* Taylor Swift?"

He shrugged. "It's fine. She saw the funny side."

"You had a chat with Taylor Swift?"

"She's a friend. I can introduce you if you like."

I had to do everything in my power not to squeal. He shrugged out of his peacoat. The most hideous sprout-green Christmas pajamas hung from his slender frame. It was the most ridiculous thing I'd ever seen, but more ridiculous was that he still managed to look sexy. How could any man look sexy covered in tiny reindeers?

A laugh burst out of me. "Why has somebody vomited Christmas on you?"

He frowned and looked down at his outfit. "Frankie told me it was a Forster tradition. We all have to wear Christmas pajamas for Christmas dinner. I thought she was winding me up, but then Elliot confirmed it."

I tried to contain my laugh. "Oh God. They were having you on. The bastards have teamed up to prank you. I warned you not to listen to anything my family says."

Frankie appeared behind us and burst out laughing. "Well, don't just stand there, come in and do us a twirl. Show us your runway technique."

I shook my head. "Why are you like this? This is why I can never bring a boyfriend home."

My face heated. Gabe's eyes slipped away. Oh shit. This was just sex. One night of sex and one weird night in a private theater box, which had felt like a date but couldn't be a date because my entire family had also been present. Great. Now he probably thought I was some obsessive stalker. But then, he was the one who wanted to eat Christmas dinner with my family.

I fumbled, looking for a change of subject. "I'm so sorry. Reece will have something else to wear, or you can go home and change if you want . . . or if you want to go, you can go. This was cruel of Frankie. I'm sorry."

"It's a joke," Frankie cried.

"It's not funny, Frankie. Gabe will never set foot in this house again."

Her eyes went wide. "It was Elliot's idea too."

"It's fine." He held out his arms and sent a rueful glance down his torso. "I'm styling it out."

I couldn't help my smile. He was styling it out. This man looked like a god even dressed like an elf.

He shrugged. "Let's eat. I'm sure you've waited long enough."

Frankie clapped him on the back. "You're a good sport. You're going to fit in well around here." She took him by the elbow and led him into the kitchen. "You'll definitely fit in better than Miri, anyway."

Chapter 30

MIRI

Later that evening, after Christmas dinner and arguments over board games, we decamped to the lounge to watch a movie together. Everybody took their usual spots. Elliot and Reece on the couch with Mum, and Frankie on her favorite beanbag next to the Christmas tree. I sat at the foot of the armchair in the corner of the room farthest from the TV.

We didn't have enough places to sit, and as much as it would have amused me to see Gabe's face when I offered him a spot on the floor at my feet, he wouldn't be impressed by my hospitality skills. Frankie held the remote toward the TV, lazily channel-surfing. She flicked the light switch. The TV screen and the colorful Christmas lights glowed bright in the darkness.

I patted the armchair behind me. "Your throne, Mr. Rivers."

Gabe planted himself in front of me and extended a hand to pull me up.

"No. You're the guest. You sit on the chair."

He sat down and patted his lap. "There's room for both of us."

I threw a wary glance across the room, but everyone had gone back to squabbling over what to watch. Would it be too much to sit on his lap with everyone here? Jed had never been a PDA kind of guy. It would have been weird to cozy up with him, but maybe it was okay. The lights were out, and it wasn't my fault there weren't enough chairs.

I settled on Gabe's lap. He pulled a blanket from the arm of the chair and threw it over us and wrapped his arms around my waist, holding me. I melted into the heat of his firm body.

His lips brushed my earlobe. "This is nice."

It was. In fact, it was delicious to be in his arms so warm and snuggled with my family around me. The fairy lights glittered and the fire crackled in the hearth. Heat seared my skin. If we could get through the rest of the evening without my family embarrassing me further, then it would be perfect.

"I'm sorry about the trick with the pajamas," I whispered. "The twins are hazing you."

"Did I pass?"

"With flying colors."

"I'm voting *White Christmas*," Mum called.

"Boo. Too old," Elliot said.

Gabe's hand crept around my waist and under my T-shirt. He smoothed his warm palm over my stomach. Tingling lit my skin.

"*It's a Wonderful Life*," Reece said.

Gabe's fingers dipped down, teasing the waistband of my leggings. My body tensed. Was he trying to touch me? Here, in front of everyone? His fingers slid lower. I was about to whisper at him to stop when his finger moved lower. A jolt of electricity went through me. Heat blossomed over my skin. I sucked in a breath. Oh my God. He held perfectly still. My fingers dug into the chair. I froze, battling the desperate urge to grind against him for more friction. Everybody had their backs to us. The lights were out, all the chairs faced toward the TV, and our armchair was flush in the corner out of sight, but still . . . my entire family was in the room.

"Nope. That's even older," Elliot said.

Frankie folded her arms and relaxed back into the couch. "*Die Hard.*"

"That's not a Christmas movie," Mum said.

"It's set at Christmas," Frankie said.

"We have the same argument every year. *Die Hard* is not a Christmas movie," Reece said.

"Of course it is," Elliot said.

Frankie fist-bumped her twin. "Thank you."

Gabe's finger moved slowly, circling. The movement so small as to be torturous. I gripped the sides of the chair. Oh God. I had to tell him to stop. He couldn't do this with my family in the room. We were out of sight, and the blanket was covering us, but still . . .

Too much. I couldn't take it. My body responded to the slightest of touches from this man. I wouldn't be able to hold it together if he carried on, but the desperate throb between my thighs wouldn't let me ask him to stop either.

Elliot snatched the remote from Frankie. "Do we have to have this argument every year? Put *Elf* on and be done with it. It's the only one we can all agree on."

Gabe dipped a finger down, spreading my wetness up to rub firmer strokes, still too painfully slow and light. Oh God. His erection pressed into my backside. It took every scrap of willpower not to grind into him for the friction I craved.

Frankie twisted her head to look at us. "Gabe is the guest. Let him decide."

Gabe's finger froze. The aching pulse at the loss of pressure was enough to make a strange whimper leave my mouth. I tried to arrange my face into a normal expression.

Gabe cleared his throat. "Whatever you like."

Frankie shook her head. "No. Come on. What's your favorite Christmas movie?"

"I don't have one," Gabe said.

Elliot shoved a handful of popcorn into his mouth. "There must be one that you like?"

"I've never watched any Christmas movies."

Gabe pressed his finger down, the firm pressure sending a wave of pleasure racing through my core. Oh God. I gritted my teeth. This man was trying to kill me.

"What? How can you have not seen a Christmas movie?" Frankie cried.

"Christmas isn't a big thing in our house. Dad always worked and Mum goes abroad," Gabe said.

Mum's eyebrows rose. "So, what did you do?"

Every member of my family turned to look at us. Panic ran through me. I took a calming breath. They didn't know what was going on. They couldn't. The room was dark. A blanket covered us. Nobody knew what was going on underneath. I had to be like a swan—graceful on the surface despite legs kicking frantically out of sight. I was just sitting on his lap. Completely innocent.

Gabe pressed his lips together. "I don't know. Whatever. It's just another day, isn't it?"

If I hadn't been so unbearably turned on, I might have had sympathy for him. My family was weird and annoying, but we always stuck together. I couldn't imagine thinking of Christmas as just another day or spending it alone. Frankie opened her mouth and closed it as if she was going to say something but thought better of it. I shifted in Gabe's lap and the slight slip of his finger almost made me cry out. My heart hammered. I needed the attention off us because if he didn't get me off after this I'd die.

Mum cocked her head. "Miri, what's your vote?"

Gabe rubbed another smooth circle and I bit down on my lip.

I would have struggled to recall my own name with Gabe touching me like this, let alone a movie. "I don't know. I don't care.

Put something on. Anything. For God's sake. Choose something before midnight."

Frankie snorted. "Wow. Calm down. It's only a movie."

Gabe chuckled darkly and eased my knickers aside, slipping a cool finger inside me and curling upward. I smothered my moan.

"What?" Frankie said, frowning.

"*Home Alone*," Gabe said smoothly. He held his hand perfectly still. "That's one, isn't it? The little kid is left when his parents go away."

Frankie raised an impressed eyebrow. "You do know one! That's good. I'd go for that."

"Yep, me too," Elliot said.

"*Home Alone 2* is better," Reece said.

"Don't be ridiculous, Reece. *Home Alone* it is," Mum said.

Everybody turned their attention back to the TV. My body sagged with relief. Gabe's smooth circles turned to firm strokes. He added a second finger, easing in and out in painfully slow thrusts. The tension building inside of me was too much. I had to keep still instead of chasing my building orgasm. Every part of me was taut. A pressure cooker ready to bubble over.

Gabe turned his face, his stubble grazing my cheek, his warm breath fanning my neck and his expensive spicy cologne wrapped around me. I curled into his firm chest; his heart pounded against my back. It was beating as fast as mine. I needed him to go faster, but I couldn't ask, and it would have drawn attention to us anyway. The need to come was a divine, unbearable torture. A slow, delicious death by an impending climax I couldn't chase.

Just when I thought I couldn't handle another second, the most intense, shuddering release ripped through me. I bit my lip so hard it throbbed with a pulse. My fingernails dug into the side of Gabe's thighs, but he didn't flinch. I bit harder on my lip, trying to keep in my desperate whimper. He held his fingers inside of me, filling

171

me while my body shuddered in intense waves around him and I tried desperately not to make it obvious. He worked me through every quiver and tremble before my body went limp.

Lazily, he pulled his hand from under the blanket. His eyes never left mine as he put his index finger into his mouth and sucked it clean. A suggestive smile lit his face. Oh God. I twisted my head to the couch, but everybody was too engrossed in the film to notice. He nipped my earlobe lightly with his teeth and whispered, "Very good, Little Swan."

I felt the smile on his lips when he pressed a kiss against my neck.

◆ ◆ ◆

Later, after the film, Gabe poked a finger through the blinds in the living room and frowned.

"What is it?" Mum asked.

"Snow's getting thick out there. I'd better call my driver."

Snow covered the street, thick and white like icing on a perfect wedding cake.

Mum rolled her wheelchair forward. "Why don't you stay, Gabe? Give the poor man a night off. It's Christmas."

Gabe pulled out his phone. "I wouldn't want to put you out. Karl knew I'd need him tonight."

Mum frowned. "It's no problem. The boys can share a room and we can make up the spare."

I shot him an apologetic glance. "Mum, Gabe has the penthouse suite at the Beaufort. We've talked about this. He doesn't want to stay in our box room."

Gabe pocketed his phone. "Actually, it might be a good idea. The snow is so heavy. I'm sure Karl would appreciate the time off." He flashed me a smile and a glint glimmered in his eyes. "Besides, I already have my pajamas on."

Chapter 31

MIRI

The spare room was little more than a box with a single bed so small Gabe's feet would be hanging off the end, but judging by the endless stream of compliments he threw at my mum, you would have thought he was staying at the Ritz. He eulogized everything from her choice of teacups to the books on the nightstand. Mum wasn't always easy to win over, but she was about ready to kick all her own kids out of the house and adopt Gabe instead.

I shut my eyes and tried to relax the tenseness that made my muscles stiff. I'd showered before bed, washing away the traces of Gabe's touch on my body. How had I let things get so out of control? This wasn't me. I'd had one serious boyfriend and I'd waited for months to sleep with him. Jed had been a missionary-and-lights-off type. Never in a million years did I imagine myself being so turned on by a man that I'd take the risks I had. One glance from him and I lost all sense.

Gabe had woken something in me. It had all started at that club. I'd never wanted to be there, but dancing for Gabe had made me feel sexy in a way I'd never imagined myself capable of. That lap dance had been the hottest moment of my life. The way Gabe had looked at me as though he'd never be able to look away had made me feel so . . . powerful and confident. He'd helped me to explore a part of myself I might never have dug deep enough to find.

There were so many reasons why I shouldn't have let any of this happen, but I'd been unable to resist him. With Gabe in the spare room and everybody else gone to bed, I tried to relax in my own bed. A weak flash of light filled the pitch-black room. My phone vibrated on the nightstand.

Are you asleep? A message from Gabe.

I should have ignored it, but I texted back. Yes. Fast asleep.

I waited as blue dots flashed as he typed. There's something wrong with the radiator in this room. I'm freezing to death.

It's not even that cold.
I'm serious. Come and see.

Reluctantly, I got out of bed and tiptoed, in darkness, past Mum's and Reece's bedrooms, down to the little spare room at the end of the hallway. I pushed the door open as quietly as I could and stepped inside. The bedside lamp illuminated Gabe sitting up in bed. His dark, disheveled hair fell in a glorious mess and one of Reece's faded gray university T-shirts clung to his impressive torso. He looked so un-Gabe-like that I had to smother a laugh. A chill hung in the air. I rested my hand on the stone-cold radiator.

He raised an eyebrow. "See?"

I put a finger to my lip and whispered, "Keep your voice down. I'll find another blanket."

His gaze traveled over me and he bit his bottom lip. I wore an old T-shirt that skimmed my upper thighs. I pulled it down, which only served to tug it tighter over my breasts.

He pulled the duvet away and patted the space next to him. "I don't need another blanket. Get in. Come and keep me warm."

My heart pounded at the idea of slipping into that bed next to him. There were a million things I wanted to do with Gabe Rivers in a bed, and none of them were sleeping.

"Nope."

He pouted. "Why not?"

It was too late to go through it all again. "Because . . . reasons."

I tiptoed back down the hall to my room and opened the wardrobe. I scanned the shelves but there were no blankets. They were probably in Mum's room, but I didn't want to wake her up for one. I turned around and bumped into Gabe.

He towered over me, bathed in moonlight. A half smile curved his lips. He whispered, "I thought you might need some help."

"Help with what?"

His eyes dropped over my body. "To carry the blankets."

"I can't find any. You can have my duvet."

"Don't you need that?"

"I'll manage."

He studied my face, feature by feature, then frowned. "Is it just me or do you feel this?"

His free hand hovered by my cheek and he brushed a line over my jaw with his thumb. My skin tingled under his touch. My breath hitched.

He watched me with fascination. "It's electricity. Chemistry. Who knows what causes that? It feels like we're meant to be touching each other. That doesn't happen often. Not for me anyway."

He took my arm and traced a blue vein in my wrist with his fingertip. Heat washed over me in a sudden fever.

"You feel that though, don't you?" He traced his thumb down my throat and lower. "Tell me it's not just me."

My heart beat so hard he could probably hear it. Of course I felt it. I'd felt it the moment he'd kissed the back of my hand in the strip club. His unexpected kindness, and one brush of his lips had

175

been my undoing. I didn't want to feel like this, but I didn't have the strength to deny it. "I feel it."

He stepped closer, his words a hot whisper against my earlobe. "Are you going to send me back to that freezing room? You're not that cruel."

My heart drummed.

Slowly, his lips descended to meet mine. I should have told him to stop or stepped away, but I couldn't. A desperate tingling in my belly stole my breath. I pulled him roughly toward me. His hands bunched up the fabric of my T-shirt, smoothing over my stomach, my hips. He covered my throat with kisses.

Breathless, I pulled away, my voice low. "You can sleep in here with me, but we're just sleeping. I'm not doing anything with you with my family in the house. After that little stunt you pulled in the living room, I'm on guard. And you have to go before anyone gets up. Can you keep your hands to yourself?"

He smirked and held his hand to his head, saluting. "Of course. Scout's honor."

I got in the bed and he slipped in next to me. He lay on his side, keeping a distance. I reached across to my bedside table and turned off the lamp.

Darkness permeated every inch of the room. Gabe's heat and heavy weight compressing the mattress next to me made my body sing. The snow had shifted to rain that tapped the window and in the silence between us I'd never heard anything so loud. I turned to face him.

"There's no way anyone would have let you be a Boy Scout," I whispered.

I heard the grin in his voice. "I was. I had the little necktie and everything."

I should have stopped talking, but I couldn't resist. "What were you like as a kid?"

176

A pause. "Lonely."

"I would think you'd have had a lot of people around."

"The house was always full, but Dad was busy with work and I hardly saw Mother. We traveled all over the world, but I was always alone."

His thumb rubbed over my knuckles, sending tingles up my wrists. I shouldn't have moved closer, but I couldn't resist. He was quiet for so long that I thought he might have fallen asleep before he whispered into the darkness, "Your mum's not well. What's wrong? Do you mind me asking?"

"She had a stroke. She's doing better, but it did a lot of damage. We take it day by day now."

"I'm sorry. That must be tough for all of you."

"We don't talk about it. Mum likes to try and stay positive, but it is hard. I worry about her. I don't like to leave her in case it happens again. Me and Reece had places of our own, but we've all moved back in here."

The silence wrapped around us. Tentatively, I groped for his face in the inky darkness. My fingertips brushed his lips and I replaced them with my mouth, brushing a light kiss on him. The slight movement in the bed caused a creak and I froze. That was that. We couldn't get up to anything. I wanted him so badly, but it would be too noisy. Besides, we'd said one night.

I pulled away. The silence crackled around us. I felt his hand groping for me in the darkness, running over my stomach and my hips. I held still, hardly daring to breathe. His fingers found the waistband of my knickers, teasing to slip under.

"We can't. We have to be quiet," I said.

He snapped his fingers away. The pulsing need between my legs ached unbearably. Why deny myself something I wanted so badly? I took hold of his fingers and pulled them back to place his hand where it rested before on my stomach.

"Yeah?" I heard the uncertainty in his voice.

"Yeah."

"You're sure?"

"Yes."

His fingers grazed my inner thighs, teasing and stroking. Warmth rushed wherever his palm touched as he smoothed his hands over my belly and hips then slipped a cool finger between my legs, running between my folds, parting me and resting lightly. The teasing movement drove me wild. I had to resist the urge to grind against his hand for more friction. He began to move his fingers. A low moan escaped me. How could a man be so talented with his hands? I couldn't stop myself from grinding into the bed. A creak rang out from the mattress and we both froze. I dug my fingernails into the duvet.

"Fuck," I whispered. "Don't stop now."

He chuckled and whispered into my neck. "I thought we had to be quiet."

"We do, but you can't leave me like this again. Why do you love torturing me so much?"

"Because it's so fun."

He resumed his work on me and it took everything I had to keep still and quiet.

My breath came in sharp gasps. "Oh God."

"What?" I couldn't see his face, but I heard the grin in his voice. "I'm trying not to make a noise."

"Faster. Please."

He increased his pressure, setting a rhythm with his expert fingers. An intense throbbing need for release built in my core. He teased a cool finger at my entrance, dipping into my wet heat. Then he slipped in another finger, filling and stretching me, finding the precise spot that made me squirm. I dug my fingers into his T-shirt, gripping him and pulling him into me for a kiss. My breath escaped in gasps and I panted and moaned into his mouth.

"Bad Swan. You're being too loud."

I was desperate to cry out but he covered my mouth with his, smothering my desperate whimpers. In the dark silence, the sensation was heightened so that it was as excruciating as it was delicious in its intensity. A divine torment. He increased his pace, his fingers rubbing in a slippery massage. He yanked up my T-shirt and his lips found my breasts. He sucked my nipple into his mouth, hard and desperate. A jolt of pleasure shot right down from his lips to my center, as though he was sucking between my thighs. A gasp escaped me but I clamped my mouth shut and swallowed it.

The bed creaked but I didn't care and neither did Gabe. My fingers tangled into his hair. I needed to come before I died of need. My orgasm ripped through me, cresting intense waves of pleasure. He covered my mouth lightly with his free hand, muffling my cries. My body trembled in the dark silence, drowning in an ocean of sensation. He kept working, rubbing with perfect pressure and suckling my nipple hard into his mouth as my body juddered and shook. My orgasm rocked the whole of my body. Tingling electricity shot from my core to my feet, making the tips of my toes pulse with tiny aftershocks.

Slowly and carefully, Gabe rolled away from me. I lay in the echoing quiet, breathing hard and trying to regain my equilibrium. He pulled me into his arms and pressed a kiss on my shoulder.

"Did you enjoy that, Little Swan?" His whisper drifted in the darkness.

"Yes."

"I thought you were going to try and be quiet."

The back of my neck heated. "It's not easy being quiet under those circumstances."

He turned me in his arms so that we were spooning.

"I want to fuck you so badly. I've never been cock-blocked by a bed before. I'm buying you a new one in the morning."

My body tensed and I fought to react. I shouldn't have been spooning with him, but his delicious warmth engulfed me, and I let myself relax in his arms. His scent filled my nostrils; he'd washed with my mint shower gel but there was a scent to him that was all him. His erection prodded my backside. Adjusting himself, he inched away.

As slowly as I could, I twisted in his arms. "Would you like some help with that?"

The bed let out an almighty groan.

"This fucking bed," Gabe whispered.

I found the waistband of his pajamas. He sucked in a breath as my hands slipped under and gripped his hard length. "Now it's your turn to keep quiet."

Chapter 32

Gabe

Buzzing woke me up. I opened my eyes and tried to reorient myself in the unfamiliar darkness. I was in the spare room in Miri's house on the shit lumpy bed. I'd buy them all new beds today. This bed had destroyed my back. Miri had given me the slowest, quietest, most torturous blow job in the world and then kicked me out of her bedroom. The ache in my spine from this crap mattress was a small price to pay. My phone buzzed again. I groaned and swiped it from the floor. Mother's face flashed on the screen. I sighed. What did she want in the middle of the night? Had a swarm of bats gathered and carried news of tonight's misdemeanors to her lair?

I answered the phone, my voice croaky with sleep. "Mother?"

"Have you seen the news?"

I checked the digital clock and groaned. "It's 3 a.m."

"Not in Dubai, darling. A story is about to break. Another pack of lies."

"What this time?"

She drew a breath. "Our names are going to be all over the papers tomorrow. Someone is saying your father and Emma were having an affair." She gave a tinkling laugh. "Have you heard anything more ridiculous?"

Her words were light, but I sensed the vulnerability under-neath. It took me straight back to that awful night. Mother had been so devastated about Dad, and it had been a snap decision to conceal the truth about the affair. I'd considered coming clean so many times, but what would it achieve? It would cause her so much pain. Mother hurt me all the time with her lack of faith in me, but I could take it. I'd built up so many walls to bear the shit that got slung at me from the press every day. Every time the press came for me, it affected her too. We had to stick together. I wouldn't be the one to bring her more pain when so many around us were intent on attacking us.

My heart pounded. I faked a laugh. "No? Ridiculous."

Silence filled the space between us. Perhaps I hadn't sounded convincing.

"Prepare yourself, Gabe. I'm talking with PR about how to manage it. I suggest you speak to them sooner rather than later."

I needed to sort this out. Quietly, I flung the duvet off and swung my legs over the bed.

Chapter 33

Miri

I knocked on the door to the spare room. "Gabe?"

No reply.

I tried again. "Gabe?"

Carefully, I inched the door open. The small bed was made and the room was empty. I showered and headed down to the kitchen, expecting Gabe to be downstairs. Reece sat alone at the table.

"Where's Gabe?"

Reece shrugged. "Maybe he slept in."

"He's not in the spare room."

"He must have gone home."

He hadn't said goodbye. A heavy ball tightened in my chest. Was that it? He'd got me out of his system? Why would he leave in the middle of the night? I pulled out my phone to text and then hesitated. What if this was his way of breaking off whatever this weird thing was between us? Our time together last night had been different from the first time. It wasn't just raw and wild. We'd had to be quiet and slow. It had been tender and deliberate. Still, Gabe had only ever wanted sex. He'd made that abundantly clear. Maybe this was the sign he was done with me.

"Oh my God, Miri." Frankie's shout from the landing was followed by her thunderous feet on the stairs. "Have you seen the news?"

She came crashing into the kitchen, still in her leopard-print pajamas. "Put the TV on. He's on there."

Reece reached for the remote and the TV on the kitchen wall came to life. We watched the screen as Gabe shielded his face with his hand and walked up the steps to the Beaufort Hotel. The story flicked back to four women around a panel, gossiping.

I could hardly believe my ears. Micky Rivers had been having an affair with Emma Cousins? What nonsense. Gabe never spoke about his ex, but it was ridiculous.

Reece looked up from his stack of books on the kitchen island. "Poor Gabe. Why do people even give such junk the time of day? Any idiot can say anything and it counts as news."

"I wouldn't be surprised if Emma leaked it." Frankie grabbed a handful of raspberries from a bowl on the counter and shoved them into her mouth. "Her past few films have bombed. She's probably glad of the publicity."

It wasn't exactly great publicity. Emma was being accused of an affair with her boyfriend's father. "It can't be true. The press make up lies about Gabe all the time. Turn it off. I can't watch it," I said.

Frankie flicked the screen off.

Reece tapped his pen against his page. "Do you want to talk?"

"With you?"

"Yeah."

"Nope."

"Nice try, Reece." Frankie laughed and switched her attention to me. "What does Gabe say?"

"He's gone." I picked at the chipping paint on the doorframe. "This thing between me and Gabe is casual. We aren't even supposed to be together. I wanted to keep things professional."

Reece turned his full attention on me. "Are you okay with casual?"

"It's not like I could get involved with a man like this. The cameras follow him everywhere. His life is a circus. I hate all that."

I looked up to find them both watching me.

"But you like him?" Frankie asked.

I fixed my gaze on the steam dancing above the cup of hot tea in Reece's hands. "Yes. I like him, and I don't want to like him. Not after Jed. I don't know how to switch these feelings off. For him this is all . . . I don't know . . . I knew it would go like this and still I went along with it. He's not what people say about him. He's kind. As odd as it sounds, I think he's lonely."

"Give him the time he needs to deal with this and then talk to him," Reece said.

"But there is always going to be stuff like this, isn't there? If it's not this rubbish story it will be another one, and even if he does want something more serious, that means that one day the story will be about me."

Reece sipped his tea. "Then you need to decide how you feel about him and whether he's worth it. You need to protect your heart too, Miri. If you aren't on the same page about where this is going, then you're going to get hurt."

"I don't know if I want it to go anywhere. I just want to play football. This is out of control."

Frankie laughed. "Welcome to the human race. You can't control everything. Least of all your heart."

I liked Gabe. I couldn't help it. I liked his humor and his charm and the way my skin tingled when he touched me. But mostly I liked his gentleness. The way he was nothing like what the media portrayed. There were so many reasons why hooking up with Gabe Rivers was a terrible idea but my heart didn't want to listen to any of them.

Frankie and Reece exchanged a look. Frankie cleared her throat, her expression unusually earnest. "I've never heard you talk about anyone like this before. You should tell him how you feel."

"It will scare him away. I let my guard down with Jed . . ."

"Not all men are idiots like Jed," Frankie said.

"Should I tell him I like him?"

Frankie nodded vigorously. "Yes. Go now. Go tell Gabe Rivers that you can't get enough of his BDE. You love him and want to have his babies."

I burst out laughing. "Why is everyone in this family so weird?"

Frankie frowned. "I mean . . . put it in your own less poetic words, but tell him."

I turned to Reece, the only sensible member of my family. "What if he doesn't feel the same?"

My brother offered a faint smile and raised a dark brow. "What if he does?"

Chapter 34

Gabe

Mother shook her head, her eyes flashing. Even through a screen, she was formidable. "Do you know what it was like being married to your father? A man that made his money in such a dreadful industry. I knew he wasn't a saint, but this is ridiculous. You're going to have to keep out of the public eye until we sort this out and it blows over."

"Fine with me. I've got my head down with work for the women's team."

"Forget about the team. We'll get someone in the interim. You'll be under the spotlight for a while now. You need to stay out of the way."

"No. We carry on as normal. I'm not hiding. I haven't done anything wrong."

"The vultures are circling. I need the heat off this. We issue a statement from the family and then we get you out of here. We'll say you've been going through a difficult patch after the loss of your father. You can stay on the yacht. Take a holiday."

No. Unacceptable. I was making progress with the team. I couldn't leave it. Not when everything was going so well with Miri.

"You can't send me out of sight because I'm inconvenient. None of this is my fault. I'm a victim here, too."

"I'm trying to help you."

A surge of emotion made my chest contract. I'd watched my father die. I'd found him with my girlfriend and then I'd held him in my arms at the bottom of those steps after he'd betrayed me, and I'd wept for him. He was still my father. Part of me wanted the world to know. It was too much to carry the burden alone.

A wave of exhaustion passed over me. "How was your Christmas, Mother?"

"Christmas?"

"Do you want to hear about my Christmas?"

She pulled an expression of exasperated bemusement as though I was a toddler asking her to play toy trains. "We're not talking about Christmas."

"I spent it with Miri and her family. We had a huge dinner and we pulled crackers and we watched Christmas movies."

Mother wrinkled her nose. "Miri?"

"The new striker. They were laughing at me because I'd never heard of any of the Christmas movies or played Uno or Twister. No one could believe that I'd never done anything like that before."

Mother shuddered in disgust. "So? Are you complaining, Gabe? You've had the world handed to you on a plate and you're grumbling that you haven't lived a pedestrian life?"

I gripped the phone tighter, resisting the urge to hurl it at the wall. No matter the topic, Mother always found a way to try and make me feel small. Ungrateful. Spoilt. But this wasn't about my ingratitude. It was about the rest of it. The way Mother only ever saw me as a problem, so she vacillated between trying to control me and ignoring me entirely.

"I'm complaining that you've never bothered with me. That nobody in this family has ever given a shit about me. That Dad was off running his empire and having his affairs and you've been on a sun lounger in Dubai or the Seychelles for the past twenty years. I'm complaining that when I was eighteen and I overdosed and almost died, it took you a week before you visited me in hospital. That you've never once personally written me a birthday card or said one nice thing to me in your entire life and now you're punishing me over a stupid story I had nothing to do with. This wasn't my fault. Why do I get sent away?"

She shook her head in confusion. "We've given you everything. You're on the Forbes rich list. You've been on the cover of *Tatler* and *Vogue*. And you're crying because I haven't played Twister with you?"

My guts churned. "This is not about fucking Twister."

"Then what is it about?"

Silence echoed from the screen. What was it about? I didn't lose my temper. What the hell was wrong with me? I folded my arms. I couldn't be apart from Miri for that long. I hadn't even said goodbye to her. I didn't want to leave the team either. Not now. Not when I had so many ways to make things better for the team. For once, I was doing a job that made a real difference. It was all such a buzz.

I'd even enjoyed the bloody karaoke. I'd worked to win the team over, even though it meant embarrassing the hell out of myself, because I wanted so badly to see this through. These women had so much talent and commitment. They impressed me at every training session, and they deserved so much better than what Dad had given them. They deserved to be in the Women's Super League. This wasn't the time to quit.

"You can't take this team from me. Not now. I'm making a go of it. I've done everything that you've asked."

"Your father left everything to me. Until I die, I'm in charge. You can do things my way or not at all. Fall in line and you get

189

everything you want. You disappear for a while and then you do a press release. We'll reassess about the team. You can't be involved with one of the players. It looks terrible. End this thing with the goalkeeper."

"Striker."

"You can't be carrying on like this when the press is watching every move you make."

A pulse pounded in my head. "And if I say no?"

"Then you're cut off. No team. Nothing. It's my way or not at all."

Fuck that. "What's that? Sorry. I can't hear you. Bad reception. We'll talk when you get home."

I swiped the call away.

Chapter 35

Miri

Gabe answered the door to the penthouse with a bottle of beer in his hand. Dark shadows haunted his eyes and his hair looked disheveled.

"Hey," I said softly. "I've been texting. You're not answering your phone."

"I'm sorry. I'm dealing with something at the moment."

"I heard." I reached for his free hand and squeezed it. "I'm so sorry you have to put up with this stuff. I hate that people make things up about your family—"

"It's not made up," he said quietly.

"What?"

He sighed and stepped aside. "You'd better come in."

We sat side by side on the couch. My mind whirled from the story that Gabe had told me about the night his dad died. It was more awful than I could have imagined. Gabe's dad and his girlfriend together. To think that some papers had printed stories that Gabe had pushed his dad while he carried all this guilt about his death.

The last words they'd spoken to each other were cross ones, and not through any fault of Gabe's. No wonder he felt so awful about it. No one knew the real story because he'd tried to protect a father who had betrayed him in the cruelest way. It was so heart-wrenching that the press had made Gabe a villain, when he hadn't done anything wrong.

He scrubbed his hand over his face. "I can't believe it's got out like this."

"Nobody believes it. It will be old news tomorrow. It will blow over."

"You're not going to tell anyone, are you?"

"No. You can trust me."

He looked me squarely in the eyes. "I know I can, Miri. I can't talk to anyone about anything. My own staff go behind my back and give my mother reports on me. Friends leak stories to the press. It's lonely. Never trusting anyone. It's fucking lonely."

His voice was low and sad. "You don't want to be involved with any of this. My life is drama. It gets ridiculous. I wake up and I have no idea what the papers are going to be saying about me or how many people are going to be piling onto me on social media. I can't trust anybody. Every move I make is splashed all over the front pages. You want to stop this thing between us. I get it. It's fine. You can go."

"That's not why I came."

His elegant fingers caressed the neck of his beer bottle. "Why did you come?"

I took a breath. This wasn't the time for declarations. "It doesn't matter now. Are you okay? Is there anything I can do?"

His tired gaze fell on his palm in mine. He pressed a kiss to the back of my hand. "People are going to find out about us. We've been lucky so far. I don't want to drag you into my world. It's hectic."

A barb speared my heart. Was this the speech? He was getting rid of me. Of course. It had only ever been one night. What was I thinking? "You don't want us to spend time together anymore?"

Alarm crossed his face. He squeezed my hand. "No. I want to spend time with you." He studied my face feature by feature. "I can't ask it of you. It's not fair."

I chewed my lip. "What if I want to be with you?"

He took a sip of his beer. "Then one day you're going to be part of a media circus."

"What if I can handle it?"

He gazed at me speculatively. His green eyes shimmered with the light from the windows. "Can you handle it, Forster?"

Yes. No. Maybe. I took his hand. "For you, I'd try."

His voice was calm, his gaze steady. "You will?"

"It's not easy for me to let my guard down. I've been hurt, too. My ex cheated on me with one of my friends. That's something we have in common. We both know what it feels like to be betrayed by the people you trust the most."

He squeezed my hand in his. His eyes filled with sympathy. "I'm sorry."

"I'm just saying that I know where you're coming from. It's hard for me to let my guard down, but I like you, and even though it won't be easy, I'm willing to try. If I'm in this with you, I'm really in this."

Featherlike creases pulled at his eyes and his lips curved into a smile. Softly, he brushed a strand of hair away from my cheek. "I don't want any secrets between us."

Guilt prickled my neck. I didn't want that either. Except I was keeping a secret from him. I'd worn a mask and a wig and pretended to be someone else. I had to tell him. This wasn't the ideal time, but I had to.

I opened my mouth to speak, but his lips crashed down onto mine. With a hand at my waist, he pulled me toward him. He kissed me and I had no idea what this was between us or what I was doing, but he was right. This was chemistry. We had to be touching each other.

He lifted my top and his lips blazed over my chest, sucking my nipples into his mouth. His large hands gripped my waist and he yanked my jeans down beneath my hips. He dropped to his knees, tearing my jeans away and tossing them.

I grabbed his hair, stilling him. "There's something we need to talk about."

His lips blazed kisses across my inner thighs, his mouth hot through the thin cotton of my knickers. "No more talking. I need you."

He pulled the material to one side and his tongue licked and probed at my sensitive flesh. My fingers dug into the couch. I couldn't help my indecent groan.

He pulled me on top of him so that I straddled his face. Alarm went through me. I'd never felt so exposed.

"What are you doing? You're going to suffocate."

"I want you like this."

Shock flew through me. "You can't . . ."

"Why not?"

"It's embarrassing."

I tried to move away but he held my hips, gripping me hard enough to bruise. "You don't have to feel shame with me. I've got you exactly where I want you."

He pulled my knickers to the side and spread me with his thumbs before lapping a slow, hot line. My head fell back with a groan. Pleasure raced over every inch of my body. I could barely form words. I tried to get off him, but he pulled me back down so that I hovered over his face.

"Say that you'll stay with me tonight," he said.

My voice came out choked. I would have said anything if it made him carry on. "Yes. I'll stay."

My legs shook and he was half holding me up. He held my hips in place and pulled me down to his mouth. "Now shut up, Forster, and let me do what I do best."

Chapter 36

MIRI

Everything was perfect. Falling in love with a billionaire had never been my plan, but despite the fact that he lived in a hotel and owned a fleet of private jets, Gabe acted like a normal boyfriend. A week flew by and he came to watch me at every practice and cheered me on at the sidelines during the weekend match. We even worked out together in the gym, and if I'd thought that Gabe was devastatingly handsome in a suit, then I swooned when I caught him on the rowing machine in sweatpants.

I was in the changing rooms, getting ready to meet Gabe for lunch, when a familiar voice stopped me in my tracks.

"Miri?"

I turned. Jed hovered at the entrance to the changing rooms. "You can't be in here."

"I need to talk to you." He craned his neck around the door and glanced about. "Can I come in? Or . . ."

What the hell was he doing here? "No. You can't. This is the women's changing rooms. Get out."

He rubbed his arm and shuffled his feet. The look on his face made my stomach lurch.

"I came to give you a heads-up." Jed sighed, pulled off his beanie, and wrung it in his hands. "I tried to talk him out of it, but Deano doesn't listen to me."

He stepped closer. A fresh cut dissected his eyebrow. A blue bruise circled his eye.

"I know about you and Gabe Rivers."

It didn't surprise me. We'd tried to be discreet because we didn't want the team gossiping. So far we'd kept out of the press, but it was a matter of time until the story leaked. I'd had to make my peace with that. This wasn't a fling, at least not for me. It was real. We couldn't keep our hands off each other. We'd have to go public at some point. But who would have guessed Jed would be the one to break the story? What did he care?

I sighed and shoved my dirty kit into my duffel bag. "So what? You've moved on and so have I. It's none of your business. Tell who you want."

"I don't care, Miri. It's not me you have to worry about." Jed chewed his lip and shuffled from foot to foot. "Deano has a clip on CCTV from the club. You and Gabe Rivers in a VIP room."

I froze with my hand on the locker. My blood turned to ice. "What clip?"

He chewed his lips. "You're on his lap. You're . . . ah . . . enjoying yourself."

Oh my God. My stomach dropped all the way to my knees. "What?"

Jed's hands worked around his beanie. The bastard. At least he had the decency to look mortified. I put a hand on the locker to steady myself.

"So, what does this mean? What is he going to do with it? Can you get it off him?"

"He'll do whatever he can to make money off it. He'll black-mail Gabe Rivers. The guy is loaded."

197

Oh God. My brain reeled. I drew a sharp breath. Had he gone to Gabe with this, too? If he released that tape the world would see me grinding over Gabe, and that disgusting possibility didn't even frighten me as much as Gabe seeing me grinding over him. I'd tried to put it all behind me. What the hell was he going to think when he found out it was me? I should have come clean, but every time I tried, the words got stuck in my throat. It wasn't that I didn't want to tell him, but I'd been hanging on and hanging on for the right moment, and it never came.

I had no idea how he'd react. Everything had been going so well, and I'd been too terrified to blow it all up. This was entirely my fault. The guilt was destroying me, but the trouble with secrets is the longer you keep them, the harder they are to confess.

Stark, black fear swept through me. "Has he gone to Gabe with this yet?"

"I don't know."

"Tell him not to bother. It's a waste of time." My fingers trembled as I slammed my locker. Maybe I could call his bluff. "Gabe won't care. He's had more sex tape scandals than you and I have had hot dinners. That man doesn't care about his reputation. It's already dirt."

"Then Deano will sell it to the press. He'll find a way to make money from it."

"This is blackmail. It's illegal."

Jed held his beanie hat low, pulling at the loose threads. "You don't know what Deano is like. I can't do anything about these guys. This isn't a bluff."

Heat pressed behind my eyes. The shame was unbearable. Everybody would see me. My family. My friends. My teammates. Gabe would see me. Desperately, I stumbled toward Jed, gripping his hands in mine. I looked him squarely in the eyes. If I couldn't call his bluff, I'd have to appeal to his humanity. Not that he had much.

"You have to help me, Jed. Please. I'm desperate. This is going to ruin my reputation. My career. I was wearing a mask. Gabe doesn't even know it was me. For God's sake, please. My whole family will see it."

He slipped his beanie back on his head. "I came here to warn you, Miri. I'm sorry. I shouldn't even be doing this. I can't help you. It's too late."

Chapter 37

GABE

Everything was perfect. Miri was the kind of girlfriend I could only ever have dreamed about. She was so unpretentious. She didn't care about social media followers or movie premieres. We hung out in our pajamas, eating dinners in the penthouse, and it was enough. At every practice I watched her, knowing that later I'd be stripping her out of those muddy shorts and making her moan. The story would break soon enough, but until then we were having fun keeping things a secret. I was serious about this woman. Mother would have to deal with it.

I took the steps down from the Beaufort Hotel two at a time. Ruby hurried beside me, scrolling her phone and reeling out the day's appointments. I wanted to get to the part of the day where I would surprise Miri in the changing rooms after a gym session and fuck her hard and fast in the showers.

A short man with his cap pulled low stepped out of the crowd. His voice was low and rough. "I've got something you need to see."

His mean-looking face was vaguely familiar. Ruby took me by the arm and shepherded me down the busy street, but the man followed, darting ahead of us.

"You're going to want to hear this," he said.

He checked his wrist. Gold glinted in the afternoon sun. A Rolex. *My fucking Rolex.* Recognition came screeching into my consciousness. This was the prick from the strip club that had divested me of my watch. The man produced a phone from his denim jacket and clicked on a video clip. I sat on a couch while a naked woman with a short purple bob ground over me. Even behind a mask, her pleasure was undeniable as her head fell back and her mouth formed an O shape.

Shit.

My jaw set, tight and grim. "What the fuck is this?"

"It's you and your hooker girlfriend in a strip club."

"Why do you have it? What do you want?"

"What do you think I want? I'll leak your little home movie unless you make it worth my while not to."

My teeth gritted. Ruby shot me a worried sidelong glance. What about Miri? I drew a calming breath. This wasn't my first rodeo. I'd had threats like this before when my phone had been hacked. The lawyers had shut it down before it made the front pages. Okay. It wasn't that bad. It wasn't great, but it could have been worse. At least I was fully clothed. It was hardly my fault if a stripper decided to get off on humping my leg. She'd been wearing a mask and a wig. Had she leaked this? Had this been her plan all along?

I'd have to squash it. I could do without Mother getting wind of it. This would be enough to make her withdraw my chances of getting the men's club forever. Still, I couldn't let someone blackmail me. I'd call his bluff.

"Do what you want. Nobody will care. You can't make out the man's face. It's a non-story."

"The director of Calverdale Ladies is fucking a stripper who happens to be his new top goal-scoring striker. That's definitely a story."

He jabbed a finger toward the screen. I couldn't take my eyes from the bruises and scabs that marred his knuckles. His words made no sense.

"What are you talking about?"

His voice was bright with mockery. "Miri Forster has signed with you. No wonder you let her join the team. If the two of you are getting up to that in public, then I bet you're a happy man behind closed doors."

My mind reeled. "What does it have to do with Miri?"

"That's her humping your leg like a bitch on heat."

I smiled at the absurdity, but an uneasy feeling made the skin at the back of my neck prickle. Of course it wasn't Miri. She would have told me. There's no way she would have lied to me like that. It couldn't be possible. I ran through the interactions I'd had in that room. Except a little something niggled at the back of my mind. Her voice. It had sounded so familiar. But I'd brushed it off because everyone sounded like that round here. It was a coincidence. My heart pounded. A sick feeling gripped me. Miri wouldn't betray me like that.

Would she?

Miri had her back to me, brushing her straight golden hair in the mirror in her locker door. She was beautiful. Powerful. Charismatic. Determined. This woman was so under my skin. I couldn't lose her. The words piled in my mouth, but I didn't dare speak them. I wanted to watch her a little longer, savor her.

She cocked her head. She must have caught my reflection in the mirror because she swiveled on the spot, a beaming smile lighting her face.

"Gabe?"

"Hi."

Her smile faltered and she wrapped her towel tighter. "Is everything okay?"

"Is it true?"

"Is what true?"

It sounded so ridiculous. "Are you Violet?"

Her eyes widened. "What?"

"Violet Delights."

"Look. Gabe." She pulled the towel tighter with trembling fingers. "I can explain. You need to give me the chance to explain. It went too far. I wanted to tell you."

My throat ached with defeat. No. What? No. She'd been grinding in my lap pretending not to know me. I'd opened up to her. She had a piece of me I hadn't knowingly given. It wasn't an outright lie, but it was deception. A secret she'd kept from me. My stomach plummeted, and it was the feeling I'd had when I'd walked into Dad's office and caught him with Emma. I was out of control again. Being made to look stupid. A person whose feelings didn't matter. Someone so easy to cast aside.

I'd trusted Miri and she'd treated me like a fool. How could she do that to me after I'd told her everything that had happened with Dad? I didn't open up to anyone, but I'd given her everything, and she'd repaid me by keeping me in the dark. For the first time, it had felt like I had someone completely in my corner. I'd been kidding myself. It was as humiliating as it was heartbreaking.

The torment gnawed at my gut, but I kept my voice level. "Why?"

Her eyes brimmed with tears. She moved toward me and I stepped back into the corridor.

"It was stupid, Gabe. I'm sorry. That first time in the club . . . I didn't know you then . . . I was scared. I wanted to tell you. I'm so sorry."

She reached for me and I snapped my hand away.

"Please, Gabe. Let's talk about this. I want to explain myself properly. I never meant to hurt you. Everything got out of hand."

Everyone I cared about betrayed me. My father. Emma. I couldn't trust anyone, but I'd been stupid enough to believe that Miri was different. She was as bad as everyone else. How had I let myself get close to this woman?

My blood turned to ice. "Did you do this to me on purpose? Was this a set-up from the start?"

She paled and ran trembling fingers over her face. "Of course not. How can you say that? Do you think I want this tape out there? I can't believe you would even suggest—"

"I have no idea who you are anymore."

"No. You know me. I wouldn't hurt you on purpose."

"You kept a secret from me. I can't trust you. We're done."

I turned on my heel. Last time, Emma had run away from me. This time it would be me leaving first.

"Wait, Gabe. Wait. Let me get dressed. I want to talk."

I kept my voice casual but I didn't turn around. "This was all a mistake. Mother's right. I need a woman in my own tax bracket. I should have known I couldn't trust someone like you."

"Someone like me?" She followed me out into the corridor, barefoot and wrapped in her towel. She gazed at me in despair. "What's that supposed to mean? Someone poor, Gabe? Is that what you mean? Someone normal. Not an actress or a model. Someone who lives in the real world. Yes. I had to strip to get money. You have no idea what I've been through. It was demeaning, but I was desperate. I hated it, every second of it . . . apart from when you were there. Because you were kind to me."

My resolve hardened. She was turning this round on me? "Have you been laughing at me this whole time?"

"Of course not. I'm devastated because I've hurt you and I didn't want that."

Her expression was tight with strain. Her wet hair dripped onto the floor in sharp splats. "I'm sorry. I was desperate and embarrassed. You can't even imagine what it's like to be that desperate. Your whole life has been money and privilege. You have no idea what it's like to live in the real world. It's different for people like you. You start on the board a hundred places ahead of everyone else."

"Right. I'm spoilt and pampered. So, I don't have any feelings? I don't have any problems. You can betray my trust and what does it matter because I'm so rich it won't affect me?"

She shook her head. "No. of course not. I didn't mean that. I don't think that . . . I'm asking for some understanding, Gabe. Please. I care about you."

"People that care about each other don't keep secrets from each other. We're done, Miri."

Her voice trembled. "You don't mean that."

I nodded woodenly. "Yes. I do."

She swallowed. "What about the recording? My mum doesn't know. I didn't tell her . . ."

"I don't have a lot of control over these things. I'll put the lawyers on burying it. I'll do everything I can."

Her eyes widened with panic. She grabbed my hand. "You're pissed off with me, but please don't throw me under the bus, Gabe. Please don't let that clip get out if you can stop it. This is my career. I've worked my whole life to play football. It's everything to me."

Exhaustion overwhelmed me. That was the part she cared about. Not me, but the tape. I couldn't do this anymore. I walked away without looking back.

Chapter 38

GABE

Mother sashayed in and took a seat on the chaise. She smoothed her skirt over her knees and a little white Pomeranian jumped up into her lap. A knot ground in my chest. This whole time, Miri had kept a secret from me. Why? Actually, fuck that. It didn't matter why. It was a betrayal. I'd trusted her. I hadn't trusted anyone in so long, but I'd trusted Miri Forster.

Mother raised an eyebrow. The Pomeranian on her lap cocked its head, watching me with expectant, beady eyes. Even the fucking dog had it in for me today.

"Ruby has filled me in."

I darted a glance in Ruby's direction. Thanks for nothing. It didn't matter anymore, anyway.

Ruby raised a rueful eyebrow and held her hands up in surrender. "I work for Joyce. I'm sorry."

That was it then. No chance of the men's team. Not without some serious arse-kissing. Maybe with time, but no time soon. A strange numbness suffused me. It should have bothered me more to lose my shot at the men's team, but the truth was, the men's team were doing great in the Premier League anyway. They didn't need me. I wouldn't be able to drive forward any real changes. It wasn't like the women's team. Everything I did here mattered. I'd be making a real difference.

Mother was wrong about women's football. Of course it was the same game that the men played, but women's football mattered in a way that was different, too. These women were so passionate because they were doing something so important. They'd had to fight to be taken seriously in a male-dominated sport. Every time they stepped out onto the pitch, they inspired other young women.

"Can the lawyers keep this out of the news?" I asked.

Mother pressed her lips. "Everybody is working round the clock to sort out this mess."

"That tape can't ever see the light of the day."

Mother smoothed a palm over the Pomeranian's fluffy head. "It doesn't look good for you, Gabe."

I'd had worse. Still, that clip needed to stay out of the press. I was angry at Miri, but not petty enough to drag her name through the dirt. I'd had a lifetime of this shit, but Miri didn't deserve it.

"Whatever it takes, that clip needs to stay out of the press," I said.

Ruby shook her head. "It's not that easy. Unless we give them something else to be excited about."

I held my head in my hands. What could we do? "What's more exciting for them than this monumental fuckup?"

"There is one thing more exciting." Mother's level gaze met mine. The Pomeranian on her lap cocked its head, watching me. "Get back together with Emma."

My jaw clenched. "Don't be ridiculous."

"A few dates. Give the press some photos. Make it look real. The media loved you with Emma. Put to bed those silly rumors about Emma and your dad. You wouldn't go near her if that was true. This is the story the press will jump on."

My stomach hardened. "No."

"Gabe Rivers and Emma Cousins. The billionaire playboy and the Hollywood actress who tamed him, back together. You're the nation's love story. This is the way to redeem your image."

I couldn't contain my eye roll. My own mother telling me to redeem myself with the woman who had fucked my father, Mother's husband, behind both of our backs.

"Under no circumstances is this happening. Besides, Emma would never go for that either."

"She's on board."

Anger lashed in my gut. So they'd already discussed it?

Mother continued casually, "She's had those ghastly movies. Emma is becoming a nobody. You can go to the *Daily News* and give them an exclusive about your reunion. It's the only story big enough to cover this up."

"I won't do it."

Mother cocked her head to appraise me. She flashed a cold smile. This is what she'd always wanted. Everything was falling into her lap. "Emma's family are our oldest friends. You're perfect together. Be sensible. You know the best way to bury something is distraction. It's a magic trick. You wave your hand over there so nobody knows what your other hand is doing."

My neck flashed hot. I could tell her the truth. All I had to do was open my mouth. But Mother would be devastated. I'd be ruining Dad's memory for her, and also Emma's. I needed Mother on my side to sort out this mess, not weeping over Dad's betrayal. This wasn't about me or Emma or my mother. This was about Miri. She had the most to lose if that tape hit the tabloids. I had to stop it.

Whatever the cost.

Mother held the squirming Pomeranian up in her arms and kissed the tip of its nose. "Everybody loves what you're trying to do with the women's team. I can't let you embarrass us and throw this all away. I'm not asking you to do this, Gabe. I'm telling you."

A cold knot formed in my stomach. "If I don't?"

She spread her hands regretfully. "Then I can't help you with the tape, and perhaps it's best I stop helping you at all. If you want to turn your back on this family, then maybe it's time you go your own way."

My jaw clenched. Of course this was more palatable than the truth. Emma had fucked my dad and now told a pack of lies painting me out to be a villain. Now I had to parade around with her like the hero in a new Taylor Swift song.

"There must be another way. Anything else," I said.

Mother laced her elegant fingers in her lap. "Get back together with Emma and the lawyers bury the tape so it goes away for good. And if you do a good enough job, maybe I'll throw in a sweetener. You slipped up with this tape, but I can't deny how well you're doing with the women's team. You need to distance yourself from this stripper who plays for you. She needs to go, and you can move on to the men's team."

Alarm went through me. "What do you mean, she needs to go?"

"She betrayed you, Gabe. You didn't even know that you were with a stripper. She's a liar. If she lies about that, what else has she lied about? Aren't you angry?"

Yes. Of course I was angry, but Miri had earned her spot on the team. She didn't deserve to get kicked off for this. Blood pounded in my ears. I could hardly focus on Mother's drone.

". . . You do a few photoshoots with Emma. You never know, if you spend some time together, you might rekindle the flame. Play the game, Gabe. The tape goes away. The girl goes away. You get the team. All you have to do is smile for a few photos and you get everything you want. Take control of the narrative. Weave a story that everybody wants to see."

"That *you* want to see, you mean?"

A smile stretched Mother's lips. "That benefits all of us."

Miri had deceived me. Still, I had to do whatever it took to keep that clip out of the wrong hands. The clip looked worse for Miri than me, and despite everything, I still cared so deeply about her. How the hell was I supposed to switch all these feelings off? I didn't want her career smeared. No matter what went on between us, Miri was an exceptional talent, and she deserved to play at the highest level. I'd promised Miri that nothing between us would impact her career. It was too important. She'd already been held back for so long, and she had family relying on her. All that mattered was getting rid of the tape for Miri's sake.

A barb of pain speared my heart. "Fine. I'll do it, but Miri stays with the women's team. She's still the best striker we've ever had. I'm not letting you punish her over this."

Mother ran her hands through the Pomeranian's fluffy fur. "Very well. Do a good job with Emma and I'll turn a blind eye to the stripper."

◆ ◆ ◆

In the limousine, I pressed my nose to the humming glass. Paris flashed by in a blaze of dark city and bright lights. The car pulled up and a suited driver opened the door for me. A light drizzle misted my face as I stepped out onto a moonlit cobbled street. A little row of bistros and cafés sat in front of us. Snatches of French conversation and music drifted from the doorways.

How fucking romantic.

This was where I'd taken Emma for our first date. She'd been unimpressed by all of it. All she'd cared about was getting the perfect shot of the extortionately priced food to put on Instagram. Miri would have thought all this was too pretentious. She'd be right.

Emma was waiting for me inside in a cozy little alcove in the empty bistro. She stood when she saw me. Her hair was set in beautiful auburn waves and a blue dress clung to her willowy frame. She looked incredible. She always had. The sight of her left me cold.

Emma threw her arms around me and pulled me into her embrace, forcing me to breathe in her tangy citrus scent. "Gabe, it's so good to see you, darling."

She released me and I slipped into the seat opposite. The candles on the table bathed us in a golden glow. Flashes glanced off the dark windows. The paparazzi were shooting us from outside. It looked more authentic like that. A secret moment between reuniting lovers. Her hand was warm on my neck. She leaned across and whispered in my ear. "Thank you for doing this, darling. This has been so hard for me, too." She moved her face away, her lips brushing my cheek. "I hated the way we left things. I've never stopped thinking about you."

She shuffled closer and rested her hand on my thigh. She was so close she might as well have crawled onto my lap. "We're here now. Let's put on a show."

I gave her a tight smile. "You always were a good actress. I have no idea why your latest movie was panned."

Her eyes were like pieces of stone. Lights flashed in the corner of my vision. The paparazzi were lapping it up. Emma smiled indulgently and cupped my cheek. Before I had a chance to react, her lips covered mine. Her mouth moved against mine and her tongue poked through my lips. She tasted foul, like an ashtray full of cigarette nubs. I steeled myself not to flinch.

"No tongue," I whispered against her lips.

"We need to make it convincing."

Her fingers snaked through my hair. She kissed me; her nose bumped against mine.

She pulled away and a smug smile twisted her lips. "I missed that."

211

Chapter 39

Miri

The scent of freshly baked cakes wafted from the kitchen. Normally I loved the smell when Reece was baking, but today it turned my stomach. I couldn't eat. I couldn't sleep. Gabe hadn't let me explain myself. The thought of how we'd left things made my chest ache. How was I supposed to carry on like this? I couldn't go out on the pitch and pretend nothing had happened between us. I'd have to make him understand. He couldn't shut me out. He was angry, but how could he not even give me a chance to explain?

Reece put a batch of muffins on the counter. "Banana and raisin. Your favorite."

Nausea turned my stomach. "Maybe later."

Frankie dropped down on the couch next to me. "Fancy popping to the Drum and Monkey for a pint?"

"Maybe another time. I'm not in the mood."

Elliot looked up from his phone. "I brought some weights home from the gym. We can do some work on your conditioning if you want?"

I looked up to find everyone watching me. An uneasy feeling settled in my stomach. Something was going on. Everyone was being so nice to me. Too nice.

"What's going on? Is something wrong?" I asked.

"Haven't you seen the news, Miri?" Frankie asked.

"What news?"

Frankie looked between Reece and Elliot, her expression weary. "I told you. She doesn't know."

My jaw set. "She doesn't know what?"

Reece rubbed his eyebrow, smearing flour on his face. "Miri, there's been something in the news. It's about Gabe . . ."

Panic made my brain reel. "Is he okay?"

Frankie bowed her head and murmured, "He's back together with Emma Cousins. There are pictures all over the news."

A deep pain stabbed my heart. "What?"

How could it have happened so quickly? Gabe had only confronted me about the tape yesterday. How could he have moved on a day later? Unless they'd never truly broken up. Unless they'd still been in contact when he'd been with me. No. He wouldn't do that. Gabe had been cheated on. He knew how bad it felt. It was wrong to even suspect him of it after all those conversations we'd had about our exes, but then I'd never suspected Jed either. Jed had been so convincing all those times he'd lied to my face about why he'd had to stay late at work, or why he'd needed all those weekends away. Maybe this was just what men did, or maybe it was something men thought they could do to me. Maybe I was just easy to dupe. I had some sort of sign on my head.

I pulled out my phone and swiped through dozens of Gabe's new Instagram stories: Gabe and Emma strolling down a busy street, Gabe and Emma in front of the Eiffel Tower. But one image made my breath hitch. It had been taken through a window. A stolen moment of intimacy between lovers in a café. Emma's hair fell in beautiful glossy waves. Gabe wore a smart suit. His hand rested on her neck as they kissed.

Reece's dark, feeling eyes met mine. "If you need to talk, I'm here. We're all here."

Silence wrapped around us. I didn't want to be around any of them. I needed to get in the shower and cry where no one could hear me. Gabe was back with Emma. It was all so quick and convenient. What the hell? After everything that had happened with his dad?

Frankie exchanged a grim look with Reece before she cleared her throat. "Perhaps it's innocent?"

It wasn't innocent. This was England's most notorious fuckboy being a fuckboy. He'd been so angry at me. He hadn't even given me a chance to explain. I'd been such an idiot to fall in love with a man like him. He had every right to be angry and upset, but he hadn't given me a chance to explain, and he hadn't even asked after my welfare. He'd got back together with his ex-girlfriend a day later. He was every bit as cold and ruthless as his reputation. I'd been an idiot to think he was anything better. What mumbo jumbo had Reece spurted? A womanizer, not even capable of emotional intimacy.

I offered my family a weak smile. They'd welcomed him into our home. He'd let us all down. "I'm sorry. I need to be alone."

On the frost-hardened pitch, I warmed down with the other girls, but I couldn't relax. I'd had to walk past Gabe's office to get out here. Mercifully, it had been empty. A week had passed. It was a new year, but I'd hidden away in my room when the clock had struck midnight, and my family had been celebrating. They'd tried to cajole me to join in, and I'd pasted a smile onto my face and tried, but the heavy knot in my chest hadn't loosened a notch. I couldn't speak to him after those photos. My breath made clouds in the freezing air. Claire blew her whistle to gather us in and we huddled together, pink-cheeked and sweating.

"Great training session, ladies. Same time tomorrow."

Exhausted and limp, I turned and made my way back to the changing room. Claire fell in step beside me.

She shot me a sidelong glance. "Strange to have a training session without Gabe here."

I nodded but held my tongue.

She kept her voice low. "Is he coming back?"

A pulse pounded in my head. "How should I know?"

"I've heard some rumors."

"Oh?"

"People are saying he might be moving to direct Calverdale United. We're going to need a new director."

My stomach dropped. "He's ditching us?"

Claire flashed a placating smile. "You don't have to worry. We'll keep up the changes that Gabe implemented."

"I thought he cared about this team."

Claire's eyes were skeptical. "I was there when his mother asked him to do this. The men's team was always his dream, I'm afraid. But we don't have to let this put us back. We've made excellent progress." She put her hand on my shoulder. "We're going to be okay without him."

Tears pressed behind my eyes. I wasn't okay without him. This was bullshit. The promises Gabe had given about taking this team to the top weren't just for me. They were for everyone. Gabe had been offered something better and jumped at the chance. He had not only been lying about his feelings for his ex. All the promises he'd made to us were bullshit, too. He'd only ever cared about the men's team.

"We're better off without him. If he doesn't care enough about this team to stick it out with us, then who cares? Good riddance."

"I care about the team." A familiar low, clipped voice drifted from behind.

Gabe stood tall and composed in his dark suit and immaculate peacoat. A scarf circled his neck. The bitter cold made his cheeks glow, and his chestnut hair was gloriously disheveled. My traitorous heart leaped at the sight of him.

Claire spun. "Hi, Gabe. We were just . . . ah . . . talking about you."

"I got that." He inclined his head in greeting. "Do you mind if I have a word with Miri?"

I pressed my lips together. I had nothing to say to Gabe, but I didn't want to make things weird for Claire.

Claire flashed me an odd look and left us. "I'll leave you to it."

I watched Claire head in the direction of the changing room. "You're back from Paris, then? Looks like you've had a nice time."

He stiffened and tipped his face to the weak winter sun. "Looks can be deceiving. Anyway, you don't have to worry about that tape anymore. We've made it go away. I thought you might want to know."

Relief went through me and I dared a glance at him. "For good?"

He nodded woodenly. "These things are never easy, but we've had everyone on it. We've paid the guy off. Got the copies. The lawyers have squashed it. It's done. It's more complicated online, but we have a team scanning. Nothing has come up yet. If it does, we're getting an injunction in place so the press can't run with it."

My shoulders sagged. "Thank you."

He nodded. I rubbed the spot in my chest where it ached. It was too painful being with him. I'd told him I loved him, and now the distance between us was so wide he was a stranger. I shook my head and charged off to the changing room.

"Miri. Wait." He jogged beside me. "You're angry with me? You were the one who lied to me."

Tears burned my throat, but I wouldn't cry in public. I saved my tears for the showers. "True, and you were the one who wouldn't let me explain. I was desperate for the money. I was frightened. I borrowed money to help my mum. They beat my brother up. It was a mess. I didn't know what to do. I shouldn't have lied to you, but I was embarrassed and ashamed. You have no idea what it's like to be that desperate."

He paled. "Miri, I'm sorry. I've been lied to before and my mind went to the worst place."

"You got back together with your ex-girlfriend one day after things went wrong with us. Is it true about the men's team? You're ditching us?"

His eyes held genuine remorse. "Calverdale United is the number-one team in the Premier League. You have to understand, this is all I've ever wanted. I played for the Academy. I've wanted the men's team for so long. This is what I was destined to do. I want to explain what's happening with Emma. Come and get a coffee with me. Let me explain."

I spun, flinging my arms open. My heart thundered. I must have looked crazy, but I didn't care. When I'd asked Gabe for a chance to explain, he'd denied me it. Why should I listen to a word? "What is there to explain? Every day this week there has been a picture in the papers of you with your tongue down someone else's throat. We had an argument and you ran straight into the arms of your ex-girlfriend. You brought me onto this team with promise after promise and now you've ditched us. We have nothing left to say to each other."

"An argument? You lied to me, Miri. You made me look a fool." He pressed his lips flat and shook his head. "Anyway, I don't care about Emma. Not the way I care about you. It's not real. I miss you." His compelling eyes met mine, his voice as soft as a caress. "I wish . . . that everything could go back to how it was before."

A knife twisted in my heart. I swiped at my cheeks with trembling fingers. So much for saving my tears for the showers. Things couldn't go back to how they were before. Not now.

I stiffened my spine. "If you're not the director of this team anymore, I can't see a reason for us to have any further interaction. This is a professional relationship."

A shadow crossed his face. I hardened my heart and headed for the changing room. For the first time in his spoiled, pampered life, Gabe Rivers wouldn't be getting what he wanted. Tears fell down my cheeks. I wiped them away and ran.

Chapter 40

GABE

I sat on a bench in the park near Calverdale Stadium. A group of teenagers had made a makeshift BBQ on the grass and the smoky scent of hot dogs and burgers made my stomach growl. The private investigator dropped down on the bench next to me.

"Mr. Rivers." She gave me a tight smile and handed me a file.

I took a deep breath. "I'm not going to like this, am I?"

She smoothed her dark bun but made no reply.

The first section of the report covered Jerry's misdemeanors and the list of women willing to give testimony about his behavior. Plenty of damning evidence to secure prosecution. Miri would be pleased with that. I'd managed to disappoint her in every other way, but at least I could keep my promise about holding Jerry to account.

I flicked to the next page and my mouth went dry. None of this was about Jerry. It was about my mother. The more I read, the more my stomach dropped. She'd been up to no good with the pension funds. There was enough incriminating evidence here to lock her up for a long time.

I flashed a glance at the investigator. Somehow I kept my voice level despite my rising panic. "Who else knows about this?"

She kept her gaze fixed ahead. "No one."

"I can sort it out. I can fix this and make sure nobody further down the chain is affected."

The chirrups of the birds and chatter from the park filled my ears. Breathe.

She inclined her head to me. "What about Jerry Reynolds?"

"I told you, I'm just trying to do the right thing here. I have no loyalty to Jerry. After what he's done, they can lock him up and throw away the key for all I care. I'll take all of that to the police, you have my word. But my mother is different. She's had to pick up Dad's mess. She's been grieving. If she's made mistakes, then I will fix them if you give me a chance."

I filled my lungs. The air smelled as though it was about to rain. A heavy, sour feeling settled in my stomach. This report was damning. Mother had spent a lifetime blackmailing me to get her own way. I could turn this information over to the police, or I could wave this report in her face and she'd be at my command, but then we'd be over. There would be no chance to repair our relationship. Despite the way she'd treated me, I'd always wanted better. Dad was gone. I had a choice whether to build a bridge with my mother or blow it to smithereens.

Not that I could let Mother off the hook entirely. This was serious. It was about pensions, and that affected employees in every part of the company. These were real people who would be harmed by her actions. I'd take responsibility for sorting out the finances, and make sure that none of our employees were out of pocket, but I'd still have to hold Mother to account. I'd give her the chance to make this right. She could start by selling the mansion. Maybe we could bump up our charity efforts. Mother could put some of her schmoozing efforts into fundraising. We'd figure out a way to put this right. If she refused accountability, I'd have no choice but to hand her over.

The investigator cleared her throat and laced her hands neatly in her lap. "As long as Jerry Reynolds is held to account, I don't see any reason to share the rest of the report. The work I've done for

220

you is confidential. You can proceed however you wish with the information. I have no further interest."

I inclined my head to take in the cherry blossoms that lined the path. The blush-pink petals spiraled in the stiff wind like snow, littering the black puddles. Relief filled me in a warm rush. Maybe if I threw Mother a lifeline with this, we could have a better relationship in the future. Even if we couldn't, at least I could be the better person. I wouldn't stoop to her level when I could take the higher ground. If Miri were here, that's what she would tell me to do. Even if she didn't want me, I could still be a better person.

With trembling fingers, I closed the report. "Thank you."

The investigator nodded. "Good luck, Mr. Rivers. You have my word, we'll say no more about it."

A knock sounded on the door to the penthouse.

"Go away." I rolled over in bed.

Emma barged in. Her gaze passed over me before she crossed to the window and pulled back the curtains. Sunlight pierced my eyes and I groaned.

"Come on. Get up. We're going for lunch at a delightful little spot by the river. Very photogenic. My publicist arranged it."

"I don't feel like it."

She moved to my wardrobe and pulled out a shirt. "Stop moping. You need to get outside and get some sunshine and some fresh air."

"I don't like sunshine or fresh air."

She sighed. "You're miserable. We all get it. You're wallowing. Warthogs wallow, not grown men."

She plucked a few strawberries from the breakfast trolley. "You've got more followers than you've ever had on every platform. My agent is texting me all day. The work is pouring in. Whether

221

you like it or not, we're good for each other, Gabe. Everybody wants us together. This is how this works."

I turned over in the bed. "Leave me alone, Emma."

She ripped the duvet off me and clapped her hands in frustration. "Babying you isn't part of the deal. Get up. We have to do the photos. Your mother said you were going to keep up your end of the bargain."

She dropped down on the bed and walked her fingers over the duvet with studied disinterest. "I've been thinking about the press conference for when you announce the news that you're taking over Calverdale United. I should be there. Maybe you could even mention me in your statement. Something about what a support I've been . . . I could write something if you like . . ."

"Why are you still talking?" A pulse beat at my temple. I pulled the duvet back. "I've got a headache."

She cupped my face, running her hands over my stubble. "You need to shave." She wrinkled her nose. "And shower."

I shrugged out of her grip. "Save it for later. There are no cameras here. Touching is not part of the deal."

She pouted and looked up at me from beneath long lashes. Slowly, she walked her fingers up my arm again. "But it could be? Couldn't it?"

My skin prickled under her touch. "You cheated on me."

"I made a mistake. I've apologized. I thought maybe, with enough time, we could work things out between us? That day was awful for me, too. For a long time, I blamed myself for what happened with Micky . . . but we can't live with guilt. Life's too short. Can't you find it in your heart to forgive me, Gabe? We're good together. Anyone can see that."

I pulled the duvet up to my chin. "You don't care about me, Emma. You never did. You like the idea of us. You and my dad were made for each other. He was only capable of loving himself, too."

She pressed her lips together. "You and I make sense, Gabe. We just fit. You can't tell me you don't recognize that?"

I sat up and looked her in the eyes. "Do you love me, Emma?"

She smoothed her hand over her auburn waves. Her eyes slipped away. "Yes."

"I don't believe you."

She gave an affronted laugh. "What can I do to prove it?"

Emma moved to the wardrobe and pulled out a suit jacket for me. "You might not be on board with us yet, Gabe, but give it time. I'm going to win you back. You're going to have everything you wanted. The best football team in the country and a woman who loves you on your arm."

I'd had a woman who loved me and I loved her. I wanted to be with her, even if it was just watching her on the pitch, because she was so spectacular that I didn't want to be anywhere else but in her orbit. Miri didn't care for my status. She didn't crave the cameras. She didn't care about my money.

Ever since I'd walked away from her, a horrible ache had taken root in my chest. I missed her. Miri had accepted me. Her family had accepted me. I thought I'd wanted the men's team. How was it possible to get everything you wanted and feel the worst you'd ever felt? The price had been too high. I'd lost Miri. I was supposed to be happy now, but I couldn't muster a smile.

"Do you want children with me? A family?"

Emma wrinkled her nose and gave a tinkling laugh. "Children?" Then her face stilled. "Oh? You're serious. Yes. Well. Maybe not quite yet, but one day . . ."

Miri put her family above everything. She'd make a wonderful mother. I'd always put kids off as something for the future, but with Miri I could see it. I wanted to watch her belly swell with my child. I wanted to be part of a family.

I sighed. "I can't do this with you, Emma. You can't want this either."

She frowned. "What?"

"This is a lie."

"It's a lie for now, but it could be real."

"It's never going to be real. Even if I could get past what you did to me, I've moved on."

Emma watched me with a grim expression. "It's all fallen into your lap, Gabe. You've wanted this team for as long as I've known you. We can work on things between us. My therapist says—"

"I've met someone else. I can't be in a room with her without needing to touch her. I don't know what it is, but it's beyond my control. I can't put this longing into words. Are you happy with that? You want to be with me, knowing that I can't love you? Knowing that I am so in love with someone else it makes me sick that I've lost her? She betrayed me too."

Emma's face darkened. Silence stretched between us.

After a while, Emma spoke softly. "I didn't think you were capable of it."

"What?"

"Falling in love." She shook her head, a sad smile on her lips. "But it turns out you are. Just not with me. You didn't ever love me, did you? It always just felt like going through the motions, like there was something missing."

True. There had been so much missing. I'd never even known what love was until Miri. Trying to settle down with Emma had been a misguided attempt to show my dad I was capable of maturity. I'd wanted to show him that I had my shit together and I was ready for the team. In reality, I'd been far from that. With Emma, I'd been working so hard to change into someone else, someone stable and ready for more responsibility in my life. It had never been that way with Miri. The irony was, being with Miri had changed me into someone better, and it was effortless.

I shot Emma a sidelong glance. "I'm sorry. I mean it. I really am."

"No. I'm sorry for what I did to you. I'm so sorry. Your dad was . . . you know how he was . . . so charming . . . so charismatic. I got swept away, even though I knew it was wrong. I knew it would hurt you." She nodded sadly and hugged herself. "No. You're right. I don't want this. I thought there was a chance that you might forgive me, but I don't deserve it . . ." Her eyes slipped away. "It doesn't matter." She chewed her lip.

Guilt prickled the back of my neck at the pain etched into her face. "I forgive you, Emma, but I can't have a relationship with you."

Emma nodded sadly. "I know. Of course I know. Your mother won't be happy. She was the one who wanted this."

"I'll handle her."

"You'll lose the team."

"I'll handle that, too."

She stood, smoothing her hands over her dress. "I'll get my publicist to draw up a statement."

She walked to the door. With her hand on the knob, she paused to look back at me. "If you love this girl as much as you say you do, then don't walk away from it. Fix it."

"She won't even talk to me."

"But you love her?"

A tight knot twisted in my stomach. "Yes."

Warmth crept into Emma's smile. "Then it's fixable."

A crescent moon hung in the sky by the time I got to Miri's mum's house. I hoped it wasn't too late to disturb her, but I was desperate. I had to explain myself. I couldn't allow Miri to think I'd got back together with Emma. She wouldn't talk to me, so I'd have to do things the old-fashioned way. I clutched the envelope in my hand.

Writing a letter with a pen had been strange at first, but then the words had poured out of me.

I knocked on the door. No reply. A light shone from the living room window. Miri's mum was in there. Maybe she'd nodded off in front of the television. I moved to the neat front garden and peered through the window. Confusion swept over me before my heart dropped to my knees. Pam Forster lay on the living room floor, her limbs at odd angles.

Oh God. No.

"Karl," I shouted over my shoulder to the limo. "Call an ambulance."

Pain shot through me as I slammed my body against the front door. It didn't budge. I took a breath and put my full weight into ramming the door. With a loud crack, the door gave way, flying off its hinges. I stumbled forward into the hallway and raced into the living room.

I dropped down to my knees next to her. "Pam?"

Her skin was a deathly gray. My fingers slipped to her neck, searching for a pulse. Memories of my father slammed through my mind, but I had to keep a clear head. My heart pounded in my chest. I wasn't religious, but a prayer went through my head.

Please let her be okay.

Pam was such a lovely, kind woman. I didn't want this pain for Miri, for any of them. I'd learned CPR. After Dad, I'd vowed I'd never be so unprepared again. Panic rioted inside but I shoved it away. There would be time to fall apart later.

I dropped down on my knees next to her. I pumped on her chest, alternating firm compressions with breaths into her mouth. Adrenaline coursed through me.

"It's okay. You're okay. Help is coming. Please come back. Miri needs you to be okay. They all need you. I'm here. I'm not letting you go."

Chapter 41

Miri

I headed back to Mum's house after sleeping at Phoebe's place. I hadn't meant to stay over, but we'd opened a bottle of wine, and I'd poured my heart out over Gabe. Phoebe had always been my shoulder to cry on. We didn't play for the same team anymore, but we would always be teammates.

From the top of the street, I caught sight of the limo parked outside. For goodness' sake. What was he doing here? Did he think harassing my mum was a good look? As I walked down the street, a little prickle lifted the hairs on my arms. Something wasn't right. Wooden boards covered Mum's front door. My stomach dropped to the floor. I ran up the drive.

"Miri?" The voice stopped me in my tracks.

I spun. Gabe's driver emerged from the car.

"Gabe asked me to wait here in case you showed up. He's been trying to call. You're not answering your phone."

"It's out of battery. I stayed with a friend last night and lost track of time. Why? What's the matter? Isn't my brother in? He's supposed to be here."

He held the passenger door open for me. "Get in. I'll take you to the hospital."

My blood turned to ice. "The hospital? Why?"

"I'm sorry." The driver toed the ground with his shiny brogue. "It's your mum."

Please. No. Please let this be okay. God, if you're listening. If anyone is listening. Please let her be okay. I'll do anything. Please let her be okay.

Heart hammering, I raced through one brightly lit hospital corridor after the next until I burst through the door of Mum's side room. Mum lay asleep in bed, thin and pale, wearing a blue hospital gown. A plastic tube led from her nose to a feeding bag on a stand next to the bed. Gabe sat in the chair at her side, his face pale and exhausted. I stiffened my spine, trying not to break apart.

"It's okay. She's stable. She's going to be okay." He stood and moved toward me before stopping.

My breath came in sharp pants. "What . . . happened? Karl said a heart attack."

"I found her last night in the living room. I tried to call, but . . . I couldn't get hold of you . . ."

Confusion made my head pound. Last night? It's what the driver had said, too, but it was so hard to contemplate. Mum had been in the hospital all night and none of us had realized. I'd stayed over at Phoebe's last night, but where the hell had Reece been? Mum shouldn't have been alone.

I took Mum's limp hand in mine. My eyes filled with tears but I blinked them back. I had to hold it together.

"It's so hard to see her like this, but she's going to be okay, Miri." Gabe's voice was softer than usual.

Reece burst through the door, red-cheeked and breathless. "What happened?"

"It's okay. She's okay. She's stable," I said.

Reece moved to Mum's side. He took her other limp hand in his. "She was fine yesterday morning. I saw her." His voice cracked. "She was fine. I'm so sorry."

"Where were you?"

He lifted his glasses and rubbed his eyes. "I was at a . . . friend's. I fell asleep. I was meant to be home. It wasn't planned."

"You should have told me. I wouldn't have gone to Phoebe's last night if it meant leaving her alone."

Mum's eyelids flickered and she groaned. Everybody stilled.

I squeezed Mum's hand gently. Her eyes opened and she blinked, adjusting to the light. A relief so overwhelming raced through me that it made tears press at my eyes.

"We're here, Mum. You don't have to worry about anything. You rest. We're all here."

She stared straight ahead, her face gaunt and white. Her fingers shook as she reached up to swipe at my face. "Miri?" Her voice was thin and tired. She brushed my cheek with her thumb and a faint trembling smile lifted one corner of her mouth.

Frankie burst through the door. "Mum," she cried. She flew toward the bed.

Gabe stepped back out of the way. He squeezed my hand. "I'll leave you. It's getting crowded."

He picked up his peacoat and moved to the door. My feet carried me out after him into the corridor.

"Gabe. Wait."

He stopped and turned.

"Your driver said you saved her life."

He brushed his fingers through his messy hair and smoothed his crumpled shirt. "It's a blur. I did my best until the paramedics got there."

"You stayed here all night?"

He nodded.

My eyes filled with tears. None of us had been here, but at least Mum hadn't been alone. "Thank you."

He took a step closer and halted. "Things are not right between us, and you must have a million thoughts going through your head right now, but if you need anything, anything at all, let me know. I want to help."

He turned around and I grabbed his hand. "What were you doing at my mum's house?"

He glanced at where my hand gripped his wrist. I released him.

"I wanted to give you a letter. I want to apologize and explain."

I couldn't have this conversation now. Not with Mum so ill. I bit my lip, holding back tears. "I can't do this now, Gabe. I can't."

Gently, he brushed the tears from my cheeks with his thumb, his fingers cool and soothing on my skin. "I know. You need to focus on your family now. I'm here for you. Whatever you need. I want to be here for you. If you'll let me. Just as a friend. I want to be your friend, Miri."

I nodded woodenly, too tired to argue. None of the stuff we'd argued about mattered now. He turned on his heel and strode away.

I called after him. "Gabe?"

He threw a glance over his shoulder and raised a questioning eyebrow.

I wiped my cheeks with the back of my hand. "Do you still have the letter?"

◆ ◆ ◆

Later that night, in the hospital canteen, I sat in a quiet corner and opened Gabe's envelope.

Dear Miri,

I'm so sorry for the hurt I've caused you. I know I've fucked up. This thing with Emma was so stupid. I was angry. It's so hard to trust when your whole life is on show and up for public debate.

I made a plan with my mother. If I staged a reconciliation with Emma to distract the media, then Mother would do everything she could to bury the tape. I needed to be certain that this didn't get out, not for me, but for you. I couldn't care less if people see me but I couldn't stand the thought of your name being dragged through the dirt.

It made me sick to think you would see those photos of me and Emma. It was all pretend. There was never anything physical between us. We didn't sleep together. I don't have any feelings toward her anymore. There is no one else for me. I only want you.

I wasn't angry about the stripping. I understand that you must have been desperate, and I hate that you felt like that. You kept a secret because you needed to. That should have been enough. You didn't owe me an explanation. I wish you'd felt like you could be honest with me but I understand that you couldn't. It was only the secret that hurt.

If you give me another chance, I promise I'll do everything to make you happy. There has been so much missing from my life for so long and being with you has opened a door. I see now. I want to commit to this, Miri. I want it all with you, a home, marriage, and children. My child-hood was fucked up. I never saw myself as capable of commitment, but I'm tired of the way things have been. I remember what you said to me in that room at the club and I agree. You know what's better than a bad boy? A grown-arse man with his shit together. You make me want to get my shit together. I'm ready.

I love you, Little Swan. You entranced me the first time I saw you on the pitch. I want our love story to have a happy ending. I'm waiting if you still want me. I understand if you don't want to be with me but I needed to explain myself. Thank you for letting me do that.

Gabe

Chapter 42

GABE

Reporters had turned up in droves for the press conference. My mother sat on my right-hand side and Rob, the manager of the men's team, sat on my left. I'd spent a lifetime waiting for this moment. The room bustled with activity as people took their seats and set up their equipment. Only ten minutes to go before kickoff.

Mother squinted into the crowd, a fake smile on her face, her voice a low hiss. "Where's Emma? I told her to be here."

"Emma's gone."

Mum's smile faltered. "What do you mean, *gone?*"

"I told her I could never love her and that I couldn't carry on with such a ridiculous farce."

Mother frowned. "I hope that's a joke."

"It's not a joke."

Mother turned to face me. "We had an agreement."

I pushed the file across the table toward her. It had taken all my resolve to wait for this moment. "The report on Jerry Reynolds is complete. I didn't trust anyone within the organization, so I hired a private investigator."

Mother flicked through the file before she paled and her fingers froze. She swallowed and lifted her gaze to the reporters settling in their seats.

"Jerry was a lecherous old pervert. He's guilty as sin, and I'm handing everything about him to the police. But the things you've been getting up to make Jerry Reynolds look like Mother Teresa."

Mother swallowed.

I leaned in to whisper, "There's enough in here for an entirely new podcast on the Rivers family. If you're lucky, you might even get a Netflix series."

She fiddled with the Peter Pan collar of her pristine blouse. "That's all your dad's dealings. It's nothing to do with me." She gritted her teeth. "You wouldn't blackmail your own mother, darling."

"No. I know how it is to be controlled and manipulated."

Red lights clicked on all over the conference room. Silence fell.

I covered her hand with mine. "Jerry won't get away with what he's done, but your sections in this report are going to disappear. Nobody knows. I'm going to sort out this mess. None of our employees should suffer because of this. We'll get everything straight again. I want to work on our relationship, Mother. I want better, but you have to let me live my life. Do you want to fix this? All of it? The company? Me and you?"

Mother's hand trembled underneath mine. Her eyes shone. She drew a breath. "I made a terrible mistake, but I can put this right, darling. Your father's death has had an impact on all of us. It's been a huge adjustment."

"You abused your power. I didn't stand for it with Jerry. If I'm going soft with you then I need to see some accountability."

She paled. "Tell me what I need to do, and I'll do it. Anything."

Time would tell whether she meant it, but I'd give her the benefit of the doubt. Being with Miri had taught me that, more than anything, I wanted family around me. I hadn't realized how lonely I'd been until the day that I wasn't.

I squeezed Mother's hand. "Good. I'd like to introduce you to some friends of mine. We'll have you playing Twister yet."

Chapter 43

Miri

I plucked a grape from the overflowing fruit bowl next to Mum's hospital bed.

Frankie scrolled her phone and Elliot stood at the window, staring off at goodness knows what in his usual quiet, intense way.

Mum sat up in bed. "How long is this going to take?"

Reece's dark eyes met hers. "As long as it takes. We're in no rush. Why don't we play a game or something?"

Frankie groaned. "No more I-spy."

We'd been waiting for the doctor to organize the discharge all afternoon. Nobody could wait to get Mum home. We were all going to be living on top of each other again, but it didn't matter. The twins would be off to university soon. Reece and I could manage between us. Neither of us wanted to leave Mum alone.

My phone buzzed in my pocket with a message from Gabe.

Put Sky Sports News on.

I hadn't spoken to him since the night he'd brought Mum in. I'd read his letter. It was hard to believe his mother could be so manipulative. It was terrible that he'd had to put up with that for so long. I wanted to talk to him, but my head had been too full of Mum to think about us.

I nudged Frankie and held my hand out for the remote control. I flicked through the channels until Gabe's face flashed on the tiny TV screen that hung above Mum's bed. He sat behind a long table, flanked by his mother and the Calverdale United manager. Gabe's mouth moved soundlessly. Subtitles flashed on the screen.

Gabe Rivers, the new director of Calverdale United.

It was an incredible move for Gabe. He would be directing the biggest team in England. I didn't want it to leave such a sour taste in my mouth. He'd said he was going to take us all the way to the top, but I couldn't blame him for this. It's what he'd always wanted. I didn't begrudge him.

"What's this all about?" Frankie asked.

"It's a press conference to announce that he's taken over the men's team," I said.

"Well, turn it up then," Frankie said.

I increased the volume. Rob Butler's voice drifted out from the screen. Gabe looked down at the phone in his hand.

Frankie gave an incredulous chuckle. "Gabe isn't even listening."

My phone buzzed in my pocket with a message from Gabe.

Are you watching?

I texted back. Yes.

I want you to know that I keep my promises.

He looked up from the phone in his lap and directly into the camera. My heart lurched as though he was sitting right in front of me, looking at me. He laid his phone flat on the table in front of him.

Confusion pulled at my brow. What was going on? I'd read his letter. He'd told me that he wanted me back. It wasn't something I could have put any thought into this past week. It had all been about Mum. But now the sight of him made my heart pound. He'd

237

put on a show with Emma to protect me. He'd saved my mother's life.

On the screen, Rob's gaze flicked to Gabe. "And now I'll hand over to the man himself."

Gabe flashed an easy smile full of white teeth and straightened in the chair. He smoothed his tie.

"Thank you, everyone, for coming. This is a big day for me and one I've been waiting a long time for. I played for the Junior Academy as a boy. My dad loved this squad. It meant everything to him. It's a wonderful team and an honor to have this opportunity. However, sometimes the thing we want isn't the thing we need; we just don't stop to question it." He paused and looked directly into the camera. "I made a mistake. A lot of mistakes . . ."

Rob coughed and whispered something in Gabe's ear.

"Yes. I'm fine. I'm grateful for the offer, but I'm turning down the men's team."

The smile on Joyce Rivers' face didn't slip, but something flickered in her eyes. Leisurely, Gabe poured himself a glass of water from a jug on the table. He took a sip and continued.

"These past couple of months I've had the pleasure of directing the women's team. Our women's team has been scandalously underfunded for a long time, and I set about changing it. We have an incredible manager in Claire Easterly, an incredible squad, and every one of them has overcome huge personal challenges to play. They don't do it for money or success. Women's football is grassroots. I've seen the commitment, the talent, and the passion firsthand. These women don't do it for anything other than the love of the game and the joy of being part of a team. I respect that, and it's been an honor and a privilege to be part of it. I'm not willing to give it up. I made a commitment to the team. I promised I will do all I can to take them to the top, and I keep my promises. I don't want the men's team. Why would I, when I'm already working with such an incredible bunch of athletes?"

Shock flew through me. He couldn't be serious.

Joyce Rivers flashed a tight smile. "Yes. We have made a commitment to our women's team. This is not lip service. We are a modern organization. I've been so inspired by my son's work with Calverdale Ladies that I'm stepping up my fundraising efforts with the Rivers Foundation. Charity has always been very close to my heart. I'm sure that's one way I can put more good into the world. I'd love to see what we can do to encourage future generations of female footballers." She shot Gabe a hesitant look, as if trying to read his reaction.

Gabe inclined his head in his mother's direction. His voice was calm and composed but steel glinted in his eyes. "That sounds like a wonderful idea, Mother. I know you're as committed as I am to impacting people's lives in a positive way."

Gabe's mother kept the smile on her face.

"Whatever makes you happy, darling. If that's what you want, then that's . . . delightful. You have my full support and encouragement."

Gabe smiled. "I know I do, Mother. Thank you. I'm glad to hear it."

Chapter 44

Miri

I went to him when I was ready, when Mum was home and we had more stability. Any sooner and I wouldn't be able to think straight. Gabe opened the door to his penthouse, dressed casually in a thick ribbed blue jumper and jeans. My heart took a perilous leap. All I wanted to do was throw myself at him. I needed his touch. It had been too long.

For a moment we drank each other in, before he coughed and spoke in a soft voice. "We've missed you at training."

"I needed some time to get Mum settled at home. Claire said it was okay . . ."

He nodded. "Of course it is. How's your mum? She's back home then?"

"She's doing better."

"I'm glad." His relieved smile wrapped me in warmth.

I stepped forward, needing to be closer. "I saw your press conference. I love that you want the women's team, but I can't stand you giving up your dream. You always wanted the men's team—"

"And now I don't. I meant every word of it. The women's team is real football. It gives me a buzz to be part of what you're doing together. It's an honor. Besides, I want to be there the day you get scouted for England. I said I'd do all it takes. Nothing matters more to me." He raised a sardonic brow. "Don't you want to be on top, Forster?"

A tingle raced over my skin at his nearness.

He bit his lip and stepped forward hesitantly. "We have so much to talk about."

I didn't want to talk anymore. We'd said all the things that mattered. "I'm tired of talking."

"Me too." His eyes dropped to my lips. "I lied before at the hospital. I can't be your friend."

My heart hammered. I raised a questioning eyebrow.

"I need to be more than that. I'm going to die if I don't touch you."

With his hand at my waist, he pulled me toward him. His lips found mine and he kissed me deeply. Entangled, we moved into his suite and he kicked the door closed behind us.

He broke off from my lips, breathless and panting. "I'm never letting you out of my bed again. Can you deal with that, Forster?"

I laughed. "If you think you can handle me, Rivers."

Epilogue

GABE

ONE YEAR LATER

"Park Place? Is that one of yours, Gabe?" Mother sat stiffly at the kitchen table. She studied the Monopoly board in confusion, as though it was about to grow legs and walk off.

"No. It's mine." Frankie shook the dice and rolled them onto the table. "Come on, Joyce. Keep up. I thought you'd be used to all this."

Mother flashed a tight smile. "I still don't quite understand it."

Miri's mum dipped her head in encouragement. "You'll get there. It won't take long before we're beating these youngsters."

"Exactly. You boomers should have the upper hand. The strategy is to buy all the property and milk the plebs for rent. It shouldn't be that much of an alien concept for you, Joyce." Frankie held her hand out to receive Mother's cash. "Pay up."

Miri flashed me a smile from across the table. Warmth filled my chest. She frowned and stood. Something was wrong. I was out of my seat in seconds and by her side.

"What is it?"

Miri rubbed her expanding stomach and smiled. "Nothing. I need to stretch. My back hurts if I sit down for too long."

Reece turned his head to watch her. "Do you want me to do the hot-water bottle? Heat at the base of the spine will help."

I moved behind Miri, rubbing her back in a gentle massage. "Here. Let me help you."

She groaned with pleasure. "Oh. That's good, but you don't have to do that. Carry on playing."

"You're carrying our child. It's the least I can do." I took her by the elbow and led her to the hallway. "Come on. Let the children play. I'm going to run you a bath."

She relaxed back, leaning into me. "I can't wait until the new place is ready. Will everybody be okay without us?"

"The nurses are 24/7. We'll only be down the road."

"I feel so bad for Reece sometimes. I don't want to leave him to do all this on his own."

I kissed the top of her head. "He said he'll be fine. We'll be here if he needs us."

She groaned and looked up the narrow staircase with trepidation. "I'm sick of waddling. I miss playing football."

"You'll be back out there in no time."

"It's not going to be that easy. This is going to have a huge impact, you know that, don't you? Trying to maintain a career with a family . . ."

"I know, and I'm going to do everything I can to support you. The plan has always been to get this team into the Women's Super League, and when we're there, we're going to need our best striker. I won't let anything hold you back again. I made a promise." I held out my arm to escort her. "Soon we'll have our own football team and we'll be coaching them."

She laughed and swatted my arm. "Let's have one baby before we think about the next one."

I squeezed her lightly. "No pressure. We can have one baby or a football team. As long as it's with you, I don't care."

She returned my smile with a glint in her eye. We'd had to get creative with positions as Miri got bigger, but I knew what that grin meant.

I whispered low in her ear. "I want you to strip for me tonight. The way you did in the club."

She hooted with laughter. "What? Look at the size of me."

"You're perfect. There's more of you to love." I wrapped my arms around her.

It was true, watching this woman's belly swell with my child brought out my inner caveman. I couldn't get enough.

I kissed the tip of her nose. "You've never been more beautiful."

She sighed. "I've never been more uncomfortable."

I took her by the elbow and helped her up the stairs. "Fine. Time for a bath. Let me watch you in there and I'll pay you back with a foot massage."

"You're good to me, Mr. Rivers."

"Because you're mine, Little Swan. All mine."

THANKS FOR READING!

Ready for more Calverdale Ladies? Check out the next book in the series! I can't wait for you to get to know Miri's brother, Reece.

Would you like to find out what happened on the night that Miri went to see Gabe at the hotel after his TV announcement? Bonus epilogue here: https://dl.bookfunnel.com/62f4xjt9uf (This link will subscribe you to my newsletter, but you can unsubscribe at any time.)

Have you read the prequel novella, PITCHING MY BEST FRIEND? Sign up to my newsletter here, and get it for free! https://BookHip.com/RVXCHSB I send newsletters once a month with book updates and recommendations of other books you might like. I promise to keep the boring photos of my garden and my dog to a minimum.

LET'S HANG OUT!

All I've ever wanted from life is a crew to hang around with so that we can all wear sunglasses, look cool, and click our fingers in an intimidating fashion at rival crews. We can chat all things romance and occasionally you might be called upon to become involved in a choreographed dance fight. I will also be your best friend forever. NB: Dance fighting skills not mandatory (but encouraged).

Join my reader group:
www.facebook.com/groups/979907003370581/
Follow my author page:
www.facebook.com/profile.php?id=61553872688253
TikTok: Sasha Lace Author (@sasha_lace_author)
Instagram: www.instagram.com/Sasha_Lace_Author

Psst! Hang on! I'd love a review if you've got a sec? If you enjoyed this book, please consider leaving a review wherever you like to leave them. Amazon, Goodreads, or BookBub. Reviews are the life-blood of authors, and are very much appreciated! Thanks so much.

ACKNOWLEDGMENTS

This is my second run at writing these acknowledgments. The first time, I was a fresh-faced indie author leaping into the unknown. I had no idea if anyone would pick up my story, or whether (more likely) it would be lost in a pile with a million others. What I didn't expect was to find so many people willing to take a chance on an unknown author.

Writing has brought so many wonderful women into my life. Thank you to all the readers who have supported me, whether it was taking the time to message with words of encouragement, leaving a thoughtful review, or shouting about my books. You helped me find my confidence as a writer. You made me feel like my words have value. It means the world, truly.

Thank you to everyone in the Montlake Romance team for all of your hard work on these books. It has truly been such a brilliant experience, and I've loved every moment. I'm so excited to relaunch these books with an amazing team of professionals. Thank you to Victoria Oundjian for giving me this chance, for your passion and enthusiasm for the series, and for making my lifelong dream to be traditionally published a reality.

Thank you to Victoria Pepe for taking this series on and bringing so much energy and enthusiasm to it. I feel so confident that it is in wonderful hands, and I'm so grateful. Thank you to Lindsey

Faber for your brilliant development editing insight, and for helping me to dig so much deeper with these characters. To Jenni Davis, thank you for giving these books such a beautiful polish, and helping me to banish the word 'quirked' from my vocabulary. I don't know how many books it will take before I can rid myself of it completely, but I live in hope.

Thank you to Laura and Clare at Liverpool Lit. You are amazing agents and lovely human beings. It is genuinely an honor to be represented by an agency so committed to breaking down barriers in publishing.

To my beta reader/editor/mentor Angela, I sent out a plea for help with my first story and the universe overshot the net and sent me you—the best friend I've never met! You have always been so accepting, so generous, and so insightful. You understood what I was trying to say with that weird first story (better than I did) and you helped make sense of it. Not only did you help me become a better writer, but you showed me that people can be miraculously kind.

To my lovely writer bestie, Heather G Harris. I have long suspected the 'G' stands for genius. You've always believed in me, and encouraged me, and you've been so generous with your time and knowledge. Thank you for being my very first beta reader, and for giving me the confidence to go for it with this story. I appreciate you.

To Jo, Tamymanne, and Kat. You are a wildly accepting bunch of fellow smut-butts. Thank you for all the laughs, and the log-ins. Jo, seriously, thank you. What would I do without the log-ins!? Please don't ever change your password, or this is all over for me.

To Helen, I'm so grateful to have a lovely friend to share this writing and publishing journey with. I really appreciate your talent for finding the perfect shocked-doll expression for every occasion, and your dedication to uncovering Rhysand fan art. Whatever happens, we'll always have the Willywahs and that street team of Ken dolls from Sainsbury's.

Thank you to my precious friend Katie. You have always brought so much joy into my life. Whatever I'm doing, no matter the hour, I'd always rather be on a boat with you, playing table tennis, and stuffing my face with free sushi and peanut M&Ms at 5 p.m., directly before our five-course meal is about to be served.

To Ruchi, my twin flame, all my literary aspirations began with you. Your West Midlands project spoke to me of beauty. The letter to Thom Yorke helped me to refine my prose. All that time spent doctoring BT phone bills honed my attention to detail. The environmental rap taught me how to dig deep. The hole in the ozone layer isn't even an issue anymore. Coincidence, or the power of rap?

Thank you to my mum for always encouraging my passion to read. Even when we had so little, you made sure I always had books. Thank you for your unconditional love and support. The past couple of years have been tough, but your selflessness and strength leave me in awe. Better times are coming, I know it. Thank you for being you. I love you.

To James, your support makes my writing possible. Your support makes everything possible. You've made me laugh every day for the past twenty years. The best part of writing about football is that I get to talk about these books with you. Why are you so randomly good at plotting? It's like that time we went windsurfing and you just knew how to stand up and do it straight away, and I was covered in goose shit and crying. It makes no sense, but I'm into it. You're better than all the book boyfriends put together. They should make a trope about you.

Last, thank you to my kind, beautiful, bright, funny, smart, wonderful boys. I became a writer when I became a mother. You gave me the will to be the best version of myself. Please know that you are the greatest joy in my life, and I love you more than anyone has ever loved anyone EVER. Now get out of here. Go on. Clear off! Do not read these books. Not even when you're grown-ups. I cannot afford the therapy you will need from reading your mother's sweary, spicy books. I have given you fair warning.

PLAYING TO SCORE

Turn the page for an exclusive teaser chapter from *Playing to Score*, the next book in Sasha Lace's Playing the Field series . . .

Chapter 1

SKYLAR

Sean's hard body covered mine. A faint odor of mud and cut grass hit my nose. The scent of the pitch always clung to him. Once, I'd loved that smell. Not so much anymore. His hot breath fanned my ear and his hips snapped hard and fast. My limbs ached from practice, but I tried to muster some enthusiasm to match his rapid thrusts.

My mind wandered to the day's events, no matter how hard I tried to rein it in. The team manager, Claire, had made us do extra laps after discovering a couple of the younger players were hungover. Claire wasn't happy until she'd had some of the girls throwing up on the sidelines. I'd called her out afterward, but she'd doubled down. If we were serious about promotion to the Women's Super League, then this was the time to knuckle down and work.

As the captain, I wanted to keep the girls happy, but Claire was right—this year was too important to fuck things up. We had to be tough on them. Calverdale Ladies finally had everything we needed to succeed: a great team and a billionaire director who wouldn't stop until we got promoted to the Women's Super League. We were two points ahead of our closest rivals in the league table. Three wins would do it.

This was our year.

Sean planted his elbows, panting and grunting as he increased his pace. The ceiling needed to be painted. Dust lined the top of the lampshade. We could do with another one. In fact, the whole bedroom needed redecorating. We'd moved in together five years ago and we still hadn't got round to putting up new wallpaper. I flicked my gaze to the eggshell curtains. It was time for a change. A new color scheme entirely. Maybe lilac. I was definitely having a lilac moment after I'd found those perfect lilac football boots to match my hair.

Sean groaned and buried his face into the pillow next to my head. The bedframe rattled against the wall. Maybe we should get a new bed, too. One with a more stable headboard.

Sean's voice was ragged in my ear. "You like that, don't you? You're filthy, aren't you? A dirty girl."

I patted his clammy back. Sean's idea of sexy talk always left me cold.

His huge arm stretched over me as he gripped the headboard. "Are you close?"

Everything inside of me tensed at those dreaded words. No, I wasn't *close*. I was never *close*.

He groaned. 'Fuck, Sky. You're going to have to hurry up. I can't last . . ."

I squeezed my eyes shut, trying to clear my mind. A rush of thoughts swept in.

Just switch off.
Stop getting in your head.
Try and relax.

My fingers dug into the covers. All I wanted was to be clawing the sheets with pleasure for once, and not frustration. This should have been the most natural thing in the world. I wanted the kind of sex the girls in the locker room talked about—the excitement, the connection, and the bone-melting orgasms.

There had been times when I'd almost been able to relax enough—on the nights when Sean was out, and it was just me, a glass of wine, and a hot bath—yet still something always held me back. Sometimes your greatest opponent wasn't any of the players on the pitch, it was you, and the bullshit in your own head. Knowing that didn't make it any easier to let go.

Sean grunted in my ear. "For fuck's sake, Sky. Come on . . ."

It always came down to this moment. It had been terrifying that first time I'd faked it. Drama had been my worst subject at school. I'd been so certain that Sean would roar with laughter at my exaggerated moans, but he hadn't. He'd looked pleased with himself, puffed up with male pride, and although I'd expected to feel guilt, there had only been relief. Faking saved me from the awkwardness afterward. The recriminations. The name-calling. It was just so much . . . easier.

Sean's voice quivered with frustration. "Sky! Are you done?"

No point dragging it out. I took a few deep gasping breaths and readied myself to put on a show. Sean held perfectly still atop of me, panting. He was always so easy to read, but his tense demeanor gave me a rush of anxiety.

"You're not even close, are you?" His breathless voice was loaded with irritation.

My mouth filled with the usual lies, but the intimacy of the moment caught me off guard—he was still inside of me, his hot breath fanning my face, his critical eyes burning into me.

"I'm . . . I'm trying."

"Trying?" His frustrated expression slipped into mockery. "You're not supposed to *try*. It's supposed to just . . . happen. I thought you were going to talk to someone about this?"

"I did. The doctor said there's nothing wrong with me."

"And you let them fob you off again?"

Sean's weight on me felt suddenly like a sack of bricks. His sweaty tang filled my nose, overwhelming me.

"I'm not letting them fob me off. I just don't know what I'm supposed to do if they tell me there's nothing physically wrong with me—"

"Of course there's something fucking wrong with you. This isn't normal. You need to stop being so pathetic. Go back to that doctor, and tell them you want answers. How am I supposed to enjoy this if I'm not getting anything back from you?" He pulled out, and lifted away without looking at me. "Not good enough. You need to do better than this with me, Sky. I deserve better."

He barked his words as though I was a junior on his team who didn't have what it took to make the cut. I stared at him in disbelief. This is why I'd started faking, to dodge these conversations. If I'd been quicker off the mark with the act, we could have avoided this whole discussion.

He gave me his back. The silence rang loud. He stretched and admired his impressive muscular frame in the mirror above the dressing table.

"You remember I'm going to my parents' for dinner tonight?"

I smoothed my expression at his abrupt change of subject. Fine. I was done with the conversation too. The whole thing made me feel so shitty about myself. Talking about intimate stuff had always been awkward for me. I didn't even talk about these kinds of things with my friends. After a few pints in the pub, no topic of conversation was off limits with the team, but I always held back on the personal stuff. I was there to lead. The girls needed to see me as someone sensible to lean on. A bit of distance on personal topics didn't hurt.

"What time are we going to your parents' place?"

I watched his face in the mirror as a small frown creased his brow and then disappeared. "Don't worry about it. It's a family thing."

Sean's parents had always disapproved of me. It was fine for their son to be a football player, but they'd never liked the idea of him dating a female footballer. I wasn't blind to their narrow glances whenever I went round for tea. With my tattoos and piercings, I wasn't the kind of girl Mr. and Mrs. Wallace wanted for their superstar son. God knows who would be suitable. The Virgin Mary, maybe?

I fiddled with the silver ring in my nose and pasted a smile onto my face. "Fine. I have plans tonight anyway."

He didn't even try to mask the relief in his expression. The powerful muscles in his back rippled as he strode to the bathroom. I moved to the mirror and pulled my faded lilac hair into a ponytail that revealed the shaved edges of my undercut. The sound of the shower filled my ears.

I rested my palms on the dressing table and let my head drop. What the fuck was wrong with me? Sean was the captain of the top football team in the Premier League. Teenage girls throughout England had posters of my boyfriend on their walls. If I couldn't have an orgasm with a man that looked like Sean Wallace, what chance did I have?

A harsh buzz made me jump. Sean's phone flashed and vibrated on the bedside table. Strange that he hadn't taken it into the bathroom. Sean was surgically attached to his phone. Sometimes it made me nervous, but I trusted him. Sean had girls throwing themselves at him. It came with the territory when you dated a famous footballer, but we'd been together since school. He always told me I was the only girl he could trust to want Sean Wallace the *man* and not the football icon.

Unease gnawed my gut, and I always trusted my gut. It only took two attempts to crack the passcode and unlock the phone. Sean had never been creative. I read the first message.

Last night was amazing. When can you get away again?

The sender had no name, just an initial, M. I scrolled through an endless slew of messages until I reached a bunch of faceless nudes. The messages dated back a year. A fucking year!

Sean strolled back into the bedroom, naked and toweling his golden hair. He raised a questioning brow. "Everything okay?"

I held up the phone. I managed to keep my voice level. I even managed not to throw the phone at his face. "No. Everything is not okay."

He paled. The towel dropped from his hand. "She messaged me first. They always message me first."

They.

He swiped his towel from the floor. A cold, dark expression settled over his handsome face. "I've got needs, Sky. If you're not going to give me what I need, I have to look elsewhere."

His nonchalant tone made my voice harden. "I'm not enough for you?"

He wrapped the towel around his waist in a violent movement. "Don't try and make me feel guilty. This isn't on me. You should have tried harder to fix whatever it is that's wrong with you."

A lump of anxiety rose in my throat. Sudden heat pressed behind my eyes. That's why he'd done this. He wanted a woman without my issues in bed. A better woman. He turned back to the mirror and scanned his row of expensive skincare lotions, selecting a bottle.

"I mean, look at you." He pumped moisturizer into his hands and slathered it over his face. "How am I supposed to take you to my parents' house when you embarrass me every time? It wouldn't hurt you to tone it down a bit. Wear something more respectable. Your hair is a mess. This is what happens when you dye it so much."

My chest felt like it would burst. "Get out."

He raked a comb through his hair, angling his chin to admire his reflection. "I'm not going anywhere. You just need to cool down. We'll talk about it when I come home."

My fingernails cut into my palms. "Get *out*."

"You're acting crazy. This is what you do. You blow everything out of proportion. This doesn't have to be a big deal."

I choked back a cry. Fine. If he wouldn't leave, then I would. I scrambled around the room, picking up clothes and throwing them on.

Sean watched me. "Where do you think you're going?"

"I'm leaving."

A muscle quivered in his jaw. I braced myself for whatever nasty words he was about to spew, but a tense silence enveloped the room.

He sighed, and his voice took on an unbearable softness. "You're being ridiculous, as usual. Come on, Sky. We get each other. We can find a way through this."

We had understood each other once. We both knew what it meant to dedicate your life to football, to give everything to your team, and to deal with all the nonsense that came with a life in the public eye. I'd put up with so much from Sean over the years—the nastiness, the name-calling, the moods—but this was too much. This was a betrayal, and a humiliation. If word had got out to the press, it would have made headlines.

We'd have to find a way to handle a separation discreetly. If things got messy on social media, it could affect the teams. The logistics was a conversation for another time. For now, I needed to put all my efforts into not falling apart.

"It's over, Sean."

He shot me a look of amused contempt. "Over?"

"You cheated on me." I stormed to the door.

"I'm not the problem here. I've never been the problem." The bitterness in his tone held me frozen. "This has never been enough for me, but I stuck it out with you. You're broken, Sky."

His words landed like fists in my gut, stealing my breath. Maybe I was broken, but I was also tired of being treated like dirt. Enough.

Sean spritzed himself with his overpowering cologne. He stared at his reflection, as though enthralled by what he saw. His voice was soft and mocking. "You think you can do better than me? No man would be willing to put up with you the way I have."

I forced the words through gritted teeth. "I'll take my chances."

ABOUT THE AUTHOR

Sasha Lace used to be a very serious scientist before she ditched the lab coat and started writing kissing books. Sasha lives in the North of England and is a mom of two young boys. Everyone in her family is soccer mad, so she knows way more about soccer than she ever wanted to know. As a scientist and mom, her hobbies include: mulling over the complexities of the universe, treading barefoot on Lego, chipping dried Play-Doh from fabric surfaces, dried flower arranging (because you can't kill something twice), and writing about herself in the third person.

Follow the Author on Amazon

If you enjoyed this book, follow Sasha Lace on Amazon to be notified when the author releases a new book!

To do this, please follow these instructions:

Desktop:

1) Search for the author's name on Amazon or in the Amazon App.

2) Click on the author's name to arrive on their Amazon page.

3) Click the "Follow" button.

Mobile and Tablet:

1) Search for the author's name on Amazon or in the Amazon App.

2) Click on one of the author's books.

3) Click on the author's name to arrive on their Amazon page.

4) Click the "Follow" button.

Kindle eReader and Kindle App:

If you enjoyed this book on a Kindle eReader or in the Kindle App, you will find the author "Follow" button after the last page.